"A fabulous gothic treat of a book fill........ ...... ancient vampires, dark vendettas, and star-crossed love."

—Deborah Harkness, #1 *New York Times* bestselling author of the Discovery of Witches trilogy

"This book knocks over genre and swirls it into an addicting mix of mystery, romance, and fantasy. With nearly lyrical prose and magical characters that step right off the pages, *The Raven* is going to make SR diehards and newcomers alike nurse an epic book hangover."

—Christina Lauren, *New York Times* bestselling author of the Beautiful Bastard series

"Reynard never disappoints, especially when it comes to creating well-developed characters and granting readers an invitation to use their imaginations. This dark, sexy tale is nestled in the mysterious city of Florence and will amaze and enchant readers throughout. The author tries the paranormal genre on for size and, not surprisingly, it's a perfect fit."

—*RT Book Reviews*

"I'm loving this series . . . Sylvain Reynard's writing is exquisitely beautiful and it evokes such emotion and vivid imagery . . . Compulsive reading as the reader is swept away in an intriguing sensual romance set in the heart of Florence. Raven and William's story is addictive and mesmerizing as new meets old with humor, passion, danger, and mystery."

—Totally Booked Blog

"Sylvain Reynard's dark and mysterious world of the Florentine and its vampires is sensual, passionate, and deadly." —The Reading Cafe

Books by Sylvain Reynard

GABRIEL'S INFERNO
GABRIEL'S RAPTURE
GABRIEL'S REDEMPTION
THE RAVEN
THE SHADOW

Novella

THE PRINCE

The Shadow

Sylvain Reynard

BERKLEY BOOKS, NEW YORK

BERKLEY

An imprint of Penguin Random House LLC
375 Hudson Street, New York, New York 10014

Library of Congress Cataloging-in-Publication Data

Reynard, Sylvain.
The shadow / Sylvain Reynard.—Berkley trade paperback edition.
pages ; cm.— (Florentine series ; 2)
ISBN 978-0-425-26650-2 (softcover)
1. Vampires—Fiction.   2. Paranormal romance stories.   I. Title.
PR9199.4.R4667S53   2016
813'.6—dc23
2015034299

PUBLISHING HISTORY
Berkley trade paperback edition / February 2016

PRINTED IN THE UNITED STATES OF AMERICA

10 9 8 7 6 5 4 3 2 1

Cover photos: Man © Roman Seliutin / Shutterstock; Pont Vecchio © Ermess / Shutterstock.
Cover design by Lesley Worrell.
Text design by Tiffany Estreicher.
Frontispiece image of *Judith and Holofernes* © Pietro Basilico / Shutterstock.

Penguin
Random
House

To my teachers,
with gratitude.

Judith and Holofernes,
circa 1453–1457, by Donatello

Prologue

1268
York, England

William wasn't running.

For some time, he'd been waiting in the shadows near one of the lesser gates of the walled city of York, his horse tethered nearby. His beloved Alicia hadn't appeared. The bells for Compline had long since rung and so, impatient and irritated, he left their secret meeting place and led his horse in the direction of her father's house.

Alicia's father was a good man. He was a successful trader who'd clawed his way to the top of the merchant class. But he was Anglo-Saxon. His ancestry, coupled with his trade, made Alicia an unsuitable match for William in the eyes of his aristocratic, Norman parents.

But William wanted her. He'd courted her in secret and they'd made plans to meet and flee north. There they would marry and, with the few jewels and household items William had stolen from his family, they would make their life together.

He was young, strong, and extremely intelligent. Alicia was beautiful, kind, and industrious. Together, they would live a happy life.

Despite her promise, Alicia had not come.

William cursed in Anglo-Norman, his mother tongue, assuming Alicia's father had discovered their plan to elope and confined her to the house.

He loved her. He would have her even if he had to fight her father sword to sword. Even now, his blood sang in his veins and his body tensed with desire for her. They'd agreed to wait until they were married before lying together, but that hadn't kept them from kissing and enjoying little indulgences whenever they could. He was looking forward to uncovering her for the first time and learning the secrets of her body.

With such pleasant, sensual thoughts in mind, William tripped.

"God's bones!" he swore, dropping his horse's lead and pitching forward.

A low moan resounded from the ground.

When he'd recovered his balance, William bent over what looked like a bundle of clothing. A shaft of moonlight fell from behind the clouds, illuminating his stumbling block.

What he'd thought was a bundle of clothing was, in fact, a woman. She was wearing a dark, hooded cloak, and her skirts were pushed up to her waist. The lower half of her body was naked; blood was spattered on her legs and in between, where her maidenhood had rested.

William recoiled.

He couldn't leave her like that, even to find help. He pulled her heavy blue skirt down, covering her.

The woman shuddered and twitched.

He tugged at his horse and was about to mount him when the woman began whispering. She moved her head from side to side, her long, wavy locks of hair falling free of her hood, sweeping across her shoulders like a torn curtain.

Something about the sight of her hair stopped him.

Still holding the reins, he bent forward.

The woman had been beaten badly. Both eyes were blackened and one of them was swollen shut. Her face was bloody, her lip torn.

She lifted a shaking hand as she blinked at him from her single usable eye.

William felt the earth drop from beneath his feet.

He threw the reins aside and sank to his knees. "Alicia? Alicia, what evil is this?"

She closed her eye and coughed.

He lifted her in his arms, cradling her against his chest.

Alicia cried out from the movement. She shifted in his arms, too weak to struggle. A single, trembling hand sought the fabric of her skirts, tugging at them as if to cover herself.

The sight pierced him.

"Alicia." His voice broke. "Who did this?"

"Strangers." Her breathing was labored. "I called for help. No one came."

Her fingers pulled at his shirt.

"Will," she managed, burrowing against him. For a moment, she seemed to hold her breath, then her body slowly grew limp.

William clutched her to his heart, as his beloved's life seeped out of her body.

He lifted his eyes to the dark sky above and cried out.

Chapter One

July 1, 2013
Umbria, Italy

The Prince of Florence stood outside a house in Umbria, conflicted.

He'd already paid his respects to the Princess of the region, managing to avoid her romantic overtures. He'd enjoyed her body on previous occasions—she was beautiful, intelligent, and vibrantly sexual, as were most of his kind. On this night, however, he'd found her charms wanting. Having politely declined her invitation to fornicate, he hunted on Umbrian lands with her begrudging permission.

Locating Professor Gabriel Emerson and his family was easy. He and his wife, Julianne, owned the house that stood majestically on a hill, the lights from its windows cheering the darkness. The Prince's conflict was not in finding the Emersons or in escaping the embrace of the Princess. No, his conflict derived from a promise.

Raven Wood was human, beautiful in an unconventional way, and very brave. She was also protective of others, including strangers. In a tender moment, she'd exacted a promise from him that he would spare the lives of the Emersons. He'd made the promise in good faith, not just because he wished her to confide in him about her mysterious past, but because he cared for her and longed to make her happy.

Since she'd quit him, making it clear she could not accept the fact that he was incapable of love, he'd been tempted to go back on his promise and punish the professor for having the audacity to claim rightful ownership of stolen works of art. That he did so unknowingly was no excuse. The Prince desired revenge, and now that the only human in the world who could persuade him to indulge in mercy had rejected him, he had no reason to forgo it.

That was how he'd come to stand outside the house, listening as Katherine Picton, an older friend of the family, bade her hosts good night and Clare, the infant daughter of the Emersons, was put to bed in her parents' room.

He waited impatiently while the Emersons pursued their pleasure in a hot tub that was placed on the balcony off their bedroom.

The Prince wrinkled his nose as their marital union dragged on and on. It seemed every time he encountered the couple, they were engaging in intercourse. He tapped his leather-clad foot on the garden floor, willing them to couple faster.

It was a starless night, dark and still. The sky was a velvet arc above him while the summer breeze whispered in his ear. As he heard Julianne cry out in pleasure, he remembered Raven doing the same, while he gently loved her.

His jaw clenched.

Love—a polite euphemism for the joining of bodies for physical pleasure.

And yet he could not be scornful of the term when applied to her.

It had been almost a month since he'd known the pleasure of a woman—almost a month since he'd had Raven in his bed. He could still feel the warmth of her skin beneath his hands, the soft curves of her figure as he caressed her, the scent of her blood as it filled his nostrils.

But it was the memory of her green eyes that kept him still as Julianne kissed her husband and returned to their room. Raven had large eyes that brimmed with feeling.

Don't you ever tire of death?

Her voice interrupted his thoughts.

The truth was that he did tire of death. Even now he felt conflicted. But the Prince tamped down his misgivings and scaled the wall of the villa, eager to surprise the professor while he was alone.

And surprise him he did.

"We meet again." The Prince's conversational tone belied his menacing figure.

Startled, Gabriel stood in the hot tub, his wet, naked body shining in the dim light that shone from the bedroom.

"What do you want?" he barked, fingers curving into fists.

"I want you to cover yourself, to start with." The Prince tossed a nearby towel toward the man, regarding him with distaste.

The professor wrapped the towel around his waist and stepped out of the water. He placed his body between the Prince and the door to the bedroom, which he quickly closed.

"I said, what do you want?" The professor's posture was decidedly defensive.

"I want what's mine to remain mine. I'd like you to stop taking things from me and parading them in public as if they were your own."

The professor regarded the Prince with incredulity. "I have nothing of yours. Leave. Now."

The Prince's gaze flicked over the professor's shoulder, watching through the windows as Julianne cradled her daughter in her arms.

"You have many riches. You'd do best to attend them and not grasp after what is not yours."

The professor scowled. "Again, I'm asking you to leave."

The supernatural being shook his head, regarding the man with cold gray eyes. "I'm told you have difficulty listening to instructions. I perceive this to be true."

"I told you to leave. You don't seem to be listening, either," the professor rejoined.

"You stole my illustrations."

At the first sound of the professor's protest, the Prince lifted his hand, silencing him. "I know you didn't steal them personally. But the illustrations belonged to me before they fell into the hands of the Swiss family who sold them to you. I have taken them back and they shall remain with me. Forever."

"You lie. The family owned the illustrations for almost a century."

"Yes." The Prince gave Gabriel a challenging look. "Before that, they were mine."

The professor blinked in confusion.

When he'd regained his composure, his sapphire eyes narrowed. "You were the one who came to our hotel room in Florence. I couldn't see you but I could feel your presence." Gabriel lowered his voice. "What are you?"

"What I am is inconsequential. Let's simply say I'm not human. I am also not accustomed to arguing with human beings or offering second chances."

Once again the Prince's gaze was drawn to the figures of the mother and child inside the house. "Do you love your wife?"

Gabriel's spine stiffened. "Yes."

"Enough to die for her?"

"Without hesitation." Gabriel took a courageous step forward.

A long look passed between the Prince and the professor. The Prince was the first to break the silence.

"I have more respect for a man who is willing to live for his family than one who is willing to die for them. Protect your wife and child. Abandon any attempt to recover the illustrations and persuade the Italians to do the same."

"I paid a fair price for them. Your story sounds like a comic book."

The Prince's eyes flashed and he snarled.

The professor went back on one foot, his face a mask of terror.

The vampyre resisted the urge to attack, to exercise his power and dominance. He gazed at Gabriel, noting his tenseness, the smell of adrenaline rushing through his body, his quickened heart rate, and wondered why he hadn't fled.

Gabriel pressed his back against the bedroom door, signaling to the vampyre that he would have to go through Gabriel and the door in order to attack his family. He was willing to give his life to protect the wife and child who remained blissfully unaware just inside.

The Prince thought of another human being who was a protector; a woman who'd almost given her life to intervene in the beating death of a homeless man.

He didn't like being reminded.

"Your wife is ill," he announced abruptly, adjusting his shirtsleeves.

Gabriel's features shifted. "What?"

"You're an intelligent man, or so they say. By now I'm sure you realize I have certain—abilities. One of them is sensing human illness. I can't identify the problem, but there is something wrong with your wife, something causing her blood to lack iron.

"When I first met her at the Uffizi two years ago, I scented the illness. Whatever it is, it still threatens her."

The professor appeared noticeably shaken by the revelation and turned his head to gaze at Julianne through the window.

"You acquired illustrations that were stolen," the Prince continued. "Since I'm the original owner, I've taken them back. I should have destroyed you, but instead, I've gifted you with vital information about your wife's health. I think you'll agree I've been more than generous."

Gabriel turned his attention back to the Prince. It was clear he was struggling with what to believe, but his desire to protect his family won out.

"I'll drop the investigation and speak to Interpol personally." Gabriel spoke through clenched teeth. "I shouldn't be held accountable for the actions of others. If the Italians choose to pursue you, that's their misfortune."

"If your involvement ceases, we have no quarrel." The Prince gave him a sustained glare, then approached the edge of the balcony and turned.

Gabriel was still standing in a defensive posture outside the bedroom. He'd clapped a hand over his mouth, as if restraining himself from raising the alarm.

The Prince fixed him with a stony gaze.

"Be sure to live long enough to ensure your daughter has a good life. Things happen to children when they lose their father."

He vaulted over the railing and flew to the ground, before disappearing into the darkness.

Chapter Two

They stood for what seemed like an age, the young woman and the centuries-old vampyre, holding one another desperately on a rooftop of a loggia, overlooking the Uffizi.

They were the most improbable of lovers. Yet it was manifest to both they were a perfect match.

Raven's heart was full, her mind relaxed, her body sated.

William extricated himself from between her legs, placing her on unsteady feet. He righted his trousers and withdrew a handkerchief from the pocket. Supporting her with an arm around her waist, he lifted her skirt to press the linen gently between her legs.

When he was finished, he tossed the handkerchief aside and carefully lowered her skirt.

"Now that you've given me your gift, I must give you mine." William stroked her cheek, his eyes alight.

Raven flattened her hand against his chest, over his heart. She felt the strange rhythm under her palm and the almost frightening silence.

"This is my gift," she said quietly. "The way you touch me, I can tell that you love me."

He lifted her fingers and kissed them, one by one. "But you'll want the other gift I'm about to give you."

"This is the only gift I want, but I'm happy to have the words."

"I love you," he whispered. *"Defensa."*

She smiled against his shoulder. "I'm no longer wounded; I'm a protector."

"You've always been a protector." He kissed her forehead, before tracing the faded scar that marred it. "You told me once no one ever defended you. Tonight, I will."

"What?" She pulled back, confused.

"I promised to give you justice. I keep my promises."

A wave of anxiety passed over her. "William, what have you done?"

He smiled at her slowly. "It's what I am going to do. Come."

He pulled her tightly against him and they climbed to the roof, their bodies disappearing into the night like a wisp of smoke.

❦ ❦

Raven paused expectantly at the foot of the grand staircase in William's lavish villa.

"This way." He gestured to the hall.

She looked up at the second floor with longing. "I thought we were going upstairs."

His gray eyes danced. "We are going to the library."

Raven had expected him to lead (or carry) her to his bedroom, where they'd spend the rest of the hours before sunset making love. She frowned. "Why?"

"Come and see." He took her hand, escorting her down the hall.

The library was a beautiful room, featuring floor-to-ceiling bookcases, an immense wall of windows, and a high, domed ceiling formed entirely of glass. Pale light shone from outside, but Raven nearly stumbled in the semidarkness.

William lit a candle for her benefit. Vampyres had perfect vision in the dark.

"This isn't our destination," he explained. "It's merely the vestibule."

He turned to one of the bookcases and pressed on the spine of a large volume penned by Virgil. With a groan, the bookcase swung inward, revealing a dark passageway.

Raven peered into the narrow space. She hadn't enjoyed their last journey into the underworld, when he'd introduced her to some of his fellow vampyres. She had no wish to repeat the experience.

"I was looking forward to spending the night with you in your bed."

William gazed at her hungrily. "I'm looking forward to that, as well. But I haven't given you your gift yet."

She eyed the passageway. "I don't like surprises."

"This is a surprise you will enjoy, I assure you." He led her down a spiral staircase, carefully supporting her weight since she was without her cane.

The space beneath the villa was damp. Raven felt her skin begin to crawl and she tugged at William, stopping him.

"Can't you give me the gift upstairs? In your room?"

"Patience, Cassita." He released her to smooth her long black hair. "All will be revealed."

They continued down a long corridor that was punctuated by a series of heavy wooden doors. Raven could swear she heard rats scratching and scurrying behind them.

She clung to William until, finally, they stopped in front of a large, primitive-looking door. It was barred from the outside. With practiced ease, he lifted the bar and pulled the door open. The hallway echoed with the groans of rusted metal hinges.

He entered the room before her, using the candle to light torches that were suspended on the walls. Soon the cold, dank space was bathed in warm, flickering light.

Raven hesitated at the threshold. At first she thought the room was a wine cellar. But a glance at the interior revealed nothing like wine bottles or casks.

There was an old wooden table and a chair that sat to one side. There were iron sconces on the walls that held the now-lit torches and a pair of rusty iron manacles affixed with long, heavy chains. It was only the absence of weapons and other instruments that kept her from believing she stood outside a torture chamber. Then she saw the cell.

On the far side of the room was a small jail cell made of stout iron bars that ran from the floor to the low ceiling.

The cell wasn't empty.

She entered the room, her shoes crunching on a few small rocks that were scattered over the stone floor. Dampness seemed to lift from it, seeping through her soles and up her bare legs. She shivered.

Inside the cell was a man, lying on the ground. His garments were dirty and torn and his hair was matted. In the dim light that shone through the iron bars, she could almost make out his face, but not quite.

Raven wrinkled her nose at the stench that emanated from his direction—as if he hadn't washed in days. As if he'd used the ground of his cell for a toilet. Curious, she approached him.

The prisoner chose that moment to move, revealing his face. Raven's eyes widened.

"Oh, my God," she whispered, ceasing her forward movement.

William materialized at her side, bringing his lips to her ear. "Happy birthday."

With a curse, Raven stumbled toward the door. She only managed three steps before the contents of her stomach splattered on the floor.

William wrapped his arm around her waist. "That is not the reaction I was expecting. Are you all right?"

She pushed him away, heaving a second time. When she'd finished, he tried to pull her in the direction of the chair.

"No." She shoved his hands aside.

He looked puzzled. "What about your gift?"

"What gift?" Shakily, she wiped her mouth with the back of her hand.

"I promised you justice." He waved a hand in the direction of the prisoner. "This is justice."

Raven's eyes met William's. "How?"

William smiled, his teeth white and gleaming in the torchlight.

"I brought him here so you can kill him."

Chapter Three

Raven's world ground to a halt.

"Of course, I can kill him, if you'd prefer." William's eyes twinkled. "You don't need to decide now. Take some time to reflect on the details. I took the liberty of exacting a measured amount of justice already, but nothing approaching what ought to be done."

He stretched his hand toward her face, wearing an intense expression. "Happy birthday, Cassita."

Raven avoided his touch, her heart thumping in her chest. She gazed around the room, feeling as if the walls were closing in. She had to escape.

Skirting the sick that had pooled on the floor, she limped toward the exit. Her right leg complained as she pitched forward, pain shooting from ankle to hip.

"Cassita?" William sounded confused.

She ignored him, continuing toward the door.

"*Help me.*" The whispered plea came from the cell. The prisoner made a series of noises, as if he were trying to lift himself up, a groan escaping his mouth as he crashed back to the floor.

Raven placed her foot on the threshold.

"Don't leave me with him!" the prisoner rasped. "He wants to kill me. He pushed me down the stairs. I think my leg is broken."

Shock prevented Raven from reacting to the prisoner's cries—shock and the creeping realization of what William had done.

The prisoner rattled the iron bars. "He's an animal. Help me!"

Raven turned. "You think he's an animal because he pushed you down the stairs?" Her sudden, inexplicable anger was entirely lost on the captive.

"He kidnapped me. He says he's going to kill me!"

"Cut the shit, David," she snapped. "I know it's you."

The man blinked in her direction, several beats too long, before shaking his head. "My name is Greg. You have to help me."

Raven hobbled toward him with as much speed as she could muster. "It's Jane, you asshole." She gestured to her body. "Maybe you didn't recognize me with my *injured leg.*"

The prisoner gripped the bars with both hands, his frantic eyes meeting hers. "My name is Greg. I'm from Sacramento, California. I've never seen you before, I swear to God."

"Bullshit," Raven spat out. "You think I wouldn't recognize you? You think I'd forget what you sound like, you fucking monster?"

She stood for a moment, seething with rage.

"You molested my sister." Raven bent to the ground and picked up a rock, hurling it at him. The rock glanced off one of the iron bars; the man ducked just before impact.

"She was only five. She was a baby!" Raven scrambled to pick up more rocks, throwing them at him. A few made it through the bars, striking him in the chest.

The man fell back, lifting his hands to protect himself. "My name is Greg. I have a wife and two kids. I've never seen you before."

"Liar!" Raven roared. "I stayed awake every night, trying to protect her. But you got to her anyway. I screamed for my mother and you pushed me down the stairs to shut me up. You aren't shutting me up now, you worthless piece of shit.

"You say you broke your leg?" She bent down to his eye level. "Does it hurt? Are you afraid you'll never walk right?"

The man stared at her as if she were mad.

"Who the fuck cares about your leg? I'm crippled! I'll never run again." She spat at him through the bars. "I hate you!"

With a strangled cry, she reached through the iron bars, trying to strike him with her fists. The man dragged his injured leg behind him as he crawled to the back of the cell, evading her blows.

"You've got the wrong guy," he whimpered. "I swear to God, my name is Greg. I never hurt anyone. You have to believe me."

Raven spat again, gripping the iron bars tightly. "I hope you burn in hell. I hope you never walk again!"

William appeared to her right and touched her clenched fingers. Their eyes met. Without warning, she burst into tears.

"I'm innocent." The prisoner's voice grew more desperate. "I swear to God, you've got the wrong guy."

William bared his teeth and snarled. Wetness seeped through the prisoner's trousers and spread out beneath him. He covered his head with his arms, curling into a ball.

"One more word and I'll rip out your tongue." William gently pried Raven's fingers from the iron bars. "You don't speak to her."

The prisoner trembled in his corner, as he, too, began to sob.

With one final growl, William swept Raven into his arms. He doused the torches and carried her from the room, barring the door behind them.

Chapter Four

To say that William was concerned by Raven's reaction would be an understatement. The sound of her sobbing—a keening, soul-rending noise—tortured him.

He'd hurt her when all he wanted was to please her. Indeed, there was a part of him that wished to make the man who'd hurt her suffer. But he recognized that revenge was hers, not his. He had the power to give it to her and he did. He hadn't expected her anger to turn to sorrow.

Clearly, he didn't understand human beings.

Guilt—a very human emotion—bathed his insides. The sight of Raven's suffering also made him feel helpless, which was not a typical feeling for an old one such as himself.

A flash of memory overtook him, like a bolt of lightning across a dark sky. He was holding Alicia in his arms, watching as the very breath ebbed out of her. And there was not a damned thing he could do about it.

He'd failed Alicia. But he was a different being now, with different powers. He'd be damned if he failed Raven.

He sat next to her on the bed, placing his hand at the small of her back. "Cassita." She continued to cry, curled like a fetus on her side, as if she hadn't heard.

He rubbed at her back awkwardly, wondering if he should ring for Lucia. She'd likely suggest they administer a sedative. William wasn't sure he had a sedative on hand. Most of the medical supplies had been used in May, when he'd brought Raven back from the brink of death.

He recalled the night he'd brought a dying Raven into his home. He'd injected her with one of the oldest vintages in his collection. As the vampyre blood began to swim through her veins, she'd stared up at him with wide, frightened eyes. He hadn't known how to comfort her and had lapsed into Latin and Anglo-Norman, almost without realizing it. His whispered words had little effect. At one point, he'd had to sedate her, if only to keep her from pulling the transfusion tubes out of her arm.

Watching her cry was far more disturbing now, because he loved her.

"Cassita." He spoke firmly. "Cassita, listen to me."

"My sister," she managed between sobs. "My f-fault."

"No." William's tone was fierce. She didn't respond.

"It wasn't your fault." He grasped her biceps, pressing down for emphasis. "You protected her. You got her away from him."

Raven continued to cry. He waited, hoping she would cry herself dry, and she did. But what came next proved far more disquieting. She lay on her side, facing the wall, eyes open and unblinking.

When he spoke to her, she was unresponsive. When he tried to move her, he found that her body maintained the same posture, as if her muscles had stiffened. Even more alarming, her heart rate was uneven and her breathing was shallow. Sweat beaded on her forehead, even though the room was cool.

The physical changes in Raven frightened him. He worried he'd damaged her mind in some way, causing irreparable harm.

Minutes passed and his anxiety grew. Throwing caution aside, he placed his hands on either side of her face and looked into her eyes. "Raven, focus on the sound of my voice."

She didn't appear to see or hear him.

"You will relax your body and go to sleep. You will rest peacefully until morning, without worry or care." A moment passed without reaction, and then another, and William repeated his instructions.

His anxiety increased. He was far from confident that mind control would work; he was adept at using it, but Raven was strong-minded. And if somehow the sight of her stepfather had broken her mind . . .

Raven blinked and her large green eyes focused on his.

"Listen to my voice," he repeated. "Breathe deeply and relax your body."

All at once, Raven's eyes grew unfocused. In short order, her breathing deepened and her muscles relaxed.

"That's a good girl." He exhaled his relief. "Close your eyes."

She obeyed and he released her, pulling the covers over her dress and tucking them against her body. "Rest well, my love." He kissed her forehead, listening to her heart rate and breathing even out.

For several minutes, he watched her sleep. His sudden relief gave way to uneasiness. She was now under his control and he'd never been a more unwilling master.

A bird in a cage is never as beautiful as a bird that is free. His own words came back to him.

It was necessary to use mind control in this case, he reasoned. She was in acute distress. Something terrible was happening to her. He had intervened before it grew worse. Or irreversible.

He doubted she would view the situation the same way once he was in a position to explain himself. He wasn't looking forward to that conversation.

His gaze traveled to the version of *Primavera* that hung on his wall. The face of his former lover, Allegra, taunted him. He was seized with the recollection of her broken body on the ground beneath the bell tower after she'd jumped to her death.

Allegra's suicide was the result of revulsion and despair. Hundreds of years later, he was still troubled by the incident. And perhaps, although he would not admit it, he also felt responsible.

He looked back at the black-haired beauty who slept in his bed. They'd only been reunited a few hours before. He wasn't prepared to lose her.

William had expected her to be pleased with his gift, which he'd taken great care in procuring. He thought she'd relish the opportunity to exact justice from the man who had damaged her leg and abused her sister. Instead, she'd been horrified and upset. Even now, the sound of her wounded cries rang in his ears.

And he was responsible.

He pressed a kiss to the top of her head before placing the bracelet that marked her as his on her wrist. She'd returned the piece to him when they'd parted company. It was only right that she wear it again.

His lips fluttered over the pale skin that covered the veins in her wrist. He was hungry, it was true, but he couldn't bear the thought of feeding now. He left her to her artificial slumber and moved quickly to the first floor. Lucia and Ambrogio were given detailed instructions about Raven and the prisoner in the dungeon. Then William sent a message to Stefan, the principality's chief physician, summoning him to the private apartments at the Palazzo Riccardi.

Finally, William quit the villa, traveling to the palazzo via a series of secret passageways that lay below the city of Florence. He did not pray. God had damned him and his brethren. There was no point in cowering before him in order to ask for a favor, even for Raven.

He hoped sincerely whatever damage he'd done could be undone.

Chapter Five

S tefan of Montréal was the physician for the principality of Florence. He was much younger than the Prince and the other members of the Consilium, Florence's ruling council. But he'd been trained in twentieth-century medicine, and so his expertise in contemporary health and science was valued. For this reason, his youth as a vampyre was overlooked.

Nevertheless, when the Prince summoned him to the Palazzo Riccardi, Stefan worried his tenure had come to an end. In the past few years, the Prince had executed two Consilium members for failing to do their duty. Stefan was greatly concerned he'd become the third.

He tried to comfort himself with the thought that if the Prince wished to execute him, he'd do so at a Consilium meeting and not at one of his residences. This was a cold comfort, indeed.

"Is the vintage to your liking?" The Prince gestured to the warmed human blood Stefan was nervously sipping.

"Young and sweet. Thank you, my lord."

Stefan tried to wait patiently for the Prince to reveal the reason behind his summons, shifting his glass from hand to hand as the moments passed.

The older vampyre stood by a curtained window, seemingly lost in thought. His own glass of blood sat untasted on his desk.

Stefan found the fact curious.

"I think I broke my pet." The Prince spoke at last, keeping his back to the doctor.

Stefan placed his glass on a side table. "Is it dead?"

"What? No." The Prince turned and frowned.

"Forgive the intimate question, my lord. Has it fed from you?"

The Prince pressed his lips together. "No. And it isn't her body that's broken; it's her mind."

"Human minds, like human bodies, are easily broken." Stefan tented his fingers sagely. "It's their nature to be weak."

The Prince regarded him coolly before lifting his cup and tasting it. "Can broken minds be repaired? I've only had this pet a short time. It seems a shame to dispose of her so soon."

"The effect of vampyre blood on broken human bodies is well documented. The effect on human minds is lesser known. Who would waste their blood on a pet with a broken mind?" The physician chuckled.

He caught the Prince's narrowed eyes and abruptly stopped laughing. "I've never seen a psychiatric patient ingest vampyre blood. I admit it would make for an interesting experiment. I can't promise positive results, however."

The Prince placed his glass back on the table, his pale fingers tracing the rim. "In your medical training you must have dealt with the mind."

"Yes, when I was a student. But I'm a surgeon, not a psychiatrist. I served in the Canadian Army Medical Corps during the Great War, before I was changed. I saw men lose their minds in battle and I ordered their evacuation. Forgive me, but I was adept at removing shrapnel and amputating limbs, not treating shell shock."

"So there are treatments?" The Prince's tone was remarkably subdued.

"At that time, we used Freudian psychotherapy, convalescence, shock therapy . . ." Stefan's voice trailed off. He sipped his fortifying beverage. "Contemporary psychiatry is much more advanced. Now most disorders are treated with drugs and therapy. It depends on the condition and the patient."

The Prince nodded distractedly, sipping from his glass once again.

Stefan leaned forward in his chair. "Perhaps if your lordship were to tell me what precipitated the break in your pet, I might be of help."

"She suffered trauma as a child. Recently, she had an unexpected encounter with the person who inflicted the trauma. Her reaction to that short encounter was—puzzling."

"Puzzling in what way?"

"She vomited and screamed obscenities. She struck him and devolved into uncontrollable sobs."

"Ah," said Stefan. "Pardon, my lord, but those reactions are not puzzling to me. Clearly, the pet was upset about seeing the person and acted accordingly."

"That wasn't the puzzling part. Afterward, she lay unmoving, eyes wide and unseeing, with shallow breath. She didn't respond to my voice, and when I tried to move her she was stiff."

"How long did it remain like that?"

"Until I used mind control to put her to sleep."

Stefan's eyebrows lifted. "Isn't it normally under your control?"

The Prince smiled slowly. "I prefer my food to have a little more life in it."

The doctor lifted his glass in salute. "An old one such as yourself has no need of mind control. But I'm not surprised your pet required it in this case. What you're describing sounds like a condition called catatonia. A human physician would have run tests on your pet and medicated it. Where is it now?"

"She's still asleep."

"Have you tried to wake it?"

"No."

"You may have trouble. Catatonia, trauma, and mind control are a taxing combination. Even if you're able to wake the pet, it may not be the same."

The Prince's expression grew uneasy but he quickly adjusted it. "Do you mean the damage may be irreparable?"

"It's possible. The pet had a breakdown and you used mind control on it, which may exacerbate the mental problems. Think of it as using a hammer to repair a broken vase. All that you're left with is shattered porcelain."

"*Sard,*" he muttered. "What if you were to treat her?"

Stefan's hand shook as he guided his glass to the side table.

"I am your servant and I will, of course, do as you command. But there's little I could do that couldn't be done more effectively by a human psychiatrist who specializes in treating these kinds of cases. You'd have to remove the mind control before hospitalizing your pet, that is, if the control can be lifted. If your pet's mind is truly broken, the easiest solution would be to keep it under mind control until you tire of it. Of course . . ." He gestured vaguely.

"What?" The Prince's tone was sharp.

"Mind control works only because the conscious mind is being influenced. The pet's memories would still be intact, just not available to the conscious mind. As a physician, I'd worry your pet would still have psychiatric problems that even mind control could not eliminate. For example, it may remain catatonic."

"What if I were to execute the man who troubled her? Invited her to watch?"

Stefan restrained a smile. "With respect, my lord, you're thinking like a vampyre. If your pet is traumatized by merely seeing the man, think of what would happen if it were forced to witness his execution."

He broke eye contact and rubbed the back of his neck. "May I speak freely?"

"That is why I brought you here." The Prince leaned against the desk, crossing his arms over his chest.

"If you prefer your pets to have life in them, the level of mind control necessary to manage a broken mind would be too much. As I said, you'd be better off finding another, healthier pet. Even under mind control, the pet might be unpredictable, unstable." He gripped the armrests of his chair. "A security risk."

The Prince drained his glass. "Thank you, Stefan. I will take your opinion under advisement." His gray eyes fixed on the younger vampyre. "I assume you will keep this conversation confidential."

"Yes, my lord."

"Good." The Prince passed his thumb along the rim of his goblet, before placing it in his mouth. "Here's a remarkable piece of principality history: I've yet to execute a Canadian."

"Let me not be the first, my lord." Stefan bowed low and scurried out of the Prince's chambers.

Chapter Six

Raven's sleep was heavy and thick, like a wool blanket on a cold winter's night. She drifted through color and feeling, without dreams. Her body seemed to float untethered. It was a most unusual experience.

She heard William call her name, as if from a distance. She struggled to open her eyes and found him next to her, silently observing.

He lifted her chin with a cool finger and stared deeply into her eyes.

"Raven, I release you. Your mind is your own again."

She felt the dark haze lift and blinked confusedly against the lights in the room. Her focus moved to Botticelli's original version of *Primavera* hanging on the wall. It had always hung there, so its presence didn't surprise her.

But she was shocked to discover William had hung the sketch she'd done of him from memory—the sketch she'd left behind when they'd gone their separate ways—beside it.

Her heart rate quickened.

She surveyed her surroundings, noting the wine-colored curtains that enveloped the large four-poster bed.

"Cassita?" William's face was creased with worry. "How do you feel?" He lifted his hand to cup her face.

The joy she felt at the sight of him disintegrated when she remembered he'd broken her heart. He hadn't returned her love and she hadn't been willing to accept anything less.

She turned her head and his hand fell away. "Why am I here?"

"You're here to be with me, of course." His tone was unaccountably puzzled.

Raven gave him a dark look before shifting from under the decadent bedclothes. "We're over. We've been over for a while. This isn't funny."

"We are over?"

Raven heard something a good deal like panic in his voice. But that was impossible. William was stoic and unassailable. He would never panic.

"Yes. We broke up, remember? I can't believe you brought me here."

"Cassita." William placed his hand on her arm, his thumb brushing across her wrist next to the bracelet.

"Stop calling me that." She shook off his hand and quickly removed the bracelet, holding it out to him. "I returned this for a reason. Stop acting as if nothing changed."

When he refused to take the bracelet she tossed it on top of the bed. She swung her legs over the side and stood. Just as her feet hit the carpet, she was overtaken by an odd sensation.

Her right leg troubled her, as it usually did when she stood after lying down. But that wasn't the feeling that caught her attention.

No, she felt curiously bare beneath her dress. She smoothed her hands across her abdomen. Abruptly, she turned her back on him and discreetly slid her hand under the skirt. When she felt only skin, she froze.

"Where's my underwear?"

William was on his feet in an instant. "Raven, listen to me. We—"

"What happened to my underwear?" She turned on him in anger.

He pressed his lips together, his gray eyes clouded. "That's a pretty dress."

"I don't care what I'm wearing," she snapped. "I'm worried about what I'm not wearing. We're over. I haven't seen you in a month. Now I wake up in your bed with no memory of the night before and I'm not wearing any goddamned underwear!"

"You don't remember last night?" His voice was low, quiet, and tinged with disappointment.

She raised her arms in frustration. "What should I remember? Tell me."

He began to say something but apparently thought better of it. He stared at her for some time. All the while she clenched and un-clenched her fists.

"The color of your dress suits you," he said at last. "Was it for a special occasion?"

Raven scowled. "Gina and Patrick threw a birthday party for me. What does it matter?"

"I visited you afterward, at your apartment."

"Why?"

"Because it was your birthday." His voice grew gentle. "Because I care for you."

Raven closed her eyes and groaned. "Why are you doing this?"

"I am trying to help, Raven. I swear it. The party was last night. You can accompany me downstairs and call your friends to confirm the date." He gestured toward the bedroom door.

Raven bent her head to examine the folds of her green dress. The palm of her hand floated over the fabric the way a bird floats over a field of grass. She found the movement soothing and distracting.

"I remember the party. I gave Gina's cousin a lift home afterward."

"And then?" William prompted.

"I went home." Raven closed her eyes, seeing her kitchen in her mind's eye.

And William's beautiful figure, sitting at her kitchen table.

"I was waiting for you," he whispered.

Images crowded her mind, thick and fast.

"We flew together over the rooftops. You took me to the Duomo and showed me your city." She swallowed hard. "You told me—"

"Yes?" His tone was eager.

She opened her eyes. An incredulous expression passed over her lovely features.

"I told you I love you." He approached her cautiously and traced the arc of her cheekbone with the back of his hand. "You know me, Cassita. I think—" He paused, his ancient eyes tortured. "I hope you know I would never take you against your will."

A long look passed between them and she nodded.

He stroked her jaw. "You aren't wearing underwear because we came together, but only after I confessed I love you. I pledged myself to you and you did the same. We sealed our vows on top of the loggia by the Uffizi."

Raven's face flamed. "I remember."

"It was an act of love, Cassita, not deception."

Her mind clicked through images of the night before—his words at the Duomo, their passionate encounter on top of the loggia, and the story of Alicia, his murdered love.

Emotion bubbled up and overwhelmed her. She threw herself into his arms, pressing her cheek against his chest. "You came back to me."

"I never left."

He lifted her chin and kissed her firmly—a branding, determined kiss to demonstrate his sincerity.

His lips moved against hers as he spoke. "I never left you. I was the shadow on your wall. And even if you'd sent me away, I would have remained your shadow."

"I was so sad when we were apart. It was like I had a boulder weighing on my chest."

William's grip on her tightened and for some time they stood in one another's arms. He reveled in her softness, her warmth, her very being.

"It's almost sunset." He brushed his lips over hers once again. "You've been asleep all day."

"I don't understand why my brain was so foggy." She winked. "You didn't give me vampyre blood, did you?"

He straightened.

"William?"

"No, no vampyre blood." He forced a smile.

Raven glanced at her right leg, which still bore a scar. She moved it experimentally, finding the same limited range of movement she'd had the day before. Clearly, she hadn't experienced the healing properties of vampyre blood.

"How are you feeling?" His eyes searched hers.

She rubbed her forehead. "I'm all right. I remember our time together on the loggia. I remember you telling me you were bringing me here, but I don't remember anything after."

William hesitated, before his lips spread into a smirk. "I must have worn you out."

"Did I fall asleep on our way here?"

"I'm sure you're hungry." He kissed her forehead, then turned toward the door. "I'll ask Lucia to prepare dinner."

Raven caught his hand, tugging at him. William allowed himself to be stopped, staring down at the joining of their hands. He was of medium size and build, but extremely powerful, even for a vampyre.

He muted his strength when he was around her. Otherwise she'd never be able to restrain him.

"You're hiding something." Raven's green eyes narrowed.

He freed his hand, stretching his arm out. "Obviously not."

"You changed the subject when I asked you a simple question. And your eyes are guarded."

He stared, unmoving, like a deer that was attempting to avoid a predator.

Raven huffed. "I know you didn't give me vampyre blood. If you had, my leg wouldn't be aching. But it's difficult to believe I slept that soundly and awoke so confused simply as a matter of course."

"Sometimes oblivion is a blessing." His voice was low. "There are a thousand things I wish I could forget."

"You're scaring me."

William appeared to consider her remark. He sighed and pushed her hair behind her shoulder. "Something occurred that may have affected your memory, but that was an unintended consequence."

"I don't like feeling as if my memories are out of my control, whether it was intentional or not. Why do you look guilty?"

He withdrew his hand. "Guilt is for humans."

"You thought love was a human emotion. Yet you say you love me."

His expression darkened. "I don't simply *say* I love you—*I love you*."

She looked down, at the way her right foot turned out at an awkward angle. "We were apart for a month. You were free to pursue anyone you wished, including Aoibhe. You don't need to erase my memory in order to hide it."

"I'm not hiding sexual assignations," William growled. "Aoibhe holds no interest for me. I thought I'd made that clear. The only person I've pursued is you. The last time I had intercourse was with you, on top of the loggia. And the time before that was also with you, before you left me.

"I have not lived a chaste life in this body. But I'm not given to profligacy, especially now that I have the woman I want." William cupped her chin. "I will tell you about last night, after you've had something to eat and drink. My goal is to protect you, not harm you. I hope you will come to believe that."

Raven began to protest, but stopped. She had no reason to disbelieve him. Still, he was hiding something and, however it had come about, some of her memories had been lost.

He'd promised to tell her, though. She could give him the benefit of the doubt, at least until after dinner.

"I need to shower and change before dinner." She touched the skirt of her dress with dismay, noticing a couple of spots.

William nodded toward the closet. "There are clothes for you. Choose what you wish."

"You must have expected my return."

"Not expected." He brought her hand to his mouth and kissed it. "Hoped."

"Shower with me?"

William blinked. "Pardon?"

Raven pursed her lips. "I guess I hadn't thought about this. Do vampyres shower?"

"Of course." He sniffed. "Our sense of smell is very keen. Some of my brethren have a lax approach to cleanliness, but I make a point of shunning them."

Raven arched an eyebrow and he continued. "It's true. A few centuries back a Highlander and one of his near kinsmen applied to join my principality. I rejected them on scent alone."

Raven laughed, the happy sound filling the large master bedroom.

He appeared pensive. "I've never showered with another person."

"I haven't, either. But it sounds fun."

William chuckled and followed her to the en suite bathroom.

As she approached the threshold, she looked over her shoulder and noticed he was staring at her injured leg. Suddenly, she felt warm, and not in a pleasant way.

"I know it's ugly."

He stopped. "What is ugly?"

"My leg. The way I walk. The night those men attacked me, one of them called me Quasimodo."

"*Quasi modo?* That's nonsense."

"They weren't speaking Latin. Quasimodo is the name of the hunchback in Victor Hugo's novel *The Hunchback of Notre Dame*."

"And they called you this?" William's tone was sharp.

"I just remembered it now."

"I'm glad I killed them, for their blasphemy as well as everything else."

"I'm glad you saved me, William. I will always be grateful for that. But I'm sorry you killed them." She turned her back and entered the bathroom.

William scowled, reminded of the prisoner he held in his dungeon some floors below. He followed and turned on the shower, adjusting the water's temperature. He called her over to test it. Vampyres could sense hot and cold, but only vaguely. He worried the water would be too warm.

Raven watched as he efficiently disrobed, neatly folding every article of black clothing (with the exception of underwear, which he never wore) and placing them on the vanity.

She brushed imaginary lint from her dress as he stood in front of her, naked.

He was under six feet in height, his body lean and strong. Raven took a moment to appreciate the definition of his muscled chest and abdomen and the strong cast to his thighs. Not even a statue carved by the most talented sculptor could create a being with so much perfection. His face put her in mind of an angel, with its intense gray eyes that now looked at her expectantly.

She hid her face. "You said you loved me."

"I did. What's more, I meant it."

"Love is a peculiar thing. I've seen it. I've even cheered for it. But I never believed it was for me."

"Why shouldn't a beautiful, fierce young woman hope for love?"

"Because, as you put it, human beings are shallow."

"Love is deep." His rich voice echoed in the bathroom.

"Love is having the power to destroy another person."

William stepped closer. "Are you afraid of being destroyed?"

"Destroyed, consumed, betrayed." She fidgeted with the neckline of her gown.

William placed his hand over hers, stilling it. "Love creates; it doesn't destroy."

His lips found the place where her neck met her shoulder. He kissed her leisurely, tracing the path of her bared collarbone with his mouth. His fingers brushed her zipper. "Let me."

He undid her dress, dropping it to the marble tiles. Her bra followed. Finally, she was as naked as he, and his eyes roved her body appraisingly. "Here is a feast for my senses as well as my heart."

His pale fingers caressed her cheek, her mouth, and her neck. His strong hands cupped her breasts, her abdomen, and her hips. Eventually, his gray eyes met hers.

"The power you describe is the power you have here." He touched her forehead before moving his hand to cover her heart. "And here. It's the power you have over me. Power I haven't yielded to another since I was human." He brought his lips to her ear. "Your fears are shared."

With a slow kiss on her neck, he led her into the shower, standing behind her underneath a rainfall showerhead. Raven closed her eyes and lifted her face, like a flower following the sun. The warm water soaked her hair and streamed down the generous curves of her body.

"I've never showered with another person. What happens next?" William rested his hands on her shoulders.

She wiped the water from her face. "Whatever you want. Just don't let me fall."

William's gaze dropped to her right leg, which she was favoring. "Is the pain terrible?"

"It's worse after I've been lying down. Sometimes I topple over."

William spread his arm around her waist, drawing her back to his chest. "Then I must be sure to catch you."

She kissed him, reaching up to run her fingers through his wet hair as the water poured down their shoulders. Her motions were fraught with an eagerness born of love and affection and the relief of remembering she hadn't lost him.

He was hers.

Even now, naked, with a myriad of flaws few men overlooked, he embraced her. He embraced her imperfections.

He loved her.

His cool hands scorched her skin, splaying fingers wide over her abdomen and bringing her backside into contact with what rose between his hips. She gave him her weight and he held firm, nipping and licking at her lips before enticing her to enter his mouth.

He entertained the intrusion for a moment or two, then, with a growl, he spun her around, pressing their chests together.

Raven looked up into blazing gray eyes.

"Are you certain?"

She nodded.

"I need the words, Raven. I need to know you want this."

"I want you."

He took her mouth, his tongue alternately penetrating and re-treating in a sensual rhythm. She tilted her head, welcoming him, as the water continued to rain down. Hands roamed over slick skin as their lower bodies came into alignment. She touched his neck, his shoulders, his biceps, holding them tightly in an effort to remain upright.

William was not a tame lover. In his arms, she sensed his control, his desire, and the war that waged between the two. But he'd never harmed her and had always focused his attention on giving pleasure before taking it. Usually more than once.

"You're a dream." She sighed. "A dream of love I never thought I'd have."

His eyes burned into hers. Without warning, he lifted her, tugging her thighs around his hips. He lowered his mouth to her breasts, tasting and teasing before sucking droplets of water from her eager flesh.

She wrapped her arms around his neck, feeling him eager between her legs. He lifted her higher, hands beneath her backside, making sure he was correctly aligned.

"Breathe," he commanded, his eyes boring into hers.

Here was the vampyre, proud and powerful, teetering on the edge of control. He bared his teeth as if by instinct and his chest rumbled.

"Just don't break me," she whispered, pushing a lock of blond hair from his forehead.

William's expression grew even more fierce.

"I won't break you. Whatever harm I bring to you, I vow to heal."

He swallowed her reply with his kiss. Then with a single thrust, he entered her.

His kisses were as fierce as his movements as he pushed inside and withdrew, over and over. His grip on her backside tightened as he lifted and moved her in concert with his own motion.

Raven clung to him, her hand trailing to his lower back so she could urge him deeper. Not that he needed the encouragement.

Her breasts brushed against his chest, the friction teasing and arousing. She ignored the warm spray of the water, the scents of soap and William, and the nagging discomfort in her leg and ankle. Her focus was on feeling as he brought her swiftly to the brink of orgasm.

Before she could signal how close she was, she climaxed, her hand clutching his neck as she threw her head back. William continued his pace until she'd finished, his mouth dropping to her breasts, drawing one of them into his mouth.

When she opened her eyes, she found him staring at her hungrily.

"I have only begun," he rasped. "Breathe."

Chapter Seven

William stood from the bed, not bothering to cover himself. He'd spent two intense hours with Raven, who was now cocooned in a sheet, looking relaxed and happy.

In William's antiquated mind, none of their activities constituted making love. Love was something that either existed or not; it wasn't made and certainly not by the (admittedly exquisite) experience of joining bodies.

But he desired the curvaceous woman who watched him over the rim of her wineglass. He hungered for her, body and blood, with a yearning that bordered on desperate.

He also loved her.

He couldn't help but compare her current state with how she'd been the night before—the tears, the cries, and then the punishing silence. Stefan's assessment rang in his ears. While he was relieved she'd awoken in her right mind, he worried about how she would react when he told her about her stepfather. He was also anxious over her reaction to his use of mind control, even though he felt justified in using it. These anxieties fouled his mood.

"What are you doing?" Raven placed her wineglass next to a plate of food she'd lazily consumed after their coupling.

"Dressing," he clipped, pulling on a pair of black jeans (sans underwear). He kept his back to her as he buttoned a black dress shirt, tucking it meticulously into his jeans.

"You're finished with me."

At her tone, William whirled around. Raven looked as if she'd been smacked.

"I will never be finished with you." He gentled his voice as his eyes roved her body. "But your breasts are tender and so is the flesh between your legs. I must wait."

Raven's hand dropped to her lower abdomen. "You noticed?"

"Is that a genuine question? Or are you assuming I'd simply use you until you expired?"

She turned away, wincing at his anger.

"Forgive me." He ground his teeth. "I should have explained that I'm getting dressed because I must feed."

"You get irritable when you're hungry. So noted." Raven gave him a wry look. He sat next to her on the bed and pressed a repentant kiss to her lips.

"You could feed from me," she suggested.

"I feel the need for something stronger." His eyes darted to where her hand lay, resting in her lap. "I will feed from you again. Soon."

She pointed vaguely to where his gaze had alighted.

"Absolutely." The edge of his mouth turned up. "I think your swollen flesh would benefit from the coolness of my tongue. When the moment is right, I'll taste the blood that flows through your thigh."

Raven gaped.

William enjoyed her curious surprise. He also enjoyed the sight of her wrapped in one of his sheets. It was an image that should be captured in a painting and hung on his wall. He wondered if he'd be able to trust an artist to paint Raven in such an intimate moment, even if her nakedness was covered.

Quickly, he realized he wouldn't.

"Join me in the drawing room. Lucia will direct you."

"What should I wear?"

He gestured to the sheet.

She frowned. "I can't go downstairs like this."

"This is my home. You can wear—or not wear—whatever you like."

She pulled the fabric around herself more tightly. "Even if it was Halloween and you were hosting a toga party, I wouldn't walk around wrapped in a bedsheet."

William was puzzled by her remark but didn't bother to query her. He moved to the closet and shuffled a few hangers. "I have been looking forward to seeing you in this." He placed a long, black satin nightgown on the bed.

The gown was elegant but sensual, featuring a plunging back that would expose Raven's beautiful skin all the way to the top of her bottom. The front was almost as daring, with a deep V that would highlight her generous breasts.

Raven looked up at him with raised eyebrows. "Really?"

"There's also a robe, which in my view is unnecessary. Come to me when you're ready and I'll tell you what happened last night." He tried to keep his tone light, but knew that he failed.

Raven stared intently at the provocative satin that was draped casually across the bed and nodded.

William withdrew to the wine cellar that lay below the villa, deaf to the cries and weeping that emanated from the dungeon. He felt no remorse for holding the pedophile prisoner. He'd always despised pedophiles and had forbidden the practice in his principality.

The beast who lay in the cage down the corridor had violated Raven's young sister. William had read the reports. He'd also seen photographs of Raven's injuries.

He knew darkness. He knew evil. But he also knew there were

aspects of it that went beyond anything he could understand. He didn't waste time trying to solve the riddles of evil. Evil had its own logic and it was not something he, given his own moral code, would ever understand.

And humans think we are monsters.

He'd seen a great many things since the thirteenth century. Very little in human history surprised or shocked him, cloaked as he was in indifference. Yet he was not indifferent to Raven, or to her suffering.

He regretted not killing the pedophile when he had the chance. A death certificate would have made an excellent birthday gift. Why the devil had he hesitated?

William muttered a curse. He knew why.

As his hand hovered over the most valued vintages in his cellar, he paused. It would be easy, far too easy, to kill the pedophile and lie to her about it. But Raven had already demonstrated she could tell when he was being deceptive.

He needed old vampyre blood in order to strengthen his resolve, in order to find the words to tell Raven who he kept in his dungeon. Further, he'd have to confess to using mind control on her. He was not looking forward to that conversation or its inevitable aftermath.

His hands closed on a prized bottle, chosen for the strength its original owner had possessed. William needed the blood of an old liar, long dead, to give him the courage to tell the truth.

❈ ❈

A short time later, he sat in a large chair in front of the fireplace, scowling. The summer evening was too warm for a fire, but William liked it. Something about the sight, sound, and scent comforted him.

Raven didn't complain about the heat. She sat to his right in a matching chair, her uninjured leg curled beneath her, sipping a small glass of Vin Santo.

He'd almost finished. He tried to drink discreetly, so as not to disturb her. But he was determined not to hide his feeding from her.

"Is it good?" She gestured to the ornate gold goblet in his hand.

"Very." He lifted the drink as if in salute. "It's from the previous Prince of Florence. Would you like to taste?"

"No, thanks."

"That's probably wise. He had vice in abundance."

William drank sparingly before placing the goblet back on the table. For vampyres, blood and sex went together. Now that he'd fed one appetite, he felt another rise. Lust was certainly one of the old prince's vices and William felt it pulsing through his system.

He indulged himself in the luxury of admiring his lover's appearance. Her long black hair was wavy, having air-dried. Her skin held the luminous glow of a woman well bedded and her green eyes were bright and clear.

He found himself staring at the breasts that spilled over the deep neckline of her gown. They were ripe and tempting. He licked his lips, remembering her taste on his tongue.

Raven put her drink aside and gestured to the dark room, illuminated as it was by the fire and a single candle that burned on the table next to her.

"I'm beginning to think you don't like electricity."

Slowly, the vampyre lifted his eyes to meet hers. "We are more comfortable in darkness."

"I'm sorry."

"Bright light troubles me," he confessed, the words tripping from his tongue.

She had this way about her—this way of looking at him with those big eyes, propelling him to reveal his secrets.

"I didn't know." Raven's eyebrows crinkled with concern. "You kept the lights on upstairs."

"I wanted to see you."

She smiled half-heartedly and gestured to his drink. "Vampyre blood doesn't seem to affect you."

"That isn't true." William relaxed in his chair. "Vampyres aren't human, so blood doesn't affect us in the same way. But ingesting blood from a powerful vampyre increases my strength." *And my libido*, he added, but only to himself.

"Is that why you're resistant to relics? Because you drink vampyre blood?"

William started, but swiftly tried to cover his reaction. "No."

"You told me you don't know why you're different from the others—why you can walk in sunlight and on holy ground. But you know why you're resistant to relics?"

William forced himself to adopt a neutral expression. "I have a hypothesis, but not a demonstrated proof."

"I'm eager to hear it." She made herself more comfortable in her chair.

His gaze drifted to her neck. "Not tonight. We have more important things to talk about."

She shrugged and sipped her drink, hiding behind her glass. William was seized with the impression he'd been tested and failed.

"I've not shared my secrets with anyone." He looked down at his hands, turning them over in the firelight.

"Is that why you tampered with my memory? Because I uncovered one of your secrets?"

"No." William's response was sharp.

He lifted his goblet. "The story about relics involves the night I was changed. It was a dark time. I've never spoken of it.

"As for the blood, yes, it makes me stronger. But I am an old one and so its effects are lesser than they would be if a youngling ingested it." He drained his glass in two swallows before making eye contact with her and licking his lips.

Raven stared at his mouth, appearing both repulsed and mesmerized. "Why do I get the impression you're trying to seduce me?"

"Because there's nothing I want more than to take you now. I could beckon you to my lap and have you take your pleasure or we could couple on the floor, next to the fire."

Raven hesitated, the words of her beautiful, talented lover more than an enticement. "I asked you to let me in. You said you would."

"Some knowledge is dangerous."

"Fine." She sounded frustrated. "I'm not going to argue over every piece of information you refuse to share. Let's talk about amnesia. The last time I had memory problems was when you gave me vampyre blood."

"You had a head injury. It's possible the memory loss was caused by that."

"So vampyre blood doesn't always cause memory loss?"

"It can cause memory loss, yes, but euphoria is its most common side effect."

She crossed her arms over her chest. "I don't feel particularly euphoric at the moment. What happened last night?"

He turned his attention to the fire, as if its flames would give him the courage and wisdom he required. "Before I begin I need to know how you're feeling."

"I feel fine. Why do you keep asking me that?"

He scanned her face. "You don't feel . . . upset?"

"I'm annoyed you keep evading my questions."

He sighed. "Then let's begin. Do you remember bargaining with me for Emerson's life?"

Raven clutched at her heart and William's nostrils were filled with the scent of her sudden panic. "You didn't kill Professor Emerson, did you? Not after you promised you wouldn't."

William's gray eyes pinned her to her chair. "I keep my promises, as I shall shortly explain. I paid a visit to him in Umbria. He and his family are alive, but Mrs. Emerson is in need of a doctor."

Raven gave him a horrified look.

He shook his head. "You misunderstand. She has some kind of illness. I sensed it by smell and informed her husband. As I said, I keep my promises. You agreed to tell me about the 'accident.'" At this, he glanced at her right leg. "I agreed to spare the Emersons. The day after our conversation, I sent Luka to America to make inquiries."

"Inquiries about the Emersons?"

"No, about you."

"You thought I made everything up?" She slid her leg out from under her, placing both feet on the floor.

"Not at all. In fact, I believed you told me only part of what happened."

She grimaced. "I told you enough."

"For reasons I'll disclose in a moment, I ordered Luka to conduct a thorough investigation. He provided me with court records, witness statements, transcripts, and medical files."

The color faded from Raven's cheeks. "But they're confidential."

"Money can be a powerful motivator. When it failed, Luka used more creative means."

Raven screwed her eyes shut and turned away from him in her chair.

His voice grew soft. "I saw the reports and the photographs. What I saw more than angered me, Cassita. It grieved me. More than I can adequately express. You sustained much more than just a fall down the stairs while protecting your sister. There were bruises on top of bruises and injuries to your arms."

Unconsciously, Raven touched her left arm below the elbow. William followed her movement with watchful eyes.

"The file on your sister outstripped what you'd told me. I wanted to go to America to deal with the situation directly, but for various reasons, I had to remain here.

"I sent Luka to observe your sister and mother. As you said, your sister is successful and seems content with the man she's chosen. I assume you know about your mother's recent remarriage."

"Cara told me."

"If it had been up to me, I would have killed your mother. No reasonable adult could have been ignorant of what was going on in your household. She chose to ignore the signs and for that she should be punished. However, you asked me not to harm her. But your step-father—"

Raven rose to her feet, interrupting him. "That's enough."

She turned her back on him, lifting the robe that had been tossed carelessly over the back of her chair. She pulled it on, covering as much cleavage as possible before knotting the belt tightly.

"I find it depressing that you're only willing to share the barest of information about yourself, yet you feel compelled to send an investigator to Florida to find out everything about me and my dysfunctional family."

William watched her movements with increasing worry. He could smell the spike of adrenaline in her blood and he felt his lungs, almost superfluous as they were, constrict. It was a terrible feeling—to know he was hurting the person he loved. And he hadn't yet reminded her who was lying in a cell beneath the floorboards.

He had to tread more carefully.

"I take no pleasure in rehearsing these subjects with you," he said gently. "Far from it. Try to imagine, if you would, what it would be like if our positions were reversed. How would you feel if you discovered I'd had your experiences as a child?"

"I'd probably feel the same as you. But I wouldn't make you talk about it, because I'd know that makes it worse." Raven's shaking fingers went to the portion of her robe that opened around her neck and she pulled the fabric together, covering the base of her throat.

"There is a point to this, I promise. Something upset you last night and, for whatever reason, your mind blocked it out. I'd rather end my tale here." He hesitated. "But if you insist on hearing what happened, I shall tell you."

"I've come this far." She hobbled around the chair and picked up her glass, draining the contents.

"Would you like another?"

She set the glass down with a loud thump. "Is it that bad?"

When he didn't respond, Raven seated herself heavily in the chair. "Tell me."

William watched as she curled herself into a protective ball, pillowing her cheek against the back of the chair.

He passed a hand over his face. "I made a promise to you after our conversation. I promised I would give you justice. That's why I sent Luka to America. He discovered that your stepfather and his lawyers had manipulated the system in connection with the incident involving you and your sister. That is why he escaped punishment.

"When Luka located him, he discovered the man had used aliases before and after he married your mother. In fact, his marriage to your mother was fraudulent because he was already married."

"He was a sick fuck. That doesn't surprise me." Raven's tone was steely.

"Luka's investigation revealed a pattern. For most of his adult life, your stepfather would move from single mother to single mother, ingratiating himself into their lives for the purpose of gaining access to children."

William paused, watching Raven's reaction. She sat still, staring into the fire.

"Your stepfather has been living in California with a widow and her young sons. His marriage to her is invalid because he's still married to his first and only legal wife."

Now Raven looked at him. "The boys, is he—?"

"It seems his taste is for girls. But Luka discovered—" William stopped, for Raven's face had taken on a greenish hue. He went to her, crouching by the chair. "Cassita, look at me."

When she refused, he placed his hand on her knee. "It's finished. Luka exposed your stepfather and the group he was associated with. Many children were rescued, including those boys. All the pedophiles were arrested."

"There were many?" she whispered, her expression stricken.

William felt his lungs constrict further. He wished he could lie to her, deceive her, anything to protect her. It was quite possible she'd react the same way she'd reacted the previous evening, and all his honesty would be wasted.

He drew a deep breath, even though it was unnecessary.

"Yes. Because of you, the children were saved."

William watched as her hand covered her stomach, the fingers slowly curving into a fist.

"It's because of me they were hurt."

"That's false. You're the reason I went looking for him. You're the reason they were found."

"I let him get away. If he'd been put in jail in Florida, he wouldn't have hurt all those children."

He stood, leaning over her. "Don't take on sins that aren't yours."

"He's been doing this for years. I should have stopped him."

"Tell me what power you had as a twelve-year-old girl who was in the hospital with a broken leg. Your stepfather could have attacked your sister a second time, but you got her out of the house. You protected her."

"He got to her anyway." Raven picked at her robe, twining the fabric around her fingers.

"He's been caught now. And he won't escape."

"But I could have done more. Later on, when I was old enough, I could have filed other complaints. I could have gone to the media." She looked up at him. "Are you wealthy?"

William's brow furrowed. "Yes. Why?"

"How wealthy?"

He relaxed his posture, placing his hands in his trouser pockets. "I have property and investments. I hold a fair bit of currency in Swiss banks."

"Is it a lot?"

He paused. "Enough to destabilize Europe."

At her sharp intake of breath, he hastened to explain. "I've been acquiring assets since the thirteenth century. Apart from the theft of my illustrations, no one has ever stolen from me. At least, not for long."

"Then you can help them." She sat forward. "You can protect the children—make sure they can go to school. Give them a chance to see beautiful things."

"Why?"

"Because I'm asking." Her expression grew pleading.

"I don't intend to refuse," he replied. "But why are you asking?"

"So they can see a light that shines in the darkness."

William didn't know what to make of her—this lovely young

woman who wore her heart on the outside. This noble, fierce, generous lady who treated human suffering as if it were her responsibility to end it.

He touched her cheek. "You are the light that shines in my darkness." Then he placed his hand on her head, the way a priest blesses an acolyte. "That's why you studied art, isn't it? So you could find the light?"

"When you've been surrounded by ugliness, you can't help but want beauty. I did everything I could to make sure I'd be surrounded by it for the rest of my life. Father Kavanaugh helped me."

William froze. He hated priests almost as much as he hated God, for more than one reason. He withdrew his hand.

"I will instruct Luka to make arrangements for the children, anonymously, of course."

"Thank you."

He bowed.

Raven pointedly changed the subject. "What does my history have to do with last night?"

"There was an incident. You were upset. You wouldn't calm down and I didn't know what to do." He shifted his weight from foot to foot. "I used mind control."

"You what?" Raven leapt to her feet, forgetting the instability in her leg. She swayed and would have fallen, but he caught her. She pushed against his arm, trying to regain her footing. "Why would you do that?"

"Listen to me." He tugged on her arm, pulling her against his body. "You were crying hysterically. I had no idea what to do."

"Hysterical?" She placed both hands on his chest and pushed. "Men always dismiss women as being hysterical. It's their way of saying our feelings don't matter."

"I am not dismissing you." His grip on her tightened. "After you stopped crying, you lay on the bed, staring at the wall. You didn't move. You didn't respond. The sight of your suffering undid me. I couldn't stand by and do nothing. You, of all people, should understand."

She pushed against him a second time. "That doesn't justify screwing with my mind."

"Doesn't it? You risked rape and murder to end the beating of a homeless man. You spoke out to protect Aoibhe when those murderers cornered her." His hands slid from Raven's elbows to her waist. "You risked your life by standing between me and the hunters. Why? Because you love me.

"Don't you see? I'd cast my arm in the fire to ease your suffering."

Raven's demeanor softened. "You can't use mind control every time I'm upset."

"It wasn't just about your reaction."

"Then what was it?"

William's mouth slammed shut.

"What was it, William?" she persisted.

He made sure she was steady on her feet before releasing her. He turned his back and walked toward the fire, placing a hand on the mantel.

"Answer me, damn it!"

"I was afraid." The moment the words escaped his lips, William wished he could steal them back.

"Afraid?" Raven repeated. "You're a vampyre. You're a prince. What could you possibly be afraid of?"

"*Sard*," he swore, placing his other hand on the mantelpiece. He lowered his head, leaning heavily against his grip.

"William?"

"I was afraid I'd broken you."

Chapter Eight

Raven measured the vampyre's profile and the way the flickering firelight danced across his features. He was beautiful and terrible, a dark, avenging angel with something akin to distress radiating from his eyes.

"I broke Allegra. She climbed to the top of the bell tower and jumped." His eyes pierced hers. "I was afraid that in my quest to give you justice, I'd broken you. So I did what I could to ease your suffering. I meant what I said upstairs, Cassita. Your fears are shared."

Raven averted her eyes, fidgeting with the knot of her robe.

"How does it work?"

A pair of shiny black shoes entered her field of vision, stopping an inch away from her bare feet. A single finger lifted her chin.

"It's similar to hypnosis, I think. Not all human beings are susceptible to it. You, for example, are strong-minded enough to be resistant."

"Then why did it work last night?"

He released her. "Because you were overwrought."

Raven huffed. "Okay, I grant you hypnotized me or whatever because I was upset. But I want you to promise me you won't do it again."

He nodded.

"I need the words, William."

He clenched his fists. "I—promise."

She tensed, as if steeling herself for the next revelation. "Now tell me exactly why I was crying."

"It could start again." His voice held a warning. "You had an extreme reaction. What happens if it worsens?"

Raven rubbed her eyes with the heels of her hands. "I only remember bits and pieces of the week I spent here, after you rescued me. Even those pieces are hazy."

"You were unconscious most of the time."

"I decided I don't want to relive those moments. But I need to know what happened last night."

"Very well." William nodded in the direction of her chair.

"Just spit it out."

He took her warm fingers in his cold ones, cradling her hand in his. "I sent Luka after your stepfather because I intended to kill him. It was the least amount of justice you deserved and I wanted to give you that. When the time came, however, you and I were estranged. His execution wasn't a decision I thought I could make."

Raven's eyes widened. "William, what did you do?"

"I threw him down a flight of stairs."

"What?"

"I wrenched his arm, the way you described he wrenched yours. His leg is now broken and he sustained other, minor injuries." William's expression was noticeably absent of remorse. "I decided to reserve the true punishment for you to mete out."

Raven's face paled and she pulled away. "Where is he?"

William pointed to the floorboards. "Down there."

❀ ❀

It took some time for Raven to process what William was saying.

"He's here?" she whispered. "In the house?"

"Yes."

"I have to get out of here." She limped toward the door that led to the hall.

"He's locked in a cell, below the villa." William followed, speaking quickly. "He will never hurt you again, I swear it."

"Why did you bring him here?"

"I promised you justice."

"Justice." She laughed bitterly. "It's too late."

"It is never too late for justice. After I became a vampyre, years after Alicia was murdered, I tracked down her killers and ended them."

Raven's lower lip trembled. "Where were you when I was twelve?"

William caught her and encircled her with his arms. "You're mine now. No one touches you. No one hurts you. And everyone who has will pay."

She clung to him, hiding her face in his shirt. His arms tightened around her. "Your reaction to his presence now is about one-tenth of what it was before."

"I hate him, William. Of course I'm going to have an extreme reaction."

"I made a mistake bringing you to him. Seeing him face-to-face was too much of a shock."

Raven lifted her face. "I saw him?"

"It's a mercy you don't remember. I think it was the sight of him that caused you so much distress."

Raven began to tremble. He pulled back and began to rub her arms up and down. "Cassita, look at me." He paused until she made eye contact. "You're safe. You're here with me and you don't have to see him again."

"You're going to kill him?"

"Or we could turn him over to Aoibhe."

"Why Aoibhe?"

"She hunts and kills rapists. I doubt it would take much to persuade her to dispose of your stepfather. She'd enjoy torturing him."

Raven looked horrified.

"Cassita, I would prefer to be the one who ends him. But you're the injured party. You should decide."

"I never wanted to kill him. I just wanted Cara to be safe."

William leaned forward, his voice dropping to an urgent whisper. "Say the word and I will punish him. Leave his fate to me. You won't have to know."

"But I would know."

His gray eyes glittered. "You won't see remorse on my face. I feel none."

Raven was silent.

He rumbled in his chest. "Your stepfather deserves to be put to death. He struck you. He tried to kill you because you were protecting your sister."

"I failed, William." She disentangled herself from his arms, her gaze bending to the floorboards.

He set his teeth. "You didn't fail. You protected her—not once but several times. And in return, he threw you down the stairs. Say the word and he will breathe his last with my hand on his throat."

"What he did to the others was worse."

"Then do this for them. Do this for your sister." William's hands folded into fists, his body shaking.

Suddenly, Raven brushed past him, limping toward the door. "I can't make this decision."

"If you can't, then who can?" he called after her.

"Cara."

Chapter Nine

"*Es natural condición de las mujeres desdeñar a quien las quiere y amar a quien las aborrece.*"

A silken whisper came out of the darkness, tickling Aoibhe's ears as she trod lightly over ashes and bone fragments. She cut quite a figure, the tall, strikingly beautiful vampyre climbing the secret burial ground that lay outside the city of Florence. The air was thick with the scents of death and another, more pleasant aroma.

"Show yourself or I'll kill you, and this time, I won't lend you the power of resurrection." Aoibhe's voice was low, the Irish lilt of her speech giving the words a musical quality.

A hooded figure stepped out from behind a tree and bowed elegantly.

"Good evening, Lady Aoibhe." He addressed her in English. "You look beautiful, as always."

"This had better be important." She scanned the area, her senses alert. "It's dangerous for us to meet."

The figure laughed. "Why should you worry? Your pretty face and pretty lies will always save you. If I'm seen, my life is forfeit."

She lifted her nose imperially. "Say what you need to say and be quick about it. If they call a Consilium meeting, my absence will be noted."

"If the security system is anything like what it was, they already know you've left the city." The figure threw back his hood, exposing a mane of thick black hair.

"You look remarkably well for a dead vampyre." Aoibhe smiled.

Ibarra moved toward her, but she eluded him, retreating several feet.

"Don't touch me. I can't return to the city smelling of you. I was surprised to receive your missive. I thought you'd returned to your homeland."

He shrugged. "It's more convenient to plot my revenge here. What news from the principality?"

"Hunters managed to worm their way inside the city. A group of them attacked me, but the Prince came to my rescue."

Ibarra stared in surprise. Abruptly, his dark eyes narrowed. "Why should he come to your aid? He takes pleasure in killing members of the Consilium."

Aoibhe preened. "We are allies, he and I. He knows there are traitors amongst us. And he trusts me."

The Basque regarded her with cold calculation before slowly shaking his head. "Why haven't you found them yet?"

"They're keeping themselves well hidden while casting suspicion on others. They sold the schematics of the security systems to the Venetians, but implicated Christopher and his people. They helped the feral enter the city, implicating you and causing your execution."

"We need to find them. I won't rest until I've made them pay." Ibarra growled.

"I want my revenge, as well. After your death, they colluded with the hunters, advising them where to find the Prince and me. I barely escaped with my life."

Ibarra's dark brows lifted. "You and he were together?"

Aoibhe tossed her long red hair. "Yes, what of it?"

"Your loyalties are divided."

She spat out an Irish curse. "And your jealousy is tiresome. You pledged fealty to me, Ibarra. I saved your life and I keep your secrets. Cross me and I'll inform the Prince that you're alive."

Ibarra lunged toward her, but she leapt to the side, baring her teeth. "I'm the best friend you have, Basque. Don't provoke me."

He hesitated. Then, through a great exertion, he appeared to calm himself. "We had a pact to overthrow the Prince."

"We still have a pact. Help me destroy him and we'll rule Florence together. Oppose me, and I'll see your head displayed on a spike in the center of the great hall. *Again.*"

A long look passed between the two supernatural beings. Then, surprisingly, Ibarra's mouth widened into a grin. "You're more dangerous than he is."

"Hardly." Her posture relaxed, but she still kept her distance. "Now, to continue my report. The borders appear secure and the hunters have been killed."

"There are more. I encountered a group not fifty miles from here."

Aoibhe's eyes widened. "Are they headed here?"

"I've kept my distance, but I could be persuaded to learn more." He surveyed her features. "Who do you suspect of being a traitor?"

"Max is involved, I'm sure of it."

"Max is lazy and stupid, which is my good fortune. He couldn't be bothered to burn my corpse."

Aoibhe grinned. "Amazing how enemies so soon become allies. I agree—Max isn't intelligent enough to mount a coup. Someone is guiding him."

"Niccolò."

"He's the obvious choice," she mused. "But why didn't he seize control when we were at war with Venice? He assumed the role of prince in order to make the Venetians think their assassination attempt was successful."

"He knows he isn't strong enough to fell the Prince, even with Max's help."

"That's true." She shivered. "It would take an army to fell him. The more I've seen of his power, the more I realize we'd need the entire city to aid us."

Ibarra came a step closer. "What aren't you telling me?"

She smiled artfully. "Nothing you don't already know. He's an old one, perhaps the most powerful next to the Roman. And he seems to have a strange sort of magic that protects him and his precious villa."

"What's the source of his magic?"

"If I knew, I wouldn't need your help in killing him."

Ibarra's hand tightened on the hilt of the sword that hung at his side. "Killing the Prince will be difficult. We should start with an easier target."

"Who?"

"Niccolò."

"If he's the traitor, we need him alive so he can do his work," Aoibhe said. "We wait for him to fell the Prince, then we kill him and seize the principality."

Ibarra's dark eyes glinted. "You won't be alive to do so."

She frowned. "Why not?"

"Haven't you read his work? He speaks of eliminating threats to a principality before the transfer of power. If Niccolò is the traitor, he'll kill everyone on the Consilium except his closest ally before he kills the Prince."

Aoibhe closed her mouth with a snap. "I hadn't thought of that."

"So you do need my help, after all." He winked maddeningly at her.

"You're wasting time," she hissed. "What are we to do?"

"I agree it would be easier to wait and kill the Prince's successor, since certainly he won't be as powerful as the Prince. But a coup may fail. If we're on the wrong side, the Prince will end us. And there's the added difficulty of avoiding assassination by the traitor, if he decides to eliminate his rivals."

"I shall try my best to stay alive," Aoibhe rejoined dryly.

"We need to discover the traitor as soon as possible. And we need to be cautious, especially around the other Consilium members. Trust no one."

Aoibhe cocked an eyebrow at him. She took a moment to examine their surroundings, the city that lay beneath them, sparkling like a jewel, and the dark woods nearby.

"It's too dangerous for you in Tuscany. Return to the Basques and I'll send word when it's safe for you to return."

"How shall we seize power if I'm miles away?"

"By watching and waiting. Whoever is behind the attacks must be growing impatient. We wait for them to reveal themselves and assist them with the coup."

"That's a risky proposition. They may decide to end you first."

She smoothed the front of her dress. "I know how to protect myself."

"What about Lorenzo?"

Aoibhe waved an impatient hand. "I grew tired of him over a century ago. I'm looking forward to killing him, but only after the Prince is dead."

"And what of the Roman? Or the Curia?"

"Neither will interfere unless our conflict is made visible. So long as the humans remain none the wiser, we are safe. Let the traitors risk exposure and depose the Prince, while we wait in the wings."

Soft laughter came from Ibarra's lips. "You're far more cunning and dangerous than that pretty face suggests."

"Men have been underestimating me for centuries." Her voice grew harsh. "Don't make the same mistake."

"Oh, I won't, fair Aoibhe." Ibarra offered her an appraising look. "I won't."

Chapter Ten

Raven sat in front of her computer in her small apartment in Santo Spirito, waiting for her sister to respond to her request for a video chat.

She'd just completed a sketch of Saint Michael, sword in hand, poised to defend those in need. He was the saint she'd begged to intervene when her sister was being stalked by a monster. But the saint, if he existed, had ignored her pleas.

In this sketch, Michael figured as a warrior with the wings of an angel and the visage of a vampyre prince. Almost twenty years later, he'd come to her defense. The damage, however, was irreversible.

Her defender was, at that moment, on his way to an undisclosed location in order to take care of principality business. He'd been angry when she insisted she needed to speak with Cara before pronouncing judgment on their stepfather. But his anger had been dull, not sharp, and quickly gave way to resignation.

He was distracted, Raven thought, or he wouldn't have yielded so easily. She was fairly confident his distractions were related to her and not to the principality, because he'd intended to be at her side while she spoke with Cara. In fact, he'd refused to leave her and it was only after repeated requests from someone on the other end of Marco's cell phone that he'd relented.

Raven believed guilt and remorse were emotions William experienced, but in a blunted way. He didn't understand the burden she carried over failing to protect her younger sister. He couldn't fathom the depth of her guilt.

It was close to eleven when he'd driven with Raven to Santo Spirito. They could have traveled on foot—or rather, William could have traveled on foot and supported Raven while they ran through the dark streets. But he insisted on taking the Mercedes, as if he wanted to keep her away from prying eyes.

He'd pressed his lips to her forehead before directing Marco to accompany her upstairs. He said he'd see her soon and made her promise to call Ambrogio if she needed anything.

Raven's insides twisted as she remembered the way William had looked at her before she exited the car, almost as if he were afraid.

Something was wrong.

She was staring at the sketch of Saint Michael and his beautiful face when her computer chirped. Cara's image filled the screen.

"Happy birthday, Rave. Did you have a good time at your party?" Cara's large blue eyes surveyed her sister's face. "What happened? Did you bump into Bruno?"

Raven put her sketch aside so Cara couldn't see it. "No, I didn't bump into Bruno. I never see him anymore. And I had a good time at the party."

Cara frowned. "You don't look happy."

Raven fidgeted in her seat. "I have a lot on my mind."

"Well, I hope this will cheer you up. Dan and I are talking about coming out to see you in August. Would that be all right?"

"That would be great." Raven smiled and her smile was genuine. "It's been too long since I've seen you."

"You look different." Cara leaned closer to her computer's camera. "Have you lost weight?"

"A little." Raven shifted uncomfortably.

"I called you yesterday but you didn't answer. I sent you a present. Did you get it?"

"Not yet. The mail can be slow."

"When it arrives, let me know. I think you'll like it." Cara settled back in her chair. "What's up?"

Raven struggled to find the right words.

"Seriously, Rave. Tell me what's wrong." Cara sounded impatient.

With a sigh, Raven decided to blurt out the problem. "Someone contacted me about David."

"David who?" Cara carelessly flicked a lock of long blond hair over her shoulder.

"David who was married to Mom."

Cara's eyes met her sister's. "Why would someone contact you about him?"

Raven looked down at her sketch of Saint Michael as she frantically tried to create a credible lie. "Um, a private investigator was looking into David, and he found out about us. He said David was married to someone else before he married Mom."

Cara shrugged. "We knew that. He was a widower, remember?"

"The investigator said his first wife is still alive. They're still married."

Cara inspected her fingernails, which were painted a pale pink. "So he was a bigamist. Who cares? Mom divorced him and married Stephen. Don't let some jackass get you all bent out of shape. You're supposed to be celebrating your birthday and having fun. Were there any cute guys at the party?"

Raven studied her sister's face. "*Who cares?*"

"Yes, Rave, *who cares*. Don't bring up that old shit. It's time to let it go." Cara adopted a singsong voice and began repeating the last three words.

Raven interrupted. "David was part of a pedophile ring in California. That's why he was being investigated."

Cara examined her fingernails once again. "Is he in jail?"

"Not exactly," Raven hedged. "The investigator has him."

Now Cara made eye contact. "What do you mean, the investigator has him? How do you know?"

"The investigator told me. Someone wants David to pay for what he did to those children, and not by going to jail."

"That's crazy!" Cara exploded. "Who is that guy?"

"Forget about that. The investigator wants my opinion. What should I tell him?"

"About what?"

"About what should happen to David. About what we want to happen to him."

"Do you have any idea how crazy this sounds? Some guy contacts you out of the blue, asking what you want done to your stepfather. That is whacked. You need to call the police."

Raven studied her sister. "Is that what you want?"

"What does it matter what I want? This has nothing to do with me. I'm talking about what you should do."

"He saw the police records."

Cara turned away from the camera and began rummaging in her purse. "There's nothing to see."

"*Cara,*" Raven whispered.

Cara's eyes moved to her sister's and, for a moment, Raven thought she saw acknowledgment. Her sister retrieved what looked like a tube of lipstick and began painting her mouth with it.

"You need to call the cops. The guy who called you is a nutcase. How did he find you? You go by a different name."

Raven bristled. "He isn't crazy. He found me because he's good at finding things. He wants to hear what we think. He's offering us justice."

"Justice?" Cara laughed. "Some lunatic approaches you and says he has our stepfather, and you want advice about what he should do to him? I can't believe you haven't called the cops already."

"We weren't the only children he hurt." Raven leaned toward the camera. "But we're the oldest. The investigator wants to give us closure."

Cara tossed her lipstick into her purse and moved out of range of the camera.

"There's no *we*, Raven. There's just you. You want some stranger to do God knows what to David. Why? Because you had an accident and fell down the stairs?"

"I didn't fall down the stairs. He pushed me!"

"Yeah, keep telling yourself that."

Pain shot through Raven's middle at her sister's words. "I don't care about me." She clutched her laptop screen with both hands. "Are you listening? It was never about me. It was about you."

"It wasn't necessary."

"Someone had to protect you."

"Protect me from what?"

"From what he did to you!" Raven shouted.

"He didn't do anything!" Cara slapped her hands on the desk. "How many times do I have to tell you? Nothing happened! He never touched me. Do you hear? He never touched me!"

"*Cara*," Raven managed. Cara turned her face away and began to cry. Raven reached for the screen. "I'm sorry."

"What the hell is going on?" Dan, Cara's boyfriend, came into view of the camera. He tried to put his arms around her but she pushed him away.

"Fuck you, Raven!" She turned toward the camera, her face filling the screen. "Fuck you."

"Cara, I'm sorry. If you could just—" Raven's plea was cut off by Cara's disappearance and the sound of a door slamming.

"What just happened?" Dan crouched so he could see Raven's face on the computer.

"I didn't mean to upset her. We were talking about our former stepfather. I just found out he was part of a pedophile ring in California."

Dan cursed. "Why did you tell her that?"

"I wanted to know how she felt about it. I wanted to know what would give her closure."

He stood, facing the door. The sounds of Cara's sobs could still be heard in the background. He moved toward the computer once again. "You upset her."

"I was trying to help her."

"I don't want you bringing up that shit again."

"She's my sister." Raven felt a tear slide down her cheek.

"She doesn't need your help. Nothing happened to Cara and I want you to stop trying to convince her that it did."

"Dan, I—"

"Stay out of our lives. That's it, Raven. I mean it."

Before Raven could protest, Dan ended the chat.

For a long time she sat, staring at the computer. Then she walked to her bed and crawled under the covers, pulling them over her head.

❈ ❈

Gregor moved away from Raven's bedroom window and climbed to the roof. He leapt from building to building with the intention of informing the Prince about what had just happened to his pet.

In truth, he was confused. He didn't understand the subject of the argument or its context. However, it was clear the pet was distressed, which meant he needed to report that fact with haste.

As he dropped to street level and approached one of the secret entrances to the underworld, he quickened his pace, hoping the pet would not harm herself before he could deliver his report.

He wanted to keep his head.

Chapter Eleven

"This is disturbing." The Prince folded the handwritten report and placed it carefully on his desk.

He was seated in one of his personal rooms near the council chamber that lay at the heart of the underworld. A set of flickering candles sat to one side, the only illumination in the dark space.

"Yes, my lord. That's why I thought you should see it immediately." Niccolò stood in front of the desk. His face wore a look of intense concentration as he watched his ruler's reaction.

"What news from Rome?" The Prince placed his hand on top of the report, as if by pressing down he could lessen its threat.

"None. As usual, the Roman seems to operate without the Curia's interference. If you recall, Lorenzo was told personally by the Roman's lieutenant that Rome's support ends when the Curia's involvement begins."

"I am aware of that." The Prince's hand folded into a fist. "I am also aware of the fact that Rome is Florence's ally."

A look of surprise flitted across Niccolò's features.

"Nevertheless," the Prince continued, "we don't want the Curia here."

"No, my lord. If I may?"

The Prince waved his hand in his security adviser's direction.

"Thank you. The war with the Venetians was kept quiet. The Curia heard of it but did not interfere, probably because they were delighted two principalities were at war."

"Obviously," the Prince commented dryly.

"But the murder of the Interpol agent by a feral drew international attention. Then there were the bodies found downstream. And more recently, the incidents with the hunters."

"I am well aware of our most recent history, Sir Machiavelli. Have you anything new to contribute?"

Niccolò schooled his features, hiding his irritation. "Forgive me, my lord. Now that it's clear the eyes of the Curia are on Florence, it may be the time to enact stricter laws on feeding and killing."

"Our laws are already some of the strictest. That is how we've avoided their attention."

"True, but a gesture of strictness may ameliorate the situation."

"Our citizens have always enjoyed their liberty," the Prince mused.

"There will be no liberty to enjoy if the Curia enters the city. Remember what they did to Prague."

The Prince was filled with revulsion. He remembered the reports of how the Curia had entered Prague and slaughtered most of its supernatural inhabitants as punishment for widespread, indiscriminate killing. It was a genocide.

"My lord?" Niccolò's voice broke into the Prince's reflections.

He straightened in his chair. "Outline your analysis and recommendations. I'll review them and call for a Consilium meeting tomorrow."

"With respect, my lord, the proclamation should come from Florence's Prince and not the Consilium."

"I don't disagree. But the support of the Consilium is useful for my purposes."

Niccolò bowed. "Of course, my lord."

"You are dismissed."

The Prince stroked a hand across his chin as he watched his adviser's departing form. He would do what was necessary to avoid confrontation with the Curia. Even as he made plans on how to do so, his thoughts strayed to a certain young woman, wondering how she would fare if their most dangerous enemy ever entered the city.

He lifted a copy of one of Machiavelli's works from the desk and opened it, noting with satisfaction that the missive he'd hidden inside was still there. He reshelved the volume in one of the bookcases, not because he thought he'd ever need to produce the secret message, but simply because it was precious to him. And he wanted it to remain hidden.

Chapter Twelve

As the first rays of morning sun illuminated the city, Raven awoke to discover a naked vampyre in her bed.

It was not an unwelcome discovery.

The bed was narrow—too narrow for two persons. Somehow William had slipped between the sheets without disturbing her. His naked body was spooned behind her, his arms around her waist, his long legs entangled with hers.

It was very comfortable, despite the coolness of his skin. She closed her eyes and settled into his embrace.

"I wondered when you'd stir." William chuckled in her ear.

"You could have woken me."

"And miss the opportunity to do—whatever they call this?"

"What?"

He squeezed her waist. "I don't know what it's called, the way we are lying together."

"It's called *spooning*."

William paused. "That is an extraordinarily silly description for something this sensual."

Raven laughed and snuggled closer. He pressed a smile against her hair. "I enjoy the sound of your laughter. I can't remember the last time I heard it."

"I haven't had much to laugh about recently."

He flexed his hand against her abdomen, pulling her back against the cradle of his hips.

She sighed. "It's fine."

"Do not do that."

"Do what?"

"Lie."

"I'm not lying." Raven fidgeted with the old T-shirt she was wearing.

William's hand slid to cover hers. "I can tell when you aren't being truthful. I can hear it in your heartbeat. I can smell it through your skin."

"Which is extraordinarily creepy and annoying," she mumbled.

"Almost as annoying as humans who mumble." William nipped at her ear playfully. "Tell me about your conversation with your sister."

She twisted in his arms, but he wouldn't release her. "I don't want to talk about it."

"And her decision regarding your stepfather?" William touched the edge of her jaw, a gentle touch, as if he were trying to coax her to look at him. "I am sorry your conversation with your sister was not what you hoped."

"That's an understatement."

William was quiet for a moment. Raven could almost hear him thinking. "You—concern me."

She recognized his remark as akin to an admission of weakness. "Why?"

"I can't stop thinking about the other night. How upset you were." Raven's lips twisted. "I'm sorry."

"I don't want an apology. You have nothing to apologize for." William pushed his hair back from his forehead, his body noticeably tense. "What I want is to care for you."

"You care for me well enough." Raven relaxed minutely, thinking back to their shower together the previous evening. She felt her skin grow warm.

"I meant with respect to your heart and mind, not just your body."

"My heart and mind are part of my body," she whispered.

"Which is why I must care for them all." Leisurely, he entwined their hands. He brought their connection to his mouth and began kissing the tips of her fingers. "I thought I was giving you a birthday gift, but I gave you a burden instead. I'd like to remove that burden. But I can wait."

Raven changed the subject. "What about you? You seemed distracted last night."

"We have some concerns about the principality."

"Are they serious?"

"Yes, but they're being addressed."

"What kind of concerns?"

He began kissing her fingertips once again, drawing them into his mouth and laving them with his tongue. "I don't want you to take on the worries of the city. You have enough trouble."

"I care about you, William. If you're worried, so am I."

He kissed the back of her hand. "You honor me with your concern."

"Then honor me by telling me what you're worried about."

"Only if you agree to tell me about your conversation with your sister."

Raven swore, her body tense. "All right." She relented after a pregnant pause. "You go first."

William's body shifted next to her. He looked surprised. Clearly, he hadn't expected her to agree.

"Vampyres are prey to two groups. You met the weaker one, the hunters. Our spies informed us the stronger group, the Curia, has turned its eyes to Florence. We do not want their scrutiny."

Raven placed a hand on his arm. "When you say Curia, are you referring to the Vatican?"

"Not precisely," he hedged.

"Then who are they?"

"Our sworn enemies. A powerful group of human beings with—shall we say—supernatural abilities." William watched her reaction, cocking his chin in the direction of her chest. "This is what I was worried about. I've made your heart race."

"You can't keep secrets from me just because I'll get upset. I'm not made of glass. I'm not going to break."

His expression tightened. "Human beings are easily broken."

"I'm not."

He stroked a single finger over the scar she wore on her forehead. "Unfortunately, my sweetheart, you are only too breakable. A break of any part of you is not something I can sustain."

Raven lowered her eyes, a hesitant smile creeping across her face.

William's finger traced the curve of her lips. "It isn't something to smile about."

"You called me *sweetheart.*"

"And?"

"No one has called me that before."

"It suits you. You're all sweetness and heart. And all mine." He kissed her firmly. "You have the sweetest heart I've ever had the pleasure of listening to."

Her smile deepened. "Tell me your troubles and we'll move on to sweeter things."

William pulled back, his expression shifting. "Florence has avoided the attention of the Curia since I became prince, primarily because I enacted two laws—one that prohibited feeding on children and one that prohibited indiscriminate killing."

"What's 'indiscriminate killing'?"

"Killing a human every time we feed. Long ago, I persuaded my brethren that food would be more plentiful if we fed without killing. Further, our citizens are not permitted to kill for sport, as a disproportional murder rate attracts unwanted attention. Those who cannot abide by our laws are invited to leave. Forcefully."

"If the laws have been in place all this time, why is the Curia coming after you now?"

"They heard about the corpses found by the river and about the feral who killed the Interpol agent. They know we wiped out the last incursion of hunters. Since all these events happened in a very short period of time . . ." His voice trailed off.

"What does that mean?"

"It means if they don't like what they see in future, they'll intervene." His face grew grim.

Raven's eyes fixed on his. "How?"

"They'll send an army and lay waste to us."

Raven sat up. "They'll kill us?"

William frowned. "Not you. The Curia is sworn to protect human life, which is why they're eager to wipe us out."

"Can you fight them?"

William rolled to his back and stared at the ceiling. "We can try. We may even succeed in killing some of them. But they have weapons from which we cannot defend ourselves."

"Don't take this question the wrong way, but if they have powerful weapons and they mean to destroy you, why haven't they?"

William's gray eyes grew glacial. "They know it is beyond them to eradicate evil."

"You aren't evil."

He turned back to the ceiling.

She touched his chest. "What about the other principalities, wouldn't they help?"

He grimaced. "The last time multiple principalities banded together to fight the Curia was in the Middle Ages. We outnumbered them, which is why the war went on so long. But we could not defeat them.

"The war caused widespread panic and death. Eventually a truce was negotiated, a truce that declared vampyres would live underground, in secret, and cede control of the human population to humans. If another principality were to come to our aid in a conflict with the Curia, it would break the truce and result in a world war. No one wants that."

"If the Curia were to attack Florence, your neighbors would let them?"

"Not only would they let them, they may be tempted to assist them, if the Curia were to promise to leave them alone."

Raven's eyes widened in horror.

He lifted his hand to caress her cheek. "Before you panic, you should know that there's no guarantee they will come. Conflicts with the Curia draw public attention. The Curia prefers to operate in secret."

"At the moment, they're just watching?"

"Yes. I must be especially attentive to the principality and I must take great care to protect it."

"I understand." Raven felt cold all over. She reclined once again, burrowing under the covers.

"I hope you don't." William pulled her until she was draped over him and they were face-to-face. "I hope you never understand. The farther away the Curia is from you, the better."

"You said they're sworn to protect human life."

"Yes, but since you've become what they call a feeder, they'd take great pains to separate us. But enough of this. There's no point in you worrying about things that may never come to pass." He took her lips in a long, deep kiss.

"I don't want to lose you," Raven whispered.

He pushed her hair behind her shoulder, a smile playing about his lips. "It's strange to see a human so concerned with the fate of a group of vampyres. Then again, I should have known your protective streak was extensive enough to apply to various creatures."

"I don't believe in indiscriminate killing. And I don't care who the Curia are or who they think they're protecting. Vampyres are sentient beings and their lives should be respected."

"Spoken like a true protector," he whispered.

His hands firmly gripped her bottom as his tongue teased at the seam of her mouth. He took his time, gently tugging at her lower lip and nipping on it, only to cover her mouth with his own and stroke his tongue over hers.

When they parted, Raven felt a good deal too warm.

William began dancing his fingers up and down the curve of her spine. "Enough of my troubles. What did your sister say?"

"You're naked."

He barely suppressed a chuckle. "I can't imagine your sister saying that."

Raven rolled her eyes. "I'm talking about you."

William's hands splayed across her bottom as she lay atop him. "Yes, I am naked."

"Why?"

"Why should I wear clothes when sleeping next to the woman I love?"

Raven's heart stuttered.

Of course, he could hear it. "What is making you anxious? Nakedness or love?" His fingers sifted through a lock of hair that spilled over his chest.

"Both."

"For what reason?"

"This is all very new."

William's hand slipped from her hair to her lower back, lifting the hem of her T-shirt. "I like the way you feel. I like discovering new things about your body—how you react to my touch, to my kiss, to my body when it's inside yours. You are a book that deserves to be read over and over again."

She smiled and pressed her breasts to his naked chest, reveling in the cool smoothness of his muscular form.

"We'll talk about your sister later. Go back to sleep."

"I'm not sure I can. At least, not like this." Raven moved her injured leg, wincing.

"Sweetheart," he murmured. In a flash, he switched positions, placing her gently on her back and hovering above her, kneeling between her legs.

Raven felt herself flush.

She looked up into intense gray eyes. "Are you really afraid of losing me?"

"Without qualification." He put his weight on his forearms, at her sides.

"Then we're the same."

William bent his head so he could kiss the swell of her breasts through her T-shirt. "We are not the same. You are a soft, warm, desirable woman whose body is a wonder of divine artistry."

She drew him down so she could hide her face in his neck. "Go easy on the compliments, William. I'm not ready to hear them."

"That is a tragedy."

She clutched him more tightly.

"I am sorry about your sister." He spoke next to her ear.

"She doesn't believe me."

"That I have your stepfather?"

"No, she doesn't believe my stepfather attacked me. She thinks I fell down the stairs."

William's grip on her tightened. "She doesn't remember?"

"You read the files. She was traumatized. Over the years, I've tried to talk to her about it, but my mother always inserted her version of events. Last night it became clear Cara's memories are completely suppressed."

"I take it, then, your sister isn't interested in justice."

"You could say that."

The lovers were silent for a long time. Eventually, Raven began nuzzling his stubbled throat with her nose. "You have whiskers."

"I am male, in case you hadn't noticed." He flexed his hips as if to prove his point.

"I've noticed." She lifted her head and brushed her lips across his. "But I thought vampyres stayed the same."

"We change in slight ways. Our hair grows, as do our nails, but very, very slowly."

"Good to know." She kissed him once again, before dropping her head back on the pillow.

"What will you do about your sister?"

"I'm hoping I can repair my relationship with her. Someday."

William frowned. "Is there a chance it's beyond repair?"

"She was really upset. Her boyfriend told me to stay out of their lives."

The barest rumble escaped William's chest. "Do you want me to deal with him?"

"God, no." Raven cringed. "Dan is a good person. He's upset because Cara is upset."

"I can arrange to have the files sent to them. They'll have to admit you're telling the truth."

"No. Some grief is so great, it can't be felt; it can only be observed. Or denied. Let Cara have her denial."

"You're protecting her again." William squeezed Raven gently. "Perhaps this is a case when you shouldn't protect her."

"She has enough to deal with. I'm not going to put all of this on her. Not until she's ready."

William shook his head. "So you'll continue to bear the burden for your family, and the brunt of their anger?"

Her green eyes slanted to the side. "There's nothing else I can do. You said you wanted to take away my burden. But it's a burden I'll always carry, whether my sister believes me or not."

"Justice will release you."

"Will it?"

William opened his mouth as if to reassure her and closed it. He changed the subject. "I saw the sketch on your desk. I'm sure Saint Michael is insulted by being drawn with my likeness, but I appreciate the compliment."

"Saint Michael can't be insulted, because he isn't real."

"He is, actually."

"You've seen him?" Her tone was slightly mocking.

"Not Michael himself, but an angel, yes."

Raven squinted at him, searching for any sign of duplicity. She found none. "I don't believe you."

His hand slid down to rest on her hip. "I know."

"I wasted a lot of time praying for help when I discovered what my stepfather was. No one helped me. If there are such things as angels, why didn't they help?"

"Believe me, I've asked myself the same question over the centuries. Forget about them. Let me be the one to give you justice."

Raven smiled up at him sadly. "You are already my angel."

"If I were an angel, my name would be Death."

"No, your name would be William."

His gray eyes glittered and he took her mouth, kissing her firmly. Raven wore a wistful expression. "I wanted Cara to be the one to choose his fate. She's the one he touched."

"He touched you, too." An angry look flashed across William's face. "You deserve justice as much as she."

"What he did to her was worse. Now she wants nothing to do with me."

"You can choose for her."

"Not right now." She stared up at him, a pleading look on her face. "I just want to feel."

"Then let me love you."

William took her mouth with his, teasing her with his tongue before dipping inside.

Chapter Thirteen

It did not trouble William to keep Raven's stepfather imprisoned in a dungeon. Nor was he troubled by his treatment of the prisoner or the conditions in which he was kept. It occurred to him, however, to take Stefan's words into consideration—he needed to stop thinking like a vampyre.

Raven didn't recall her encounter with her stepfather the night of her birthday party, a fact William regarded as a mercy. He had no wish to revive her memory and he was concerned her previous reaction would be repeated.

When Raven announced she wished to confront the man, William discreetly ordered his servants to clean the prisoner and move him to another location in the villa, one that would be less alarming.

Once again, he wished he'd killed the man when he had the chance, primarily because the monster deserved it. And because he had the suspicion that Raven, given her true nature, would be unable to stomach a death sentence. There had been a time when he, too, was steeped in mercy. But that was when he was human and in the service of a saint. When the saint died, so did the mercy.

Strange how Raven had resurrected so much humanity in him.

These were the thoughts William had as he waited for Raven, who was girding herself mentally to confront her stepfather.

He stood admiring his priceless Botticelli illustrations, reexamining the figures of Dante and Beatrice. Although he could not understand Beatrice's regard for Dante, now more than ever he understood Dante's devotion.

❈ ❈

After sunset Sunday evening, Raven followed William up the stairs to the top floor of the villa. They traversed a short corridor, pausing in front of Marco, who was standing guard outside a closed door.

"You are dismissed." William nodded at Marco, who bowed and disappeared down the staircase.

Raven leaned on her cane. "Now what?"

William turned to her. "He's inside. He's restrained, which means he can't touch you. He won't be able to speak, but he can both see and hear you."

Raven's heart skipped a beat.

"Cassita." William crowded her. "You don't have to see him. Say the word and he disappears forever."

She lifted her chin. "I'm not a coward."

"Indeed, you are not." William's ferocity softened into admiration. "You've demonstrated your bravery again and again. You don't need to do so tonight."

"Someone needs to hold him accountable. Someone needs to speak for the children. I owe them that." Raven looked down at her injured leg, which was visible beneath the hem of her modest dress. "Cara should be here."

"That can be arranged."

"No."

William put his hand on the doorknob. "Whatever injuries or revenge you wish visited on him will be done. You are judge and jury here. All the power is yours."

"I don't feel very powerful." Raven bowed her head.

"Let me tell you what I see." William stepped closer. "I see a woman who opposed evil when she was a child. Who fought a grown man to protect her sister. Who told the truth when the adults in her life lied. Who, when her mother betrayed her, protected her sister a second time by fleeing the house. Those actions cost you. And still, years later, you are opposing evil and defending the weak."

His eyes grew haunted. "Unlike me, you never gave in to the darkness. Who is more powerful, you or I?"

"William, we—"

He placed a hand to her neck. "I know the answer to that question. It's you. You aren't the girl he knew. You aren't Jane anymore. You are Raven."

She leaned against him and he took her weight.

"Are you ready?" he whispered.

"Yes." She squared her shoulders and heaved a deep breath.

William opened the door. It creaked on its hinges, opening inward to a small, windowless room. The room was dark, despite the lamp that burned on a table nearby. The space reminded Raven of a poet's garret, nestled like a treasure under the sloping roof.

The only furniture in the room was a single chair. A man was sitting on it. His hands were manacled behind him and his feet were encased in irons, with a short chain running between them.

Raven noticed that he'd stretched his legs out in front of him and that one of them twisted to the side at an odd angle, as if it had been injured. She stared at the leg, recalling William's words from the previous evening. He'd pushed the monster down the stairs.

It was poetic, perhaps, but not pretty. She felt a cool hand at her lower back and she jumped, muttering an expletive. William floated around her, into her sight. "He can't speak. But he will listen."

Raven looked at the man, whose gaze was moving rapidly from

William to her and back again. His eyes were wide in his bruised and beaten face, his hair matted and dirty. But his clothes were clean, if torn.

He was gagged.

William approached the man and he began muttering excitedly behind his gag, his uninjured leg shaking and jerking.

"Silence," William hissed.

The man quieted immediately, his eyes moving to Raven. He gave her a pleading look.

"She is the only reason you are still alive." William gestured to Raven with a flourish. "I would have killed you the first night. You will treat her and her words with respect."

The prisoner mumbled more loudly against his gag, shifting and twisting in his chair. Of course, there was no escape. Raven clutched her stomach, trying hard not to vomit.

"I can't do this." She turned her back on the prisoner and began limping toward the door.

William breezed past her and stood at the door. "Instruct me on what to do with him and it will be done."

"It isn't enough."

"Then tell me what is."

"I want my father back." Her voice broke. "I want a sister who doesn't hate me and who wasn't hurt. I want my mother to love me again."

"Cassita," he whispered, "not even God himself can give you those things."

"I know."

"Then let me give you what I can."

"You can kill him. But then I'm a murderer. And I still won't have what he took from us."

"This isn't murder. This is justice."

The prisoner erupted, his muffled cries rising to a terrified pitch. Raven turned and saw him struggling in his chair, trying to escape.

"You're trapped," she said, eyeing his injured leg. Her eyes focused on his. "You're powerless to stop us from doing anything we want to you."

The prisoner continued to strain against his bonds, but in vain. Emboldened, she took a few steps in his direction, leaning heavily on her cane. "You probably don't remember me. I was Jane."

The prisoner rattled his chains, ignoring her.

"I was Jane, but I'm not anymore. I'm someone else. Someone you can't touch. How does it feel to be powerless?" She lifted her cane to point at his leg. "How does it feel to be crippled?"

He made eye contact with her and anger rose in her chest. "Why don't you ask me how it feels? How it felt to be a little girl trying to fight off a grown man. How it felt to be in the hospital with a broken leg. Why don't you ask me?"

She slammed her cane on the floor, the sound echoing in the room. "Ask me!"

The man stopped his struggling and glanced at William, who was standing behind her.

"Why don't you ask me what it felt like to walk in on you with my sister? She was only five!"

Raven lifted her cane and swung it with all her might, striking his injured leg.

The prisoner howled behind his gag.

Raven's shoulders shook. "What about the other children? What about the girls in California? Why don't you ask me about them? When you abuse a child, it can't be undone. The child will never be the same. My sister will never be the same.

"There's nothing I could do to you that would ever give us justice. Nothing will give us our lives back. Nothing will erase what happened." She leaned closer. "I could kill you." She gritted her teeth. "But I'm not a monster."

The man began to struggle once again, his eyes avoiding hers. William moved as if to intervene, but Raven caught his sleeve. Her green eyes fixed on the eyes of her stepfather. "I'm not going to kill you."

All at once, the man stilled and he returned her stare.

"This isn't mercy. I don't forgive you. I'd hope you rot in hell but I don't believe there is such a place. I choose to live a life that will let me sleep at night. While you have to live whatever life you have left knowing the girl you threw down the stairs protected you so she wouldn't become a monster like you. That's how much I hate you, you sick fucker. That's how monstrous you are."

Her body shook with anger. "I hope you live a long, miserable life with the rest of the monsters before you get there. I hope you rot!"

Raven spat in his face before turning her back on him. She limped slowly toward the door, leaning on her cane.

"Send him to California so they can put him on trial. Make sure they know about all the children he abused. Make sure I never see him again."

William took hold of her hand, halting her. His eyes searched hers.

"He should have to face the children he abused and their families," she said. "They need their own closure. I'm not going to steal that from them."

Raven opened the door and walked through it.

Chapter Fourteen

It was after midnight when Raven awoke in William's bed. The room was dark save for a pale light that shone from the gardens. Through the doors that opened onto the balcony, she could see William, sitting outside. He was holding a book.

Raven pulled the sheet around her naked body and padded out to him, not bothering with her cane.

"What are you reading?"

He looked up at her and smiled. His reaction was so spontaneous, so happy, it took her breath away.

He showed her the book. "*The Art of War* by Sun Tzu."

She wrinkled her nose. "Are things that bad in the principality?"

He tugged her hand, pulling her into his lap, and set the book aside. "Don't worry about it." His lips found hers in the semidarkness.

"It's too dark to read." She rested her head on his shoulder.

"Not for me."

"Is that what you do while I'm asleep? You read?"

"Not usually." His fingers sifted through her hair.

"What do you do all night?"

"The night is our day. Usually I'm concerned with affairs of state. The evenings are when we feed, socialize, fornicate." His voice grew rough.

"That's an awfully old-fashioned word for what we do."

"What we do together is more than that, assuredly. If you were to witness how my kind usually engage in intercourse, you'd note the difference."

Raven's stomach soured. "No, thank you."

"You are a puzzle I cannot solve."

At the change in his tone, Raven lifted her head. William was watching her with eager, searching eyes. He pushed her hair back from her face, as if it were obscuring his vision.

"I was worried you'd react to your stepfather the same way you did the first night. I was mistaken."

"I don't have an explanation for that."

"Perhaps even though you couldn't remember the incident, part of your mind remembered it. Maybe that made it less shocking."

"It was still shocking. I felt like I was twelve years old again." She leaned forward. "But you were there. And I knew you would never let him hurt me."

He touched the apple of her cheek with his finger. "You didn't need me. You were brave and fierce on your own. I have seen a great many things during the centuries I've been alive. I've met a great many people. None have resisted my understanding the way you have."

"I'm hardly a mystery. I'm just an average girl from Portsmouth, New Hampshire."

"You let him go."

Raven's body stiffened. She turned away, looking out over the extensive gardens that bordered the villa, and at the lights that shone dimly over them.

"I didn't let him go. We sent him to the police."

"Human justice is flawed."

"Is vampyre justice better?" Her eyes sought his, challenging him.

"Vampyres know little enough about justice. They know vengeance and revenge, instead."

"Then kill him. Bring him to me and kill him now."

William moved so quickly he was almost a blur. He placed her in his chair and stood before her. "Finally," he said, turning toward the door.

"And when he's dead and we're standing over his corpse, what will we have accomplished?"

He faced her. "He would be dead and his soul would be in hell."

"I don't believe in an afterlife. So he's dead. Then what?"

William peered down at her. "Your life continues, content in the knowledge he paid for his sins and will trouble you no more."

"My life didn't end because of him. That idea grants him too much power."

William's gaze fell to her injured leg, which was peeking out from under the bedsheet.

"He deserves to pay."

"Yes, he does. Can a dead man heal my leg? Can a corpse erase my memories or end my nightmares?"

William clenched his jaw so tightly Raven almost heard the bones creak. "I should think you would achieve satisfaction from his suffering. And yes, I think your nightmares would end."

"Only to be replaced by different ones—nightmares in which I'm forced to look at a man whose death I caused." Raven stood on unsteady feet, clutching the sheet to her chest. "He stole from me. What he stole I can't get back, even if I kill him."

"That's rubbish," William exclaimed. "He stole from you. You steal his life from him. Since what you steal is greater, you win."

"Winning?" She laughed bitterly. "What would I win? Money, power, my family? His death gives me nothing, but it would take away what I want most—to live a life where I can sleep at night, knowing I've done the best I could with what I have. That's the life I deserve. I won't let him steal it from me as well."

William pressed his lips together, as if he were resisting the urge to argue.

She gestured to herself. "I am not a killer. I won't let him turn me into one. He doesn't have that power."

"All humans have the potential to be killers." William's tone was glacial. "They simply need sufficient motivation."

Raven's green eyes flashed and she stood toe to toe with him. "How's this for motivation? I hate him. With every atom of my being, I hate him. If I had a soul, I'd hate him with that, too. But I love myself more."

"Forgiveness doesn't entail the negation of justice."

"I haven't forgiven him. I don't have it in me."

"Then leave him to me," William hissed, his face inches from hers. "I won't tell you what becomes of him. You can forget he ever existed."

Raven looked down at her injured leg. "You don't understand. I'll never be able to forget him."

William cursed, a string of profanities Raven did not understand.

She placed her palm over his heart. "Will you hunt everyone who ever troubled me? Will you kill my ex-boyfriend, who humiliated me and broke my heart? Will you kill my friend Gina because she hurt my feelings the other day?"

"Yes."

"I don't need you to be my angel of death." Raven withdrew her hand.

William was quiet for so long, Raven worried he'd gone into a trance. Pain flamed in her injured leg, driving her back to the chair.

He stood over her, his expression conflicted. "I was like you once."

"Before you became a vampyre?"

He nodded.

"What happened?"

His face hardened. "I watched goodness die, not once, but twice. And I lost hope."

She reached for him, closing her hand over his cool fingers. "You told me once that I was hope, dancing in your arms."

He stared at their hands, then slowly skimmed his lips over her forehead.

"Would that you had enough hope for both of us."

Her grip on him tightened.

"You remind me of someone," he whispered.

"Who?"

"A saint."

A laugh escaped Raven's throat. "I think in order to become a saint, you need to believe in God."

"I believe. I simply think God is a monster."

"I don't understand why you still believe in him if you hate him so much."

"Some things can't be disbelieved." He bowed his head. "But you—you've changed me."

"How?"

"Before we met, I wouldn't have thought twice about taking a life had I decided the life was worthless."

"And now?"

William covered their connection with his other hand. "Even though I desperately wish to end him, I would rather please you."

She brought her lips to his fingers and kissed them. "Now I know why you need to spend the daylight hours in solitude and meditation. No one could spend centuries making decisions like this and not need time to think and find peace."

He lifted her hand, lacing their fingers together. "We are susceptible to a kind of madness because of our longevity. Resting the mind keeps it at bay."

Raven's eyes widened. "Madness?"

"The madness that turns a vampyre into a feral."

She gazed up at him in horror. William continued. "I'm afraid that's not the worst of it. In addition to the possibility of madness, there's the curse."

"What curse?"

"During the war with the Curia, they cursed us with a life span of only a thousand years. When a vampyre approaches that age, he begins to go mad. I suppose it's like the senility of old age in a human. Then, on or around the one-thousandth year, the vampyre dies."

"I thought vampyres were immortal."

"They were once. But their immortality was taken away by the Curia. One more reason why we hate and fear them."

"How old are you, William?"

"I was turned in 1274. But this is a secret, Cassita. Even those closest to me in the Consilium don't know my true age."

"Why not?"

"Several of them are already covetous of my throne. I don't wish them to be able to pinpoint my weakness."

She forced a smile. "I knew you'd outlive me."

"That is one of life's greatest tragedies." He hesitated. "Unless you become like me."

She disentangled herself from his grasp. "I don't want to live that long."

"I won't let such beauty die," he whispered.

"But you'll have to, someday." Raven smiled sadly. "Art is the only beauty that never dies."

He kissed her, until she opened to him. With a growl, he plunged into her mouth. She wrapped her arms around his neck, anchoring him to her.

Without warning, he swung her into his arms and strode inside toward the bed.

Within moments, they were both unclothed and he was kneeling between her legs.

He rained soft kisses down the center of her body, pausing to pay homage to her breasts. Then his face descended between her legs.

His tongue was cool as it fluttered over her. She closed her eyes, her hands fisting the sheets at either side of her body.

William kept an unhurried pace, tasting and licking from side to side. He nuzzled the inside of her thigh with his nose before drawing the flesh into his mouth and sucking.

His palm slid up her side to cup her right breast, holding the weight in his hand. She murmured her approval, and he nipped at her thigh.

"I am going to feed from you. Here." He bit at the flesh again, if only to give her a warning.

She lifted her head, gazing down at the powerful creature that worshipped between her legs.

She nodded.

He looked up at her through his eyebrows and smiled a slow, sensual smile. "Prepare to be pleasured."

Raven watched as his head descended. But with the first touch of his mouth, she closed her eyes. He kept his slow pace, teasing and tasting her with lips and tongue.

At the crest of her orgasm, he released her, turning his head to her uninjured leg. He gripped her thigh tightly and then he was sucking the flesh into his mouth and tearing into the skin with his teeth.

Raven soared, her body shaking with mindless pleasure.

William drank and swallowed and drank some more, his grip on her thigh ever tightening. When her body finally relaxed, he released her, pressing the coolness of his tongue to the wound on her leg.

"I could drink you dry and never be satisfied." He rested his chin on her opposite leg.

Raven lifted her head but found the task too great and rested back on the pillow, her mind floating on a wave of ecstasy.

Chapter Fifteen

Professor Gabriel Emerson was like a man possessed.

William York had frightened him—not by threatening his safety, but by threatening Julia and Clare. Gabriel didn't know if what the mysterious being said about Julia's health was true. Nevertheless, he was determined to find out.

He made arrangements for his family (and Katherine Picton) to return to Boston, escorting them to Rome and waiting at the airport until they were successfully in flight. Then he returned to Florence.

He knew better than to stay at the Gallery Hotel Art. It would be easy, too easy, for the fiend to find him there. Instead, Gabriel booked a room at a convent operated by the Suore Oblate dell'Assunzione. He believed it would give him a measure of security against the agent of darkness.

On Monday morning, he was given the latest edition of *La Nazione*, the Florentine newspaper, to read alongside his modest breakfast.

He stared at the front page in shock.

His old nemesis, Professor Giuseppe Pacciani of the Università degli Studi di Firenze, was missing. According to the article, the Dante specialist had disappeared shortly after the theft of the illustrations of Dante's *Divine Comedy* from the Uffizi. The journalist suggested a connection between the two seemingly disparate events, hypothesizing that someone in Florence seemed to dislike Dante.

The article painted a dark picture of Florence and the crimes that had plagued it since the robbery. Pacciani's wife was interviewed, bemoaning the fact that the Carabinieri were unwilling to investigate her husband's disappearance, claiming there was no evidence of foul play and arguing the man had simply tired of his family and abandoned them. Signora Pacciani admitted her husband had been unfaithful, but she insisted he would never have left their children. Nor would he have left behind his rare editions of Dante, which still sat on a bookshelf in their apartment.

Gabriel dropped the paper on the table.

He was not a man given to believing in coincidences. Nor was he a strong skeptic. He couldn't express how he knew the theft and Pacciani's disappearance were related, or how he knew that William York was behind both of them, but he knew. He would have staked his life on it. And that, in itself, gave him all the more reason to distance himself from the search for his lost illustrations.

As he packed his bag and made his way to the Uffizi, he wondered why William York had caused Pacciani to disappear. He wondered why the dangerous and malevolent being had offered him mercy, instead, even gifting him with the knowledge that Julia was ill.

Gabriel Emerson had no answers to his questions, except his belief that a higher power was somehow watching over him and his beloved Julianne and that this power was greater than any darkness.

Chapter Sixteen

Later that same morning, Raven exited the elevator on the second floor of the Uffizi Gallery.

She'd stayed with William at his villa the night before. After their conversation about her decision, she'd taken comfort in William's body, taking what she needed and hoping she was giving something in return. By all accounts, William was very, very satisfied.

Returning to work Monday morning was a relief. The restoration of the famous *Birth of Venus* was almost complete. Soon the year-long project would come to an end and the beautiful painting would be returned to its rightful place on the wall of the Botticelli room.

Raven had been tasked with giving an update of the team's progress to Dottor Vitali, the director of the Uffizi. In truth, it was an honor to be sent on such an errand, with a folder of digital photographs and a seemingly infinite series of reports, but Raven would have preferred to stay in the restoration lab, continuing to coat the surface of the painting with protective varnish.

She sighed at the thought, the rhythmic tapping of her cane echoing down the corridor. The tapping was soon drowned out by the sound of a familiar voice speaking Italian.

"It's already done, Massimo. I've fired the private firm I'd engaged to assist in the investigation and I've already spoken with Interpol.

I don't expect the illustrations to be recovered and I want no part of this futile exercise."

Raven stopped. Professor Gabriel Emerson had returned to the Uffizi. And what he was saying was more than surprising.

"Gabriel, my friend, it's only been a few months. These things take time. Your illustrations will be found once the thieves try to sell them. They'd be foolish to try to take them to market so soon after the robbery." The voice of Dottor Vitali wafted down the hall.

Quietly, Raven approached the open door of his office.

"It's too late." The professor sounded agitated. "Did you know that one of the Interpol agents investigating the robbery was killed?"

"Yes, I was sorry to hear that."

"Did you see the cover of *La Nazione* this morning?"

"Not yet."

Raven heard the shuffling of papers, surmising that the director was looking for his newspaper. She stopped outside the door, straining her ears.

"There," said the professor. "See the front page? It's an article about Pacciani. He went missing shortly after the robbery. No one, not even his wife, knows where he is."

"Are you suggesting he stole them?"

"No. And I'm not suggesting—I'm asserting. Agent Savola was killed. Pacciani is missing. Both of them were connected to the illustrations in some way. And both men were also connected to me."

"My friend, surely you don't think—"

The professor interrupted him. "I will do what I deem necessary to protect my family. The streets of Florence are dangerous. The bodies of three men were found near the Arno a short time ago, and the police seem to have no clue who killed them. I'm finished with the investigation; I'm leaving Italy and returning to Cambridge. I'm not planning to return anytime soon."

"Gabriel, this is too hasty. Speak with Ispettor Batelli. He says he has several promising leads."

"That's what I'm afraid of," Gabriel muttered.

Sensing a break in the conversation, and worried about being surprised as she was eavesdropping, Raven knocked on Vitali's door.

He invited her to enter and she stepped across the threshold.

"I'm sorry, Dottor Vitali. Professor Urbano sent me to give a report about the *Birth of Venus*." Raven eyed the director and Professor Emerson cautiously. "I can come back later."

"I was just leaving." The professor retrieved a piece of luggage from nearby. "Good-bye, Massimo. Let me know when you're in Cambridge."

Vitali stood and the men shook hands, but the director was reluctant to let his friend go.

"Stay. We can discuss this."

"Julianne is ill," the professor announced, ignoring Raven's presence. "She's already returned home and has appointments scheduled for some tests. I need to rejoin her as soon as possible. The thief can have the illustrations."

Raven flinched at his final remark, but said nothing. Gabriel nodded at his friend and at Raven before marching toward the door, his expression pained.

"Professor Emerson." The sound of Raven's voice surprised even herself.

He turned toward her, lifting his eyebrows expectantly.

"I'm so sorry to hear that Mrs. Emerson is ill."

The professor's eyes narrowed suspiciously and Raven clutched her cane, stumbling over her words.

"I met her. I gave her a tour of the restoration lab. She was very nice to me."

The professor glanced at Raven's cane. "I didn't recognize you."

"I hope your wife will be all right." Raven rummaged in her jacket pocket and retrieved a small card. "This is my e-mail address. Please let her know I was asking about her. If there's anything I can do, anything at all, please let me know."

A muscle jumped in the professor's jaw. He took the card from her hand and perused it. His expression softened.

"Thank you." His sapphire eyes met hers, but only for a moment. Then he exited the office without a backward glance.

With a groan, Vitali slumped in his chair and removed his glasses, passing a hand over his face. He was quiet for some time.

"Well, Miss Wood. Tell me about the *Birth of Venus*."

Raven limped to an obliging chair and began her report, but her thoughts were fixed on the professor and his wife, and their infant daughter, Clare.

Chapter Seventeen

"The news is all over the gallery. Emerson is pulling his support from the investigation." Patrick Wong looked over both shoulders before leaning across the table toward Raven. "I wonder what that asshole Batelli thinks."

It was Tuesday. Raven was having lunch with Patrick and his girl-friend, Gina, both of whom worked at the Uffizi with her, at an *osteria* near the Piazza Signoria.

Carefully, Raven rested her fork on her bowl of pasta.

"I haven't seen Batelli since he cornered me in the restoration lab." She resisted the urge to mention that Batelli had been ordered by his superiors to stay away from her since then.

"I saw him," Gina interjected. "He and Vitali were on the second floor, arguing."

"That doesn't surprise me." Patrick tucked into his lunch with gusto. "Batelli looks like an idiot. No fingerprints, no footprints, no physical evidence at all. No wonder Emerson brought in a private firm."

Raven focused on her meal, trying hard not to think about the reason why no physical evidence was found.

"I understand why Professor Emerson is giving up." Gina shifted her dark hair behind her ear. "If you look at the major art thefts of the twentieth century, most of the artwork was either retrieved in a few weeks or it was lost for decades. Thieves took thirteen paintings from the Gardner Museum in America. It's been twenty-five years and they still haven't recovered them."

"The FBI think they know who took the paintings," Raven mused. "National Public Radio did a story about it."

"In twenty-five years, NPR can do a story about Batelli and how he harassed innocent employees while failing to find a single clue." Patrick gave Raven a sympathetic look.

"I have a theory." Gina lowered her voice, glancing between her friends. "I don't think the theft was one of opportunity, because there are other rooms that are more accessible. I think the thieves had a buyer in mind. They've probably already delivered the illustrations and the new owner is hiding them."

Raven's cheeks flamed as she thought of the elaborate display on the walls of William's villa. She began nibbling at her pasta determinedly.

"I agree." Patrick leaned over to press a chaste kiss on his girlfriend's cheek. "I think Emerson knows this, he's frustrated with Interpol and the Italian police, and he's decided to throw in the towel. For now."

Raven made an effort to sound nonchalant. "Do you think he will come back?"

"Emerson strikes me as a stubborn person. He isn't going to give up completely, but he isn't going to waste his time waiting for Batelli to grow a brain." Patrick sipped his wine and replaced the glass on the table. "I hope Vitali keeps Batelli away from us. He was quoted in *La Nazione* saying he won't rest until the culprits are found. I have a suspicion he's going to want to interview us again, since he doesn't have any other leads."

Raven kept her eyes fixed on her lunch, not knowing what to say.

"Enough talk about Batelli." Patrick's posture relaxed. "How about you, Raven? What are you going to do when the restoration project finishes?"

"I still have a position at the Opificio. But I won't be expected to return until September. As soon as the project at the Uffizi is finished, I'll be on vacation." Raven touched her gold bracelet.

"Will you go back to the States? Or are you and the rare vintages collector on again?" Patrick pointed to her adorned wrist.

"I'm not sure what I'm doing for vacation, but yes." She smiled. "He came to see me after my birthday."

"So you have a boyfriend." Patrick gave Gina a significant look.

Raven squirmed. "Yes."

"I'm happy for you." Gina lifted her glass in a toast.

The three friends clinked their glasses together and the subject of conversation turned back to their respective jobs at the Uffizi and workplace gossip.

As they approached the employees' entrance after lunch, Gina placed a cautious hand on Raven's arm. "Raven?"

"I'll catch up with you two later." Patrick gave Gina a lingering kiss before disappearing through the door.

Raven leaned on her cane, looking at Gina expectantly.

"I wanted to apologize," she stammered. "About my cousin. I was speaking with Roberto yesterday, asking him about you."

Raven chewed at the inside of her mouth, wondering what Roberto had said.

"He was angry with me," Gina confessed. "He thought I was trying to play matchmaker and that I was doing it only because he's blind and because . . . because of your leg."

She glanced down at Raven's cane and blushed.

"That wasn't what I was doing. I just thought you and he would have a lot to talk about. You're both good people who love artwork and history. I thought you would understand one another. But I didn't think— I didn't think that it was only because of your handicaps."

Gina bit her lip, her expression sorrowful.

"I'm not saying this correctly. Roberto said I was prejudiced, thinking handicapped people should only be with other handicapped people. But that's not what I thought. I just wanted you and Roberto to know each other—not to be romantic, necessarily, but to be friends."

Raven stared. Her friend was obviously in distress, and even though her explanation was muddled, it seemed sincere. Certainly, it appeared Roberto had given voice to the concerns Raven herself had had. She could hardly fault Gina for apologizing.

"Thank you," Raven said quickly. "I like Roberto. He's a good person and I know we'll be friends. So thank you for introducing us." She touched the bracelet she was wearing, almost instinctively. "But I'm seeing someone."

"I'm glad." Gina's smile was wide and happy. "I will tell Roberto this, and he will be happy for you, too."

She opened the door for her friend and held it, before following Raven into the corridor.

Chapter Eighteen

"'Transformations are strictly forbidden until further notice. Any killing of human beings within the city is also strictly forbidden. Violations of this new law are punishable by death.'" Niccolò lifted his gaze from the scroll he was reading, interrupted as he was by a cacophony of noise emanating from his fellow Consilium members.

Maximilian was already on his feet. "You're taking away our ability to add to our numbers and to defend ourselves." He leveled angry eyes on the Prince. "Your edict means death!"

"Sit down." The Prince's voice was low, barely above a whisper. Max hesitated, but only for an instant. Then he slung his large body back into his chair. The Prince stared at him, his body still, his gray eyes cold and angry.

"If I may, my lord." Niccolò looked at the throne.

The Prince waved a hand in his direction.

Niccolò turned to face his detractor. "I am eager to hear your alternatives, Sir Maximilian. But before we entertain them, I'd like you to accompany me to the principality library. I want to show you the accounts of the Curia's massacre of Prague."

The other members of the Consilium began to murmur in response. Niccolò continued to stare at Max until the Prussian giant lowered his gaze.

"We must do all we can to avoid Prague's fate. The best course of action is for the principality to exist quietly and avoid undue attention. Will you mind the new recruits? Keep them from killing when they feed?"

Max remained sullen.

Niccolò turned his attention to the other Consilium members. "Friends, the austerity measures are temporary but necessary. We must work together to promote them amongst the citizens and persuade them to obey."

"Precisely," said the Prince. "We don't know the Curia's plans. As intelligence is gathered, we may modify our response. But unless you wish hundreds of blackcoats swarming our streets, you must support and enforce the new laws."

His gray eyes moved from member to member, pausing perhaps a bit too long when they met Aoibhe's eyes. The Prince nodded at his head of security to continue.

The lieutenant bowed. "With respect to the Curia, there are wheels within wheels. It's possible they're looking to make an example of a principality in order to demonstrate their power to the Americans, who are notoriously unruly. If we bide our time, perhaps their eyes will fixate elsewhere and we may regain our former liberty."

"We could distract them." Pierre stood and bowed. "Why not send a killing party to Zurich, London, or Berlin? Have them pile bodies in a public square. Panic will ensue and the Curia will have no choice but to forget Florence and deal with it."

"The thought had occurred to me," the Prince observed. "If you were caught, the diversion would be in vain. We'd find ourselves under renewed scrutiny and at war with another principality."

"They would have to deal with panicked humans first," Pierre countered. "If the spectacle was large and public, the Curia would have to investigate it. They'd be focused on another city, not Florence."

"They're adept at dealing with more than one principality at a time. But I agree, it would attract attention." The Prince gazed at Pierre with renewed interest. "Are you volunteering?"

"It would be an honor, my lord." Pierre gave an exaggerated bow.

"The covens in Switzerland are sparse and weak. We needn't fear retaliation from them and certainly the Curia would be surprised by killings within those borders. But Switzerland is near. What about Paris? If you were caught, they'd think you hailed from the city."

"That's true, my lord." A hint of discomfort shadowed his face. "I had thought of Russia."

"The eastern covens are at war with the patriarchs," Lorenzo interjected, tapping the staff of the principality impatiently on the stone floor. "The patriarchs despise the Curia and would never let them past the borders."

"A fair point." The Prince peered down at Pierre thoughtfully. "Paris is the obvious choice, given their history with the Curia. They'll be too concerned with staving off a massacre to wage war with us, even if they discover who sent you. Who would you choose to accompany you?"

"Max."

The Prussian growled. "It's a fool's errand."

"You were just bemoaning the fact that you wouldn't be allowed to kill or add new recruits." The Prince's tone was sharp. "Pierre's suggestion will enable you to have your fill of killing."

He gestured to Max to stand. "Maximilian, you are hereby ordered to assist Pierre in his mission. I am placing you under his command."

"That's an insult!" Max spluttered. "I outrank him by over a century."

"*Audentes fortuna iuvat*. In case you've forgotten your Latin, that means 'fortune favors the bold.' Pierre will lead the mission to Paris and you will accompany him. If you fail, it will mean a death sentence. If you succeed, you will be rewarded." The Prince leaned forward on his throne. "If you refuse, I will kill you."

If Maximilian could have gone pale, he would have. His eyes widened almost to the point of bulging, his large fists clenching and unclenching. His gaze flickered to his left, but it was unclear who he was looking at. Both Niccolò and Lorenzo avoided eye contact.

Max returned his gaze to the Prince and nodded.

The Prince turned back to Pierre. "I want you to leave at once. Gregor will see that you are outfitted for your journey. Tell no one about your mission. We can't risk the news reaching the ears of the Curia."

Pierre and Max bowed and exited the chamber.

The Prince cast his eyes on the remaining three members of the Consilium. "Our numbers are dwindling. We have yet to replace Ibarra and will be without Pierre and Max indefinitely. Lorenzo, invite Stefan of Montréal to join us at our next assembly."

"As you wish." Lorenzo bowed. "But he lacks the requisite years for Consilium membership."

"He is a person of influence, despite his youth," rejoined the Prince. "Let us return to the matter at hand. Are there any further objections to the new laws?"

Aoibhe stood. "None from me, my lord. I saw what the Curia did in Paris to a coven of old ones. I came here because it was widely known that Florence was one of the only European principalities the Curia ignored." Her expression shifted. "I support the Prince and his new laws."

The Prince nodded and Aoibhe regained her seat. He waited a scant minute before turning to Niccolò.

"Remind the brethren they are free to leave the city, should they find the new laws too restrictive. Suggest they wear the safety vests we procured to protect them from hunters, but remind them if the Curia invades, the vests won't protect them. Let us hope we'll have good news from Paris in short order."

The Prince stood, as did the Consilium members, who bowed before him as he swept from the council chamber, his black velvet cloak streaming behind him.

❀ ❀

"Take this missive to Venice at once. Instruct Tarquin to hand over the delinquent tribute immediately or risk the consequences." The Prince addressed his lieutenant, holding out an envelope that had been sealed with the mark of Florence.

He was annoyed at having to deal with a minor irritation—the puppet prince he'd installed after defeating the Venetians in a recent war.

Lorenzo eyed the envelope nervously. "My lord, I am eager to serve you in all things. But if I deliver this message, the Venetians will kill me."

The Prince tossed the envelope on top of his desk. "And risk another war? I doubt it. We culled their army when we defeated them."

"Forgive me, Prince. Perhaps Niccolò would be a better choice?"

The ruler's gray eyes lasered into his lieutenant's. "Why would you say that?"

Lorenzo's lips pulled into a sour expression. "They fear him."

"If they fear him, they are more likely to kill him."

The lieutenant's expression relaxed, marginally. The change did not go unnoticed.

The Prince sat back in his chair. "If Venice is foolish enough to execute a high-ranking member of my principality, I'll invade them and execute their leadership."

"With respect, my lord, what about the Curia?"

"It's to our benefit that the Curia see us concerned with affairs of state and not looking over our shoulders. The threat of war with Venice should put them at ease with respect to their spies. Send Gregor."

"If I may, Prince." Lorenzo adopted a conciliatory tone. "Why not Aoibhe? She'd charm the Venetians easily enough. Tarquin is already taken with her."

"Yes, I know," the Prince muttered. "That was one of the reasons why we chose him. But Aoibhe is too valuable to risk losing."

The Prince withdrew a single piece of paper and scribbled on it. Then he folded it to form an envelope and melted some wax with a nearby candle. He sealed the envelope with the wax, imprinting it with the ring that held the symbol of Florence.

He placed the second envelope on top of the first.

"Tell Gregor to read the top message and deliver the second one. He is to leave immediately."

Lorenzo lifted the envelopes. "As you wish."

"Order Gregor to return with the tribute as soon as possible. Once you've sent him on his way, I would like you to meet with Aoibhe."

"To what purpose, my lord?"

The Prince frowned. "You are free with your questions this evening, Lorenzo."

The lieutenant lowered his gaze. "I beg pardon, my lord. Lady Aoibhe is, shall we say, challenging. I prefer to arm myself before accosting her."

"Too true." The Prince indulged himself in a small smile. "In view of the brewing conflict with Venice and the new edict we're enacting,

I think the principality is in need of a diversion. I want you and Aoibhe to plan a Bacchanalia."

Lorenzo's eyebrows lifted. "Yes, Prince. But given the Curia's scrutiny . . ."

The Prince was swift to interrupt him. "The time is ripe to reward my citizens for their loyalty and to inspire their fidelity. So long as there is no killing, the brethren should be free to eat, drink, and fornicate."

"Of course, Prince. I live to serve you." Lorenzo bowed and withdrew, leaving the Prince alone with his thoughts.

Chapter Nineteen

After almost a year of work, the restoration of the *Birth of Venus* was close to completion. The team had to contain their excitement so as not to rush any of the final stages.

Raven painstakingly continued to cover the magnificent painting with protective varnish, day after day. Her work was important and far from mindless, yet it led naturally to contemplation and the occasional flash of insight.

Raven had several intellectual virtues that made her an excellent art restorer. She was extremely focused and disciplined and she paid attention to detail, down to the smallest fleck of paint. However, these were not the mental powers needed to figure out why Professor Emerson had walked away from the investigation.

She knew William had interfered and that he'd done so to protect himself. He'd also interfered to protect her—using his influence to keep Batelli at bay. Having seen Professor Emerson's anger at the theft and his wife's sorrow, Raven was convinced it would take more than a survey of the past century's art heists to convince him to wash his hands of it.

He'd made much of the strange disappearance of another Dante specialist, Professor Pacciani. Raven wasn't clear on the connection between the two events, but whatever Emerson thought it was, it had intimidated him.

Raven was well aware of the antipathy that existed between the Emersons and William. She was the one who'd exacted his promise that he wouldn't kill the man. But William wanted his revenge. He'd confessed to confronting the professor in Umbria. Funny how that confrontation came only a few days before Emerson's visit to Vitali.

Raven meditated on these ideas, but as Monday became Tuesday and Tuesday became Wednesday, she was unwilling to mention them to William. She was concerned about Mrs. Emerson's health and hoped that her return to Massachusetts would enable her to receive the medical care she needed. Certainly, the farther away the Emersons were from William, the better for them.

As she packed up her art supplies on Wednesday evening, she hoped the Emersons would reach their home safely and that they would stay safe, living long, happy lives that did not incur the wrath of the Prince of Florence. And she did not give up hope of persuading William someday to share his illustrations with the world.

Chapter Twenty

On Thursday evening after work, as Raven climbed the steps to her apartment, she was surprised to see Bruno on the landing.

She hadn't seen him since she'd visited him in the hospital after he'd been attacked by the large, bearlike vampyre William called Max. Raven shivered at the recollection. It had been her fault he'd been hurt, since she'd foolishly gone out without wearing the relic William had provided for her protection. Bruno had almost died and she'd had to beg William to help him.

Looking at him, impeccably dressed as he was in a suit and tie and with a tall, thin blonde on his arm, he looked healthy.

Raven limped to the top of the stairs, pausing in front of her door to smile in Bruno's direction.

The woman on his arm was the sole focus of his attention. They stood in front of his grandmother's apartment and embraced, their mouths fusing in a passionate kiss. Raven blushed and turned away, fumbling for her keys.

"Hello." Bruno greeted her.

The sound of her key and the scraping of the lock must have distracted him. Raven turned and smiled. "Hello, Bruno."

"This is Delfina." He gestured to the woman at his side, then looked back at Raven and blinked. It took a few seconds for her to realize he didn't remember her name.

She stifled a wince. "I'm Raven, Delfina. It's nice to meet you."

Delfina smiled and returned her greeting.

"How is your grandmother?" Raven turned to Bruno once again.

"The chemotherapy is helping but she isn't eating. We just brought a dinner that my mother made, and she won't touch it."

"I'm sorry to hear that." Raven paused, looking at her door. "Would she like some company? I haven't eaten yet and I could bring my dinner over and sit with her."

"That would be generous, thank you. We have dinner reservations so we can't stay."

Delfina murmured something that Raven couldn't hear and Bruno laughed. He placed his hand on the doorknob to his grandmother's apartment. "But, please, my mother made enough for both of you. Don't bother bringing over anything."

"Are you sure?" Raven asked, watching his reaction carefully.

"Please." He extricated himself from Delfina and opened the door to the apartment, disappearing inside.

Raven could hear the dull murmur of voices. In a moment, Bruno returned.

"She's eager to see you." He stood to the side and gestured for Raven to enter. She quickly locked her apartment and made her away across the landing, nodding at Delfina as she passed.

"Have a good night." She gave Bruno a small, awkward wave.

"Thank you." He took Delfina's hand and they disappeared down the staircase.

Raven sighed. How interesting it was that a creature such as William, who was far more intelligent and handsome than Bruno, could find her beautiful, while a human like Bruno couldn't even remember her name.

William was the only one who'd ever looked at her with longing. She closed the door.

Chapter Twenty-one

Raven turned her head to find William staring at her unblinkingly, like a gray-eyed cat.

They were standing at the Piazzale Michelangelo, looking down at the radiant skyline of the city the following evening. They'd dined together, but on different food, at William's villa before walking hand in hand to the place that offered one of the best vistas of Florence.

Raven had put her cane aside and was leaning against a low stone wall that framed the *piazzale*. She'd been admiring the various landmarks and the way they were illuminated. The Ponte Vecchio and the Arno reflected the lights from the buildings that lined its banks.

It was so beautiful it made her heart hurt. She hoped she would always be able to live there and enjoy its beauty. She glanced at William and found his gaze intent on her.

"What are you looking at?"

"You."

She turned back to the view. "There are more beautiful things you could be looking at."

He rubbed his thumb across his lower lip. "I wish I had your talent for drawing. I'd sketch you like this, in profile, looking down over the city."

"I noticed you framed the sketch I did of you."

"I framed it not for the subject matter, but for the artist."

"You hung it next to your Botticelli." Her tone was slightly accusing.

"Great artists are best displayed in the company of other great artists."

She shook her head, but her smile remained in place.

He moved nearer. "Would you ever consider drawing a self-portrait, for me?"

Raven lifted her eyebrows. "Really?"

"I should like to have it."

"Then, yes, I suppose." She leaned against the railing, taking her weight off her disabled leg.

"I thought you were beautiful, even on the night I found you." William lowered his voice. "It was your scent that drew me to you—it bespoke a beautiful soul. But I was captivated by your eyes."

Raven's smile blossomed and she returned to look at the Arno.

Beyond the Ponte Vecchio, near the Ponte Santa Trinita, was the place where William had rescued her. Now when she drove over the bridge from Santo Spirito and into that area, she experienced anxiety and a feeling of dread. She wondered if she was guilty of suppressing memories of the night she was attacked, or if the memory loss had been the result of a head injury and vampyre blood, as William suggested.

She sighed and thought of Cara.

"Why the deep sigh?" William moved nearer, but didn't touch her.

"I was thinking about my sister."

"I've thought about mine over the years."

"What happened to them?"

"My sisters, as well as my brothers, married and had children. I didn't trace their descendants, but I'm sure some of them live in England still. Some of them probably went to America or Canada."

"Do you miss them?"

"Not really. I'd already severed ties with my family before I became a vampyre. After the change, I had little interest in them." He pressed his forearms against the railing. "Vampyres are egoists—only concerned with themselves and whatever pleases them. That doesn't leave much room for familial attachment."

Normally, Raven would have argued with him, pointing out that the general principles that applied to vampyres did not apply to him. But at that moment, she simply didn't have it in her to argue, so she was silent.

"What was your father like?"

"He was tall—taller than you—and big. He worked construction. He had dark hair and green eyes." Raven pointed to her face. "I look like him. He was funny. He liked to laugh. He liked to take me and my sister to the park and run around with us."

"If I had the power of resurrection, I'd give him back to you."

Tears filled Raven's eyes. She nodded, too overcome to speak.

"What were you thinking about your sister?"

Raven flexed her hands against the stone, finding the cool roughness against her skin a pleasant distraction. "I love her. She's my best friend." Raven lowered her head. "She hates me."

"If she hates you, she's clearly lacking in perception."

"William," Raven reproved him. "Since we couldn't rely on our mother, I became Cara's mother in a lot of ways. Having her break off contact with me is devastating."

William placed his hand over hers. "She still won't speak to you?"

"I've tried calling, I've tried e-mails. She won't answer."

"I'm sorry. I . . ." William shook his head.

Raven remarked his worried expression. "What is it?"

He redirected his gaze to the Palazzo Vecchio. "I see your suffering and I don't know how to end it. I'd like to give you your father back. I'd like to give you your mother and your sister. But I can't. It makes me . . ." He paused abruptly. "I don't like feeling powerless."

She rested her head against his shoulder. "Thank you."

"Why are you thanking me? I haven't done anything."

"You're here."

Ever so softly, the edge of his finger feathered over the hinge of her jaw.

A long look passed between them.

"I wish I'd found you seven hundred years ago."

She entwined their fingers together. "We wouldn't have one another now if that had happened."

Raven had the impression he wanted to say something but was choosing his words carefully.

"Is being a mother something you want?"

That was a question she had not expected.

She studied the skyline intently. "I didn't expect to find someone to love. Marriage and children weren't part of my aspirations. I wanted a life filled with beauty and friends and I was determined to be content with those things."

"You volunteer at an orphanage."

"Yes."

"Will that be enough?"

"I don't know. I'm thirty, William. I probably have ten years left in which to have a child. Maybe I'll want a biological child someday, but right now I find the thought daunting. The idea of creating a child with someone other than the man I love is repugnant."

William lifted his arm and curled it around her waist, bringing her into his side.

"Enough about me, William. I should be asking about your burdens. I'm sorry I've been so focused on myself."

He squeezed her waist. "You don't even realize how unselfish you are. You've been asking me about my troubles with the principalities and worrying along with me for days. You've done more than enough."

"I think all this deep conversation is because of the view," she blurted out. "The beauty of the city makes people reflect on life and time and secret desires."

William chuckled and pressed a kiss to her temple. "What do you desire, little bird?"

"The steadfast love of a good man."

His arm about her tightened. "I am not a good man. I'm not a man at all. But I love you and my love is certainly steadfast."

She closed her eyes and leaned against him.

"I admire you." He spoke into her hair.

"Why?"

"Because you're principled and you hold fast to those principles even when it's difficult. You're noble."

"I feel awkward and overwhelmed more than anything."

"That is not how you appear to me." He lifted her chin. "Knowing what I know about your character and your heart, I've never seen anyone more beautiful."

She turned away. "Stop."

"I love you." He kissed her cheek, the way a shy boy kisses a girl he cannot help but kiss.

"I love you, too."

William relaxed in her arms. Raven hadn't realized he was holding himself tensely until she felt the change.

"What's wrong?" She touched his face.

"I will never have your nobility of spirit, or your protective nature, but as long as I have your love, I can be content."

Moisture pricked the corners of Raven's eyes. "You're giving me a toothache."

He pulled back. "How is that possible?"

She laughed. "It's a figure of speech. It means you're being too sweet. Say something awful."

William's expression changed and he brought his lips to her ear. "I want to take you back to the house, so I can spread you on my bed and do all kinds of wicked things to you."

She nuzzled his chin with her nose. "My toothache is gone."

With another laugh, he took her hand and led her back to the villa.

Chapter Twenty-two

T wo weeks later, Ispettor Batelli watched the black Mercedes pull away from Santo Spirito. He pulled lazily on his cigarette, leaning in a doorway across the piazza from Signorina Wood's apartment.

Detective work could be reduced to one maxim—follow the money. This line of inquiry was frequently augmented by another maxim—follow the *ragazza*. He'd been doing both relentlessly for some time.

Batelli meditated momentarily on the *ragazza*'s vulgar linguistic counterpart, as he watched the lights go on in Raven Wood's apartment. She was the point at which the paths of William York, the dead Interpol agent Savola, and the robbery of the Uffizi converged.

Professor Emerson had tried to persuade him to stop the investigation, suggesting that the stolen Botticelli illustrations might emerge on the black market once the intense police scrutiny abated. His observation had merit, but Batelli would not admit defeat.

He was convinced the thieves who'd targeted the Uffizi did so already having a buyer. He suspected the artwork was still in the area, but hidden. Further, he suspected the theft was in some way connected with the mysterious William York.

He didn't know the name of the man Raven was seeing. He'd

taken photos stealthily, but his attempts at identifying her lover had been thwarted. The man seemed to appear only after dark and he usually kept his face hidden, as if he suspected he was under surveillance.

From what Batelli observed, the man roughly matched Emerson's physical description of William York. But without a photograph of the man's face, the description was useless.

The Interpol databases yielded nothing about anyone called William York. An attempt to lift fingerprints from the back door of Signorina Wood's building yielded nothing, because none of the prints could be linked to anyone matching his description.

The license plates of the Mercedes were also a dead end. The car was registered to a Swiss diplomat who did not match her lover's description.

Batelli's intuition told him he'd run into a crime lord. He couldn't identify the nature or ethnicity of the organization, but it wasn't the Mafia and it wasn't the Russian mob. He began asking questions of a friend of his who worked on an anti–organized crime task force, but his friend was as puzzled as he was.

Which was why Batelli continued to watch Raven and her patron, hoping for some kind of clue as to his identity.

Batelli had no idea that even as he shadowed Raven, a vampyre shadowed him.

Chapter Twenty-three

Aoibhe fixed her dark eyes on the Prince and wrinkled her nose. "You smell of pet."

The Prince ignored her, striding in the direction of the training hall.

He'd had precious little time with Raven that day. She'd worked her normal hours at the gallery before beginning her volunteer shift at the orphanage. He had had to content himself with petting in the Mercedes on the way from the orphanage to her apartment, after which she was supposed to spend the evening with Lidia, her neighbor.

The Prince begrudgingly bade her good night before descending into the underworld. He was bored, restless, and eager for a diversion. As always, Teatro held little interest for him, and although he was in a mood to feed, he was not inclined to drink from anyone other than her.

He'd agreed they should spend the night apart, so Raven could attend to Lidia, who was receiving chemotherapy, and so he could attend to the principality. But the separation made him irritable.

An irritable vampyre is someone all creatures should avoid. Alas, Aoibhe was not conscious of this maxim.

She trotted after him, her green velvet dress billowing behind her.

"Did she rub herself over your entire body? I can hardly breathe for the stench."

The Prince turned on her, his face a mask of anger. The truth was that Raven had, indeed, rubbed against him. They'd enjoyed one another in the backseat of the Mercedes in a way that was both decadent and heady.

The Prince didn't want Aoibhe to know the depth of his attachment to Raven—for her sake.

At the sight of his anger, Aoibhe retreated backward. She curtsied. "I beg pardon, my lord."

"There was a time when you found the fragrance of my pet to be most desirable. If that opinion has changed, I recommend you keep your mouth shut." He turned on his heel and continued on his path.

Something that looked a good deal like triumph flashed across her face, but only for a moment. She followed. "The Bacchanalia will begin in a week's time. All is ready."

"Good."

She spoke at his elbow. "In celebration of the coming festival, perhaps I could procure a drink for you. Something young? Something fresh?"

"I am well fed."

"Then perhaps another diversion?" She paused in front of a heavy wooden door. The Prince stared at the door, contemplating her suggestion.

She opened the door and held it, allowing the Prince to see inside the gymnasium. The space was very large and had an upper gallery. Vampyres young and old prepared for battle, practicing with various weapons.

He entered the gymnasium and, once again, Aoibhe followed, closing the door behind them.

At the sight of the Prince, a hush fell over the crowd. Citizens bowed their respect, pausing their sparring.

"I'm sorry Max isn't here. He could do with a lesson," Aoibhe commented.

The Prince said nothing.

She moved to whisper in his ear. "We haven't had news of Max and Pierre. I would have thought they'd have completed their mission by now."

He growled his frustration.

"Let's find you a worthy opponent." She gazed around the room quickly. "Alas, I'm the oldest one here, except for you."

"Niccolò and Lorenzo need to spend more time training."

"Undoubtedly. A youngling could probably best them."

The Prince walked to the cache of weapons and chose a large, heavy broadsword. He walked to the center of the gymnasium, tossing the sword from hand to hand. Aoibhe sought a weapon that roughly matched his and followed.

The other vampyres quickly retreated, moving to the perimeter of the hall.

At the sight of her, the Prince scowled. "You can't fight in a dress."

"I've been fighting in a dress since I was changed." She gave him a saucy look. "But since you object . . ."

She divested herself of her garment, tossing it aside. She stood in an ivory slip, her long red hair a riot of waves about her body, her hand clutching a sword. A murmur lifted from the crowd, for Aoibhe was a goddess in body as well as in face.

"Shall we?"

He regarded her for a moment, then pointed his sword at hers. "Perhaps you'd prefer something smaller."

"The size of your sword is more than adequate, my lord."

Laughter filled the hall.

"Then we'll spar until first blood."

"Agreed."

Aoibhe winked at him and took a fighting stance, her body turned sideways, her sword lifted with both hands and pointed toward the ceiling.

Before she could take a single step in his direction, he blurred toward her, then retreated just as quickly. Aoibhe stood, shocked, a small line of blood drifting from her cheek to the edge of her mouth. He'd caught her with the tip of his sword before she could even draw breath.

Her tongue peeked out, straining toward the blood. She smiled slowly. "It seems you are not as well fed as you claim."

The Prince scowled. "Are you hungry for more?"

"Indeed, my lord. Clearly, your little pet isn't sating your appetite. You'll have to take another. Or more." She resumed her stance, her white cheek still stained with the blackish blood, even though the wound had closed.

The Prince gripped his sword more tightly, the knuckles of his hand indicating that her taunt had found purchase. He beckoned to her.

This time, she moved immediately, approaching him with speed and swinging at his chest. The Prince sidestepped her at the last moment, his hair fluttering in the draft created by her weapon. He smacked her bottom with the flat of his sword, causing laughter to bubble up from the crowd.

She turned, swiping at him from the side. Once again, he sidestepped her blow.

Aoibhe was beginning to lose her temper. She swung in the direction of his head and he ducked, pushing her abdomen with his hand and knocking her over. Her sword went flying and landed a few feet away.

The Prince turned his back on her and strode to the door, to the sound of great applause. He handed his sword to one of the young-lings who stood nearby, and exited the hall.

Aoibhe picked herself up. "What are you looking at?" she snarled to the crowd, throwing her dress over her head and walking to the door.

※ ※

Later that evening, Raven sat at her desk in her bedroom, staring at her laptop. She deleted an e-mail from her mother, suspecting it would be an angry, ranting diatribe, excoriating her for upsetting Cara.

Raven also ignored an e-mail from Father Kavanaugh, who, ac-cording the visible subject line, had recently arrived in Rome. No doubt he was updating her about his new position in the Church.

Father Kavanaugh had become a father to her and, to a lesser extent, Cara. He'd taken them to Covenant House when they fled their stepfather, he'd protected and fed them, and he'd brought them to a police officer they could trust. He'd advocated for them with child protective services and the courts. And he'd made sure that they had someone in their life who cared about them and encouraged them to go to college, even to the point of finding scholarships for them.

Raven owed Father Kavanaugh a great deal, but more than that, she loved him. While she didn't share his religious beliefs, she knew him to be a holy man. And she knew that, in his way, he loved her and Cara. Should the need ever arise, he would move heaven and earth to help them.

But she didn't want to talk to him about Cara. Not now, when the pain was still fresh. For this reason, Raven decided to save his e-mail for another day.

With a pained heart, she typed another e-mail to her sister.

> Dear Cara,
> I'm really sorry I upset you. I'm sorry I upset Dan.
> Please don't cut me out of your life, especially over this.
> He took so much from us already. Don't let him take my sister
> from me.
> I love you,
> Rave

Chapter Twenty-four

The following evening, Gregor appeared before the Prince in his private apartments at Palazzo Riccardi. He stood nervously while the Prince read the message he'd delivered—a note from Counselor Tarquin, the current leader of Venice.

Since Tarquin had been put in place by the Prince of Florence after he'd defeated the previous ruler, and since Florence claimed dominion over Venice, Tarquin was not allowed to hold the title of prince. He was only a counselor. And like any black-blooded vampyre, he chafed under the title.

The Prince looked at Gregor and smiled. "It appears your mission was successful. Tarquin has apologized and, according to his letter, sent double tribute. I take it you have the tribute with you?"

"It has already been deposited with Lorenzo, my lord."

"Excellent. Are the Venetians worried about the Curia?"

"They made no mention of them."

"Did you note anything amiss in the city?"

"They resent being under the control of Florence, my lord. But other than that . . ." He shrugged.

The Prince placed the message on his desk, regarding his personal assistant carefully. "You seem no worse for wear."

"No, my lord." The Russian shifted his weight from foot to foot.

"Tarquin and his advisers considered killing me, but since I wasn't a member of the Consilium they said the injury to them would be greater than the injury to Florence."

"Wise words, but I would be sorry to lose you, Gregor."

The assistant seemed taken aback by the admission. "Thank you," he stuttered. "I have prided myself in my loyalty and service."

"I take pride it in as well, which is why I am sending you on another journey. One that you must keep secret."

"Of course. Where shall I go?"

"Switzerland. I wish you to visit Cologny, near Geneva. I'm interested in knowing how a particular family acquired a set of illustrations by Botticelli a hundred years ago."

"Yes, my lord." Gregor hesitated.

"Out with it," the Prince ordered impatiently.

"It is not for me to question you, my lord." Gregor fidgeted, his gaze on the floor.

"No, it is not. But in this case, and in view of your loyal service, I'll volunteer that I am trying to solve an old mystery, which I hope will aid in solving a new one."

Gregor appeared confused. "Of course, my lord."

"I shall also mention that I sent someone on a similar journey many years ago. He returned empty-handed. Let's hope you return with something more."

The Prince dismissed his assistant with a wave of his hand, before contemplating the shadow that first fell over his city at the time of the theft of his illustrations.

The shadow must be destroyed.

Chapter Twenty-five

On Sunday evening, after spending the day together, William and Raven stood outside his villa next to his prized Triumph motorcycle.

"I can't." Raven backed away. "The last time I rode with you, I was sick."

His eyes locked on hers. "This will be different. I swear."

"You like to drive fast."

"Yes."

"But I have trouble holding on. Sometimes it's painful for my injured leg. I may have to ask you to stop so I can stretch."

"Then we'll stop." He moved closer and caressed her face with the back of his fingers. "I won't let harm come to you. I swear by the relic."

Heat flared in Raven's middle at the sound of his words. "You must respect the relic very much. It's the only thing you swear by."

He nodded, his gray eyes dark and very intense. "We don't have time for the story tonight. I need to be sure you're deposited in your bed early enough to rest before work tomorrow."

"I'd rather listen to your story."

He brushed a kiss across her lips. "Another time."

She pressed her cheek to his chest and listened to the strange sound of his heart. "The restoration project is almost finished. I'll be on vacation until the beginning of September. We could go somewhere."

"I would like that." He nestled his fingers in her hair. "I would like to take you to York, where I was born. But I can't leave the principality when the Curia is watching and there's a traitor in our midst."

"Traitor?" Raven pulled back, alarmed. "What traitor?"

A muscle jumped in William's jaw. "For some time, a person or a group of people inside the principality have been trying to destroy me."

Raven's eyes widened. "What? You never told me that."

"I did, actually, during one of our conversations about Aoibhe."

Raven wrinkled her nose. "You'll forgive me if I've blotted out most of that conversation."

"I believe someone betrayed my location to the hunters, which is why they were outside Teatro waiting for us. If Aoibhe was the traitor, she would have avoided that area.

"Additionally, two years ago, I was attacked by would-be assassins. They came from Venice but were aided by someone inside the city. I haven't discovered whom. Yet."

"Why didn't you tell me about this?"

"It happened before I knew you."

Raven shook her head. "What happened to the assassins?"

"I destroyed them."

"What, all of them?"

"There were only ten. After the assassination attempt, we went to war with Venice and defeated them. Since then, the traitors have been too cowardly to risk open conflict. They colluded with the hunters to try to kill me. Now I believe they're trying to use the Curia."

"You defeated ten vampyres? What, at once?"

William smiled. "I am an old one."

"Why would the traitors use the Curia? If they come, they'll kill all the vampyres."

"The Curia makes treaties when it suits its purposes."

"William," she whispered, resting her cheek against his chest once again.

He wound a lock of her hair around his finger, his gaze fixing on the black strand. "This is not how I envisioned our evening. At least now you understand why I cannot take you to York." His expression brightened. "But I would like to take you with me tonight."

Raven looked at the motorcycle, her grip on him tightening. He watched her, a shadow of hope crossing his handsome face.

She could not disappoint him. "Lead on, old one."

He smiled widely and led her to his machine.

❀❀

William appeared to have chosen the darkest, most winding road that led from the city. Fortunately for Raven, his Triumph roadster had twin headlights that cut through the night.

She held him tightly, sitting as far forward as possible, her front pressed to his back, her arms clasped around his waist. The position was uncomfortable for her leg, but she ignored the discomfort, focusing on the feeling of being so close to the person she loved.

He wore sunglasses, but no helmet, much to her consternation. He liked to feel the wind in his hair, he'd said, and was indifferent to the risk of an accident.

"I won't let harm come to you," he'd promised, insisting she wear a helmet. He'd procured a black leather jacket to protect her from the wind and took great pleasure in placing it on her.

Raven clutched him more closely, shifting forward on the passenger seat at the back, her face turned to the side as the large, powerful motorcycle wound around the curves at high speed.

"Are you all right?" He lifted his voice above the roar of the machine.

"It's a little fast." Her reply was muffled by the helmet.

She lied. It was far too fast and the strain of having to hold him so tightly aggravated her injuries, but she knew how much William enjoyed speed. She could feel his joy, his wild abandon, as he revved the engine in the straightaways and effortlessly guided the bike around the curves. Excitement thrummed through his body, his muscles taut with control.

Her thighs tightened on the outside of his as they went around a corner, her arms cutting into the unyielding steel of his abdominals. William decelerated and she heard him chuckle, the sound of his amusement disappearing on the wind.

He was happy. He was free. And because he loved her, he wouldn't dare approach the speed he preferred.

"It's a lovely night." He gestured to the inky sky that peeked through the canopy of trees above them.

She hugged him in response. Her injured leg began to throb, so with regret she squeezed his right side, the signal that she needed a rest.

William slowed immediately, pulling off to the side of the road near a private drive. He removed his sunglasses, climbed off the bike, and helped her with her helmet, placing it on top of the seat before offering his hand.

When her stiff leg wouldn't cooperate, he lifted her into his arms. In the dim starlight, she could still see the joy on his face.

His eyebrows drew together under her perusal. "What?"

"Seeing you happy makes me happy."

Without warning, he pressed their mouths together. When they came apart, he whispered in her ear, "I'd forgotten."

"You'd forgotten what?" Her questing fingers sifted through the hair at the back of his head.

"What it's like to be loved."

She hugged him as tightly as she could, trying to show with her body what she couldn't communicate with words.

He placed her on the ground, winding his arm around her lower back to support her. "I rode horses when I was human. I liked them. I have a couple of fast cars, including a McLaren."

"What's a McLaren?"

William grinned. "It's a car made by a company that makes Formula One race cars. It's an exceptional vehicle, but ever since my first ride on a motorbike, it's been my favorite."

"I can understand that." She returned his grin.

He led her into a grove of cypress trees that skirted the edge of a private drive, piloting her up a smaller hill.

"Where are we going?"

"Somewhere special."

They walked for some time. Just as Raven was sure she couldn't walk anymore, the trees thinned out, revealing a beautiful terraced garden. There were small white lights wound around some of the trees and a few electric lanterns scattered across the terraces, interspersed with terra-cotta pots filled with flowers and greenery. Rosebushes and lavender perfumed the air. To the right side, a short distance away, was a grove of what looked like orange trees.

He brought her to the center of the largest terrace, next to a large, impressive fountain that featured a statue of Venus and Cupid. Potted lemon trees stood broadly around its circumference. Raven inhaled the sunny, citrus scent.

"It's incredible. What is this place?"

"The garden belongs to a villa farther uphill. It was built in the fourteenth century."

"Do you know the owners?"

"I knew the original owners. I believe the villa is still in the family."

"They were friends of yours?"

"I don't have friends, Raven. The owners were friends of the Medici, which is how I met them."

She glanced around. "We're trespassing."

"The current owners are elderly. They're probably asleep."

"Do you come here a lot?"

"I was a guest several times in the fourteenth century. Since then, I've visited only on occasion, always under cover of darkness." His attention drifted over the terraces, pausing from time to time. "I'm fond of the gardens. It's very peaceful here. And not a vampyre in sight."

"Have the gardens changed much since the fourteenth century?"

"Happily, no."

She fitted her arm around his waist. "Tell me what it was like living during the Renaissance."

William rubbed his chin. "It was fascinating. There were tremendous innovations in architecture, art, politics, and science. Florence was the center for many of those innovations. And at the center of Florence were the Medici.

"I played the part of a wealthy Englishman who was eager to spend his family's money and rub shoulders with the elite. Florentine society welcomed me with open arms. I used that opportunity to learn all I could from the intellectual innovators, and quietly began acquiring art.

"Vampyres had been driven underground by the Curia, but it was easy enough to mingle with humans between the hours of sunset and sunrise. They were suspicious enough to keep their distance but not fearful as their ancestors had been, when we lived openly."

"You knew Dante and Botticelli."

William frowned. "I did. I can't say I liked either of them. I certainly admire Botticelli's work, when he isn't trying to paint me into one of his paintings."

"You knew Beatrice."

"Not well, but I met her. She was lovely, very noble, and the kind of woman who turned heads when she walked down the street. I knew Botticelli's muse, Simonetta Vespucci. I knew Brunelleschi, Machiavelli, Michelangelo, Donatello, Leonardo, Savonarola, Galileo . . ." William waved a hand in the air. "I had the advantage of a long life and access to the circles in which they traveled."

"Were any of them killed by vampyres?"

"No." William's gray eyes danced. "But two of them became vampyres."

Raven's mouth dropped open. "Really? Which ones?"

"Guess." William appeared amused.

"Um, Michelangelo and Brunelleschi? They'd make good vampyres."

"No."

Raven frowned. "That's too bad. I would have liked to meet them."

"I can introduce you to Simonetta. She's the Princess of Umbria."

"You're kidding."

"No, I am not. I can also introduce you to Machiavelli, but you've already met him."

Raven fanned a hand to her forehead. "What?"

"Niccolò is a member of my ruling council. You were in the same room with him when I blindfolded you and took you down to the council chamber."

"I don't remember much of that meeting, apart from being scared."

William kissed her cheek. "You were very brave."

"What's he like?"

"He's very much as you might expect. However, time has taught him prudence."

Raven stared at William as an idea suddenly occurred to her. "Did he write *The Prince* for you?"

William chuckled. "No, that was for the Medici. Machiavelli was not on good terms with them and that was one of his attempts at ingratiating himself."

"Are there any famous artists who have become vampyres? Monet? Van Gogh?"

"Neither of them. But I can't speak for the entire art world. For years, I've focused my attention solely on the principality. In any case, many of my kind change their names so as not to be recognized. Or hunted."

"Yes, because art historians would be interested in interviewing them."

William shook his head. "It would be a short interview. The art historian would most likely end up an entrée."

"But what a way to die."

William laughed and hugged her, spinning her slowly in a circle.

She admired their surroundings once again. "This is lovely. But the gardens at your villa are also beautiful."

"Thank you. I took my inspiration from here."

She looked up at him. "What do you like about it?"

"Its beauty. Its location. If we stood at the top, where the villa is, we'd have an extraordinary view of the surrounding hills. There's vineyards nearby. Behind the house is the olive grove. They make their own olive oil here." His arms about her tightened. "It's what you've enjoyed at the villa. I had Lucia stock it for you."

"Thank you."

"The garden here is dissimilar to the gardens at York, when I lived there. But something about this place reminds me of home." William's face took on an expression Raven had not seen before.

He seemed lost in thought for a few moments.

Raven waited for him to return to her. "What were your parents like?"

"My mother was pretty and from a wealthy family. She was very accomplished and had been well educated."

"And your father?"

"He was a tyrant." William took her hand and began leading her away from the fountain.

"Where are we going?"

"It's a surprise."

"I think I've had enough surprises. Do you want to tell me more about your father?"

"No."

"All right," she said quietly. "I'm still trying to process the fact that Machiavelli is still alive. I studied him in a political science class in college. He could have tutored me."

"He wouldn't have. Humans are beneath him and his intellect."

"I knew there was a reason I disliked him."

They walked a fair distance through the orange grove until they approached another clearing. Once again, small white lights illuminated the space from the trees on which they hung. Electric lanterns lined the perimeter of a rectangular pool.

Raven gave William a questioning look. He smirked and led her to the side. "Test the pool. I'm not a good judge of temperature."

She leaned over and dipped her uninjured foot in the water. "It's warm. The pool must be heated."

"Excellent."

William stepped over to a deck chair and began unbuttoning his shirt.

"Wait. What are you doing?" Raven sounded alarmed.

"We are going for a swim."

She looked around helplessly. "We're trespassing."

"I'm not afraid of the owners."

"I am. We don't have bathing suits."

"I don't own a swimming costume." He gave her a look designed to tempt as he pulled off his shirt, revealing his muscled chest. "And if you owned one, I'd persuade you not to wear it." He unzipped his black jeans.

Raven muttered a surprised curse.

Without shame, William walked naked to the deep end of the pool and dove into the water. The sound of his body breaching the surface seemed thunderous. Raven strained her ears for any indication that someone had heard the noise and was coming to investigate.

William swam to the side closest to her. He looked like a god, his upper body perfect in proportion and sprinkled with droplets of water. His powerful presence was barely muted by the water, although he looked up at her hesitantly.

"Are you joining me?"

"We'll get arrested."

William inclined his head to one side. "It's a warm evening. We've taken a drive down a long, dusty road. I thought it would be refreshing to have a swim. Together."

The tone of his voice changed on the last word and Raven felt it on her skin, like a caress.

"What if someone sees us?"

"I have excellent hearing and an exceptional sense of smell. The wind is blowing such that we won't be surprised by anyone coming from the villa. Come, Raven. I want to see you." His expression grew heated.

Nestled among the greenery in the semidarkness, the pool looked inviting. Even more so when coupled with the aqua-god before her. Raven balled her hands into fists.

"Fine."

Carefully, she undid her leather jacket and placed it on a chair near William's clothes. With as much speed as she could muster, she disrobed. Covering her breasts with an arm, she hobbled to the shallow end of the pool and crept down the stairs. She only relaxed when the water came up to her neck.

William watched the entire procedure like a hawk. He remained at the side, regarding her, but made no move to approach her.

Her cheeks flamed.

He extended his hand over the surface of the water. It was an invitation. Slowly, she walked over to him.

"How does the water feel on your leg?" His expression was almost tender.

"It feels good. Over the years I've done aquatic therapy and exercise. It helps."

"But you haven't been doing that in Florence."

"No, I haven't."

"I'll make arrangements."

She was prepared to argue with him, but quickly thought better of it given his tone. "Thank you. I miss swimming."

He lifted his hand, but instead of pulling her against his naked form, he gently touched her face and smoothed her hair. She placed her arms on his shoulders to steady herself. "The water is very warm."

He nodded, still staring into her eyes.

She broke eye contact. "You've gone quiet."

"Vampyres have excellent senses. When we feed or engage in intercourse, we become distracted. To ensure we aren't surprised, I'll have to forgo those activities." His hand slid under the water to rest on her hip. "I'm finding it—difficult."

She stepped closer, her breasts brushing against his chest. William closed his eyes and groaned.

"I think it would be rude for us to pursue those activities in someone else's pool." Raven kissed his neck.

Struck by a sudden inspiration, she licked a drop of water from his skin. William's hands clamped on her hips, pulling her lower body against him. Without a word, he kissed her deeply.

"I'll take care of it," he rasped, his eyes like gray fire.

He wrapped his arms around her back and Raven forgot all about the owners of the pool.

Chapter Twenty-six

Later that evening, William piloted the motorcycle to a place near the front door of Raven's apartment building. She waited for him to help her off the bike, finding her legs unsteady.

He chuckled as he removed her helmet. "Are you all right?"

"I'm perfect." She smiled and lifted her face.

He captured her lips, pulling her against him. They kissed for some time, gently exploring one another's mouths, before William withdrew. He pecked her on the cheek.

"Let's get you inside."

They walked toward the front door, holding hands and whispering about their activities in the pool. It was, perhaps, one of the most romantic evenings of Raven's life.

As they approached the door, a figure stepped out of the shadows. William's body grew solid and a loud snarl escaped his chest. Instantly, he pushed her behind him.

Raven's gaze moved in the direction of William's. Standing a few feet away, dressed in priestly black, was Father Kavanaugh. He was staring at William with a thunderous expression.

"Release her!" he commanded.

He removed a cross from his pocket and held it in front of him as he advanced, reciting what Raven thought was Latin. She tried to get around William's body, but he pushed her back, cursing the priest in Latin, teeth bared.

"By the power of the Name, I command you to release her." Father produced a bottle of what looked like holy water. Panic ripped through Raven.

She knew holy water had only a minimal effect on William. She also knew that he was at pains to keep this information secret. She couldn't risk Father Kavanaugh throwing the water in their direction, only to learn that William was immune.

"Stop." Raven managed to lean around William, making eye contact with her former mentor. "I'm fine, Father. He won't hurt me."

The expression on the priest's face grew even more determined.

"Raven, walk toward me. Right now." His voice was low as he continued to approach the angry vampyre.

"She's mine," William hissed, blocking her from the priest's vision once again.

"William, stop it." She grabbed hold of his arm and tried to push him, but he didn't move. "This is Father Kavanaugh, the priest who saved me and Cara."

William's grip slackened for a moment and she managed to extricate herself. Limping to stand between the two men, she looked from one to the other.

"I'm safe. No one is going to hurt me. Both of you, just relax." She lifted her hands, trying to keep them from shaking.

"Raven, come here. Now." Father muttered words she did not understand. He fished in his pocket and produced a flat disk, which featured a red cross formed by two swords.

William grabbed Raven's hand, pulling her to his body. He hedged her with his arms. "We must go. Now."

"But he's practically my father," she protested. "I'm not going to run from him."

William leveled angry eyes on the priest. "What do you want?"

"I'm not here to do battle. I came to see Raven." The priest extended his hand in her direction. "Release her and we have no quarrel."

"Stop it, both of you." She extricated herself from William once again. "I'm not in danger. If you two would just come upstairs, I'm sure we can talk this out."

"I am asking you now, Cassita, to come with me." William's tone caused a chill to ascend Raven's spine.

"I need to talk to him. He won't hurt me." Raven tried to convince William with her eyes. William held her gaze, then his eyes shifted to the priest.

Father Kavanaugh had not relaxed his posture but he'd stopped moving, his pale eyes narrowed.

William spat on the ground. He turned and ran toward a nearby building.

Raven watched in shock as he scaled the wall without a backward glance, disappearing onto the roof.

He'd left her.

"We need to get inside." Father wrapped an arm around her shoulders and surveyed the piazza. "There could be more of them."

Confused, she allowed him to walk her to the front door of the building.

The priest insisted on crossing the threshold first, holding out a cross and reciting sacred Latin formulations. Raven was too distracted by her worries over William's departure to pay much attention.

When she unlocked her apartment, once again Father Kavanaugh insisted on entering first. He searched the entire space, turning on every light, before allowing her inside. He closed and bolted the door behind them, breathing a slow sigh of relief.

"What just happened?" She stumbled to a chair, anxious to take the weight off her leg. She was without her cane because William had suggested she leave it at his villa before the motorcycle ride.

"Thank God you're safe." The priest hugged her as if she'd survived a war. Raven returned his embrace.

Father Kavanaugh was in his midfifties and was two inches taller than Raven. He was wearing a collar, a black shirt, and black pants. His hair, like his carefully trimmed beard, was white. His eyes were blue and usually happy. His hands were roughened from years of hard work with Covenant House in Orlando.

Once he'd released her, he placed the cross, the disk, and the holy water on the kitchen table. He pulled up a chair and sat facing her, his skin visibly pale behind his beard.

"What just happened?" she repeated, arms crossed defensively over her chest.

"We have to get out of here. Pack a bag. I'll take you to Rome, where you'll be safe."

"I'm safe here."

The priest shook his head. "The . . . man you were with is dangerous. You need to get away from him. Tonight."

"He isn't dangerous to me."

Father's eyes narrowed. He touched her chin, turning her face to the side so he could examine her neck. "No marks," he muttered. "Thank God."

She jerked away. "Tell me what's going on. What were you two saying to each other in Latin?"

"I'm sorry to tell you this but the man you were with is not a man." The priest spoke in a low voice, watching her reaction.

"I know that," Raven huffed. "He's a vampyre."

Father sat back in his chair, eyes wide.

"You know?" he said at last.

"Of course. It's obvious, isn't it? I don't know too many humans who can climb buildings and disappear into the night."

"He's feeding from you," Father announced, reaching for his cross.

Instinctively, Raven's hand moved to her neck. "It isn't like that. He loves me. And I love him."

At the sound of her words, the priest stood, holding the cross. "We can break the connection. Come with me. I'll summon the others."

"What others?"

"The Jesuits have a house near the Duomo. I'll take you to them."

Raven lifted her hands in protest. "I'm not going anywhere."

Father Kavanaugh grew visibly agitated. "You don't understand. Vampyres are possessed by demons. You're obsessed with—"

"I'm not obsessed with anyone," she interrupted. "William isn't possessed. And neither am I."

The priest examined her closely, paying special attention to her eyes. He inhaled deeply and breathed on her.

Raven scowled. "What are you doing?"

He pressed his lips together. "It was a test. Vampyres are human beings who've become possessed by a demon. They hate and destroy. When they attack a human being without taking possession, it's called obsession."

"William would never attack me." Her tone was stubborn. "He loves me."

"William?" he whispered, shock etching his features. "That was the Prince?"

Raven nodded.

The priest crossed himself again. "We have to get you away from him—away from his control."

"I'm not under his control. Listen to what I'm saying." She tugged on the priest's hand, encouraging him to regain his seat. "William isn't like the others. A few months ago I was attacked by a group of men. William saved me."

"Vampyres don't interfere in human affairs."

"William did. He healed my wounds. I would have died without his help."

"So you've fed from him?" the priest whispered.

"No."

"Good." He sounded relieved. "But you've given yourself to him?"

Raven squirmed. "We are in love. It's not what you think."

"Raven." His tone was a soft remonstration. "Did you know he was a vampyre when you gave yourself to him?"

"Yes."

He winced. "Vampyres feed on human beings. They view us as prey, as objects to serve them and their pleasures. They can be seductive and charming, but they are liars. They can't be trusted."

His hand moved to her wrist, next to her bracelet. "Did he give that to you?"

She pulled her arm back. "Yes."

"It's a mark. You're his property. His pet."

"It was a gift. I'm not a pet." She set her chin stubbornly.

He passed a hand over his mouth. "I arrived in Rome at the beginning of the month. Your mother e-mailed me, saying you and Cara had had a falling-out. I came to see if I could help." He gave her an anguished look. "I can't believe this. I can't believe you're a feeder."

"Don't call me that." Raven's green eyes flashed. "I'm in love with him."

"Don't you understand?" The priest's eyes filled with pity. "They don't love. They're evil."

"You don't know him."

"Yes, I do. I know all about the Prince of Florence."

"How?"

The priest's eyes locked on hers. "I'm part of a group that protects human beings from vampyres."

Raven felt as if her heart stopped beating.

Father Kavanaugh moved his chair closer.

"I'm a member of a group called the Curia."

Chapter Twenty-seven

"What?" Raven croaked, her mouth and throat suddenly dry. "I take it you've heard of us."

She nodded, trying to process his revelation.

"I was recruited to join the Curia shortly after I became a Jesuit. I've been serving them ever since. They just transferred me to Rome."

"You're one of them?"

The priest frowned. "I see he's been filling your head with nonsense."

"You kill them."

"We free them."

"A polite euphemism for murder," she scoffed.

"We exorcise the demon, allowing the human being to be free of its control."

"So you say." Raven wrapped her hands around her middle, fighting the creeping ascent of nausea. "I heard about what happened in the Middle Ages. How you laid waste to them."

"Revisionist history. Did the vampyre describe what Europe was like before the Curia was formed?"

Raven pressed her lips together. "Not really."

He leaned forward in his chair. "Then let me enlighten you. They were like animals, feeding on everyone—women and children, the aged, the sick. And in every case, every single case, they violated the victim sexually. When they feed, they rape. Their victim is never the same."

Raven shut her eyes and turned her face away. "I don't believe you."

"It's true. They use mind control or force to overpower their victims, then they take what they want, leaving a damaged person behind. They're horrible, evil beings."

Raven coughed, fighting the urge to retch. "William doesn't allow them to feed on children. And he would never do what you described."

"Raven." The priest's eyes filled with pity. "Have you ever seen him feed?"

"He feeds from bottles."

Father regarded her with what could only be sorrow. "And from you. Tell me, was sexual activity part of the feeding?"

Raven's skin flamed. She said nothing.

The priest took her hand. "If you've fornicated with him, the darkness has been transmitted to you. You may not be possessed at this moment, but you're under its influence. It clouds your reason."

"Nonsense." Raven tossed his hand aside and stood. "You believe a bunch of fairy tales."

"Careful." His tone grew sharp. "I've devoted my life to those fairy tales. I would die for them. And they're the only things that can save you."

"I don't want to be saved." She huddled against the kitchen counter, her body shaking.

The priest's gaze moved to the trio of objects that sat on the table. He touched the disk briefly. "This isn't the first time I've tried to help you." He spoke gently, without looking at her. "In all the years we've known one another, have I ever deceived you?"

"No."

His eyes met hers. "Have I ever lied?"

She shook her head.

"I swear before God, I am not deceiving you. I'm trying to save you!" His hands began to shake. He stuffed them in his pockets. "The Curia was formed by the Church to keep the vampyre population in check. We protect humanity and keep the vampyres from taking over."

"If they're so bad, why don't you eliminate them?"

"Not even God can eliminate the evil perpetrated by free will."

Raven rolled her eyes.

"It's true," he continued. "We can limit their evil, but we cannot eliminate them. At least, not all of them. To do so, we'd have to eliminate the demon population that spawns them. And that is beyond our capabilities.

"Just like demons, vampyres are allowed to operate within certain boundaries and according to certain rules. When the boundaries are breached, we intervene. They fear us and they are right to do so. We have goodness on our side."

Raven resisted the urge to scoff, mostly because she happened to believe that the person sitting in front of her was a good man.

The priest changed the subject. "Tell me what happened with your sister."

Raven leaned heavily against the counter, favoring her injured leg. "What did my mother tell you?"

"I prefer to hear your version." The priest's tone grew gentle once again. His gentleness tore through her the way a sword tears through flesh.

"I called Cara and tried to talk to her about our stepfather. I asked her what would give her closure."

"How did she respond?"

"At first, she was indifferent. Then she got angry. She said I fell down the stairs." Raven's lips twisted at the memory.

"That was cruel. It was also a lie."

"I defended myself. She got upset and yelled at me. Then Dan told me to stay out of their lives and not call again." Raven bit at the inside of her mouth to keep the tears at bay.

Father gave her a sympathetic look. "Obviously, Cara doesn't want to remember. But I'm curious why you broached the subject with her now." His gaze dropped to the gold bracelet on Raven's wrist.

"I didn't tell Cara about William. But since you already know . . ." She gestured to the items on the table. "William brought my stepfather to Florence."

"Why would he do that?"

"He promised me justice."

The priest frowned. "Vampyres don't care about justice, especially justice for a pet."

"Not all vampyres view human beings as pets."

"Perhaps he was bored and looking for amusement."

"So he sent someone all the way to California to track down my stepfather because he was bored?"

The priest didn't respond.

"William gave my stepfather to me as a gift. He wanted to give me the opportunity to kill him."

The priest sat back in his chair, horrified. "Raven, you didn't—"

"Of course I didn't," she snapped. "Don't you know me at all?"

"I thought I did." The priest stroked his beard thoughtfully. "What happened to your stepfather?"

"I asked William to send him back to California and turn him over to the police."

"And did he?"

"Only because I asked. He wanted to kill him."

Father Kavanaugh looked puzzled. "Why would a vampyre, a prince, take so much interest in your stepfather?"

"I told you—he loves me."

The priest turned, facing the talismans on the table. "That's impossible."

"For someone who trades in the impossible, you're incredibly skeptical."

"I'm not a skeptic about facts. The Prince is the subject of extensive discussion in Rome. I'll grant he's more conservative than the other rulers, but that doesn't make him good."

"He's different from the others." Raven's voice grew quiet. "If only you knew how much."

"His control is slipping." The priest picked up the disk and showed it to her. "We don't want a repeat of the Black Death, when bodies lined the city streets."

"William won't let that happen."

"Perhaps not." He cleared his throat. "Finding you here, with him, changes everything."

Raven crossed over to him. "Please don't bring the Curia here. William enforces the laws. The others won't."

The priest surveyed her expression, noting her clenched fists. "Then come with me."

She took a step back. "I can't. I love him."

The priest sighed loudly. "I am not eager for war. But I am only one among many. Those decisions aren't up to me."

"But they'll kill him!"

"They'll free him," Father insisted. "And by association, you. Don't you think you deserve to be free?"

"I am free," she hissed. "I never thought anyone would love me for myself. I never thought anyone would defend me. He does."

A pained look filled the priest's eyes. "I tried to defend you. I love you, Raven. You and Cara are the daughters I never had."

Raven looked down at her shoes.

"I love you, too," she whispered. "I know you defended me."

"I still defend you. I'm defending you now."

She lifted her gaze. "Then help us," she pleaded.

He drew a deep breath. "Perhaps you love him. Stranger things have happened. But the human being you love is possessed by a great evil."

She shook her head fiercely. "That's a lie."

He pulled at his beard in agitation. "If he is a vampyre, the darkness in him is more powerful than his humanity. Even if that weren't the case, he will still be held accountable for his choice."

"What's that supposed to mean?"

"A vampyre can't enter a home without being invited. A demon can't possess an adult human unless the adult grants it entrance."

Raven's mouth dropped open. "You're telling me he wanted this?"

"I'm not saying there wasn't a seduction. But if the human rejects the darkness forcefully, the demon looks elsewhere."

"William is different."

"William is a vampyre." Father stood, picking up the cross from the table. "Do not be deceived. He's controlled by darkness, and it's darkness you see when you look into his eyes. It's darkness you take into your body when you fornicate with him. If you aren't careful, that darkness will overtake you as well.

"Reflect on that, Raven, and stay away from him." He held the cross out to her. "Take it. It will protect you."

"I don't need protection from William—he protects me from the others."

The priest held her gaze for a moment and placed the cross in his pocket. He gathered the remaining objects in his hands.

"I will return to Rome tonight. Come with me."

"No."

"It's dangerous here. He might kill you."

"He's as likely to hurt me as you are."

The priest's face grew stricken. Raven felt tears form at the sight. She wanted to go to him. She wanted to hug him.

But she loved William more.

The priest sighed and rubbed at his beard before crossing to her and placing his hands on her shoulders. "Think about what I've said. Even if you have nothing to fear from him, you have everything to fear from the other vampyres, especially if they wish to attack him through you."

The priest kissed her forehead. Then, with his thumb, he made the sign of the cross over her skin.

"May God protect and defend you."

He walked to the door and unbolted it, placing his hand on the doorknob. "I'm not giving up on you, Raven."

She nodded, her eyes wet.

"Whatever you do, don't feed from him." The priest's tone was ominous. "That is a line, once crossed, that cannot be uncrossed."

Father Kavanaugh exited her apartment, closing the door behind him.

A few minutes later, she realized he'd left the cross on the table.

Chapter Twenty-eight

William's first concern was for the safety of the principality. He ran from building to building, leaping across the roofs, searching for any sign the Curia had invaded. He made a circuit around the city, examining the borders and the patrols with an assessing eye.

Eventually, he stood high atop the Palazzo Vecchio, staring down at the city he loved, and felt fear.

Under normal circumstances, he would have gone to the Consilium, shared his intelligence, and sent out search parties to see if any other Curia members had entered the city. But he couldn't risk exposing Raven.

The Consilium would demand to know about her connection to the Curia and would likely sentence her to death, a sentence he could commute to transformation, as prince. But either outcome was unacceptable. Raven didn't want to be a vampyre. And the thought of her death . . .

William shuddered.

How was it that his love for Alicia had been reduced to a small ember in comparison to the raging fire of his love for Raven? He thought he'd known love. But the warmth and affection he'd felt for Alicia was nothing compared to what he felt for Raven.

He felt desperation and desire.

The Consilium would have to be told about the infiltration of the Curia in the city, if they didn't know about it already. The intelligence network would inevitably discover the priest's presence. He would have to conceal Raven's involvement, through whatever means necessary.

With a cry, he leapt from the top of the palazzo to the stones below, breaking into a run upon impact. He'd done his duty assessing the security of the principality. Now he needed to make sure Raven was safe. If the priest had decided to take her with him . . .

William didn't want to think about the consequences.

As he raced over the Ponte Santa Trinita and over to Santo Spirito, he didn't pray. But he spoke to his friend the saint, long dead, and begged him to pray, not for himself but for her.

Chapter Twenty-nine

Raven felt as if she were underwater; all sounds seemed distant, all sights seemed blurry.

She sat at her kitchen table, staring at Father Kavanaugh's cross, completely immobile. Her thoughts returned to the day William had revealed what he was. She recalled watching in horror as he stuck a dagger through his hand and began to bleed. She remembered trying to flee from him.

The revelation that Jack Kavanaugh, the man she'd thought of as a father, was a member of the Curia was just as shocking, if not more so. He was the best person she knew. The most saintlike. And he belonged to a group that killed sentient beings. Furthermore, he believed William to be evil.

How could someone so wise and so kind be so deceived?

Unless he isn't deceived, she thought.

A sliver of doubt burrowed its way into her mind.

Had William really chosen this life? Was he culpable for that choice?

Raven covered her eyes with her hands, unable to trace that line of thought to its conclusion.

Mechanically, she moved to the window, noting with some concern that William's motorcycle was still parked outside.

He'd left her. He'd promised to protect her but he'd left. Surely he was as afraid of the Curia as she, if not more so. And he'd abandoned her.

She wondered if he'd return.

She wondered if love could be killed.

With these worries weighing on her, Raven stood, preparing to switch off the lights and go to bed. She took a step forward, pausing when she saw the cross Father Kavanaugh had left behind.

It was small and primitive looking, a wooden crucifix with a crudely carved figure of Christ. He had been so sure it would protect her, which was no doubt why he'd left it behind despite her protests.

It must be a relic.

She examined the cross, wondering what kind of relic it was. Some crucifixes had the relic inside, visible through a tiny window on the back. This one had no such window. She was about to place it back on the table and go to bed, when a sudden realization seized her.

If this were a relic, William would avoid it. He didn't want the others knowing about his resistance to relics. He'd removed the relic he'd initially given her from her apartment when they first came to know one another, so as not to arouse suspicion.

If she wanted William to return, she needed to remove the cross as soon as possible. She grabbed her keys, tucked her cell phone into the back pocket of her jeans, and exited her apartment, locking the door securely behind her.

As she descended the staircase, clutching the railing in the absence of her cane, her heart beat quickly. She moved through the back door and walked to a neighboring building, which also faced the piazza. She wasn't sure what kind of radius a relic projected, but she decided that three buildings away should be far enough.

She placed the cross in a small alcove next to a shuttered window.

At least it would offer her neighbors some kind of protection. She turned around and was just approaching her back door when she felt a sudden gust of wind.

She opened her mouth to scream, but a hand closed over it, muffling the sound.

Chapter Thirty

Raven struggled, but only until her eyes met William's.

He motioned to her to be quiet before lifting her in his arms and sweeping around the side of the building to his motorcycle. He placed her on her feet, his arms wrapped like iron bands around her waist.

"I thought I'd lost you." His normally neutral facade had cracked, revealing intense emotion.

"I thought I'd lost you." Her voice was tremulous.

His kiss was fierce as he squeezed her body tightly. He placed the helmet on her head and mounted the bike, pulling her to sit behind him. Soon they were racing across the Arno and up the winding road that led to the Piazzale Michelangelo and beyond, to his villa.

Raven clutched his back like a drowning person, eyes screwed shut. This was not like the journey they'd gone on hours before. William drove like a madman, taking the curves at an inhuman rate of speed, the motorcycle screaming its acceleration.

Raven's stomach lurched into her throat and she fought back the urge to vomit.

He pulled through the gates that protected his villa and shot down the driveway toward the freestanding garage. When he stopped, he had to pry Raven's arms from around his waist.

"We're safe," he said, lifting her helmet.

"I wish I could believe that," she managed, clutching her middle. Without ceremony, she leaned over the side of the bike and promptly emptied her stomach's contents on the ground.

❀❀

The library was dark despite the dim light that shone through the windows and the panes of glass that formed the high, domed ceiling. William had eschewed electric lights, as he was wont to do, opting instead to augment the starlight with a few candles.

"I forgot." He crouched in front of Raven's chair and wiped her mouth with his handkerchief.

"Forgot what?"

"I forgot to temper my speed. It's my fault you were sick." He tossed the handkerchief aside and pressed a glass of water into her hand.

Raven's hand was shaking so badly, the water sloshed over the sides of the glass.

With a curse, William placed his hand over hers. "We're safe here. I swept the city, looking for any sign of the Curia. I think your priest is the only one."

"What if there are more?"

"My patrols will raise the alarm. We're safe inside the villa. The relics will confuse the Curia and cause them to look elsewhere."

"You aren't thinking of leaving?"

William pressed his lips together. "I cannot leave my people."

Raven took a few sips of water before pushing the cup aside. She curled into the chair, leaning against the armrest.

William cupped her face. He pressed his lips to each cheek, slowly, as if he were savoring the contact. "It's been a long time since I felt fear."

"You left me." She gripped his arms at the wrists, holding his hands to her face. "Why?"

His gray eyes bored into hers. "If I'd stayed, it would have meant death."

"For you or for him?"

William pulled away and stood, running his fingers through his hair. "He had a powerful relic in his possession. If I hadn't fled, if I'd been drawn into battle with him, he would have realized my strength." William clenched his jaw. "I would have had to kill him."

Raven turned her face away.

"I have no compunction about killing him," William continued quietly. "I've killed members of the Curia before. But to do so would be an act of war."

He sighed. "Also, I am not eager to kill the man who rescued you and your sister. I hate the Curia. Their aim is to destroy us; my aim is to defend myself and my people. To remain this evening would have meant the death of one of us—your priest or your lover. I made the choice to leave, saving us both. I doubt your priest would have done the same."

Raven looked over and found William watching her. He was standing some distance away, in front of his desk, his posture ramrod straight.

She cleared her throat. "Father Kavanaugh left for Rome. I tried to reason with him. I asked him not to bring the Curia here, but he said he doesn't make those decisions. He also said the Curia knows you're conservative in your rule, but they don't want the existence of vampyres exposed to the world."

"The Curia is always eager to preserve its power." William spoke bitterly. "I must find the traitor. Quickly."

He maintained his distance, his posture growing increasingly defensive, as if he were preparing for a blow. "What else did you tell him?"

Raven approached William slowly. She picked up one of his fists and cradled it in her hands. "I told him I love you. I told him you wouldn't hurt me."

William's upper lip curled in derision. "Love is a myth to them. They understand power and control, but little else."

"He was relieved I haven't fed from you."

"Of course," William scoffed. "We can't have his pristine Raven sullied by the monster's blood." He sighed. "But he's right to be worried. Once you've ingested a certain amount of blood, you begin to change." William paused, his eyes appearing to darken. "And there's the bond that exists when blood is exchanged."

"I have a difficult time believing we could be bonded more than we are already."

He lifted her hand and pressed his lips to the back of it, as if that were an answer.

"At the moment, your soul is in peril because you're fornicating with a vampyre. No doubt he believes I'm controlling you. But what he truly fears is that you'll become a vampyre, because then he'd be obligated to kill you."

Raven shivered once again. "I don't think he'd do that."

William's hand moved to her shoulder. "Do not underestimate his loyalty to the Curia. They have one mission and one mission alone, and that is to destroy us. Any affection he has for you will be pushed aside if you oppose them."

Raven lifted her chin. "I don't believe it."

"Try." William crossed over to the large wall of windows on the far side of the library, turning his back on her.

"Funny how you're so sure you know him and what he'll do,"

Raven called to William. "He's so sure he knows you and what you'll do. I'm caught in the middle, convinced you're both wrong."

A flexing of his shoulders was William's only response.

"Father Kavanaugh is wrong about you. I can't help but believe you're equally wrong about him."

"That's a dangerous inference." William spoke without turning around. "He gave you a powerful relic to ward me off."

"Which I removed from my apartment." She leaned the hip of her injured leg against his desk, needing the support. "He said you chose this life."

"He knows nothing," William spat out, turning around.

"He said he wants to free you."

William strode toward her, his body almost a blur. "You've known him since you were a child. Did you know he was part of the Curia?"

Raven scowled at his accusatory tone. "Of course not! I didn't even believe in vampyres before I met you. You know that."

William continued to glare at her, his eyes blazing.

"He asked me to go to Rome with him. I refused. And even though you aren't asking the question, I'll answer by telling you that I didn't reveal any of your secrets or any of your troubles in the principality." She cursed. "I'm your lover, William, not your enemy."

His posture relaxed somewhat and he lifted a hand to trace the arc of her cheek.

"I know," he whispered.

"Father thinks you're possessed."

"Undoubtedly."

"Why does he think that?"

William dropped his hand. "I tried to explain it to you once, while we were in this room."

"All I can remember is you talking about light and darkness."

Raven moved to sit on top of William's desk in order to take the weight off her leg. She exhaled her relief.

"Just so," William mused. "You can see the possessive power of the darkness in ferals. They lack rationality. They behave like animals. Vampyres maintain their rationality, but there are times when the darkness clouds it. Or overtakes it." His gaze dropped to one of the candles that sat on his desk, and he stared at the flickering flame.

"The darkness is a demon?"

"The Curia thinks so."

"What do you think?"

William's eyes met hers. "All I know is my own experience. I feel the presence of the darkness; I feel its power and its influence. But I am able to overcome it, at least, on occasion."

He cleared his throat. "When I came upon you in the alley, I was tempted to feed from you. I was tempted to share you with Aoibhe and the others."

"But you didn't." Raven clasped her hands together.

"No, I did not. I remembered how I felt when I found Alicia. I failed her, but I would not fail you."

Raven touched his sleeve. "Your humanity saved you."

"No." William jerked away from her. "Humanity has its own darkness. You of all people know that. It was the memory of goodness and the resolve to preserve it that enabled me to save you. I'd do it again, and again, without regret. If I lived a thousand years, I would make the same choice."

His profile appeared resigned and vulnerable.

Raven blinked back tears. "Did you choose to become a vampyre, William?"

He pretended not to hear and approached the desk. He made his hand pass through the candle's flame, over and over again, the movements rhythmic and hypnotic.

"William?" she prompted.

"Yes."

Raven felt a tightness in her chest. She pressed her hand over her heart, as if in an effort to release it. "I thought for sure Father Kavanaugh was wrong about that. I thought someone forced you into this life."

"Sadly, no. Once again, I can only speak from my experience, but I have the suspicion that transformations only occur when the humans are willing to give themselves over to the change."

"Was that how it was when you transformed someone?"

"I don't know," he confessed, holding his hand in the flame. "I've never changed anyone."

"Stop." Raven grabbed his wrist and pulled his hand from the fire.

"It doesn't hurt." He held his palm in front of her face. "See? No harm done."

"You've harmed me by doing that in front of me. And you've self-harmed by treating your body with indifference."

William placed his hand palm up on her thigh. "I didn't mean to harm you." His voice was like a child's.

She lifted his palm to her lips and kissed it, surprised by the heat that radiated from his unmarked skin. "I'm glad you're all right."

His gaze flickered to the surface of the desk. "I remember when I tried to prove to you I was a vampyre. I stuck a dagger in my hand." William's eyes lifted to hers. "You were so upset. You wanted to use your white sweater to stem the bleeding."

"I love you, William. Of course I don't want to see you hurt."

"There's very little on this earth that can hurt me," he whispered, his expression solemn. "But I shall be more careful, my little lark with the large heart."

"Only when it comes to you."

"Ah, but that's not true, *Defensa*. And we both know it."

"Why haven't you transformed someone?"

He pulled his hand back. "Transformations require a certain level of responsibility. The maker becomes responsible for the vampyre he creates. I didn't want that kind of responsibility. I didn't want to exploit a human's momentary weakness and condemn him to a long life of this." He gestured to himself.

She reached for him, pulling him to stand in between her parted knees.

"Tell me why you chose this life for yourself."

William buried his face in her neck before he began his story.

Chapter Thirty-one

"I've already told you I lived in York in the thirteenth century. I was the eldest son in a Norman family. I fell in love with an Anglo-Saxon's daughter, Alicia. We made plans to elope but she was attacked on her way to meet me."

Raven tightened her embrace.

"After Alicia died, my family arranged for me to marry a Norman girl from another aristocratic family. I fled the arrangement and traveled to Oxford. While I was there, the Dominicans took me in. I lived with them and continued my studies, later taking vows as a novice.

"I moved to Paris to continue my education. It was there I became a student of a famous teacher of theology."

William cleared his throat.

"He was a quiet man—contemplative and studious. But he was kind to me. I confessed to him about Alicia and how I'd left my family. He put his hand on my head and prayed for me, with a look of sorrow on his face. As if he was truly sorry I'd lost her. As if he felt my grief."

"I'm glad he was kind to you."

"He was very kind. And very wise."

"What year did you go to Paris?"

"Twelve sixty-nine."

"How old were you?"

"Just turning nineteen."

"So young," she mused.

He smiled. "I've kept my true age a secret, but I will tell you. I was born in 1250."

"And you became a vampyre in 1274?"

"Yes."

Raven touched his face. "So young. So beautiful."

He closed his eyes as she tenderly traced his eyebrows and his jaw.

"I'm so much older than you." Her voice sounded regretful.

He opened his eyes. They shone in amusement.

"Have you been alive for eight centuries?"

"You were only twenty-four when you were changed. I'm thirty."

"Actually, I was twenty-three. I was changed in March but my birthday is in November." He pressed his lips to the side of her hand, as it rested against his cheek. "I didn't realize I would have to wait seven hundred years to find my soul mate."

She smiled, withdrawing her hand. "I didn't think my soul mate would be a younger man."

He laughed and the sound echoed about the dark library. "Age should mean nothing to us. What matters is that we've found one another. Finally."

"I agree. Your eyes look old sometimes, but your face always looks young."

"It's part of the curse—trapped in a body that never ages while our mind slowly decays."

She shuddered. "That's morbid."

He rubbed his thumb against his lower lip. "That is my reality. But I was telling you about my time in Paris. I lived, worked, and studied with my fellow Dominicans. My days and nights were structured around prayer, time at the university, and Mass. I was respected for my ability to reason and my facility with languages. I became an assistant to a friar called Reginald, who was the confessor and assistant of my teacher. When they were transferred to Naples, I went with them."

"When was that?"

"Twelve seventy-two." He pulled away, running his fingers through his hair once again. "My teacher helped me regain my faith in God. I found comfort in the Mass. I began to believe that Alicia's death, while unjust, served a holy purpose, because it enabled me to find my vocation. I prepared for the priesthood, surrounded by intellectual and spiritual titans, working in the service of a saint."

Raven watched William's expression change. "What happened?"

"What always happens—injustice and evil eat away at goodness. The teacher I was serving became ill. At the time, we weren't sure what was wrong with him, but he grew feeble. A couple of months later, we were on our way to a church council and he hit his head. This seemed to worsen his condition. We brought him by donkey to a monastery in Fossanova, about a hundred kilometers from Rome. He rested for a few days and then, against all our prayers, against all our hopes, he died."

Raven took William's hand and squeezed it. "I'm so sorry."

"Today his death would have been preventable. We would have taken him to the hospital and they'd have scanned his brain and found the injury."

"Or you could have helped him as you helped me."

William shook his head. "He was a saint. He would have chosen death rather than taken the alchemy I could have offered him."

"You loved him."

"Yes." William's gray eyes burned in the darkness. "When I

needed wisdom, I went to him. When I struggled with doubt and guilt, I went to him. He was my brother, my friend, and my teacher."

"He was your Father Kavanaugh," she whispered.

"Hardly. He was a saint, not a killer."

William turned toward the window, facing away from her. "He died in the morning. We were all in shock. It happened so suddenly, we weren't prepared. Two of us thought we saw an angel standing over the body, poised to take his soul to paradise."

"Was it an angel?"

"It wasn't a demon. Now that I am well acquainted with darkness, I can state with certainty the being was good. He certainly wasn't the black angel Guido da Montefeltro speaks of in Dante's *Inferno*. But it doesn't matter. The angel wasn't there for us; he was there for our teacher. And our teacher was already dead.

"We cared for his body, preparing it for burial. We turned his papers and books over to Friar Reginald, who'd been cataloging them. We divided his possessions. There were several crosses, one of which had been a gift from his wealthy sister. That cross came to me, along with a couple of other smaller ones.

"I didn't tell the others, but I prayed for a miracle—a resurrection. I spent hours prostrate in front of the high altar in the church, begging God to raise my teacher from the dead. By nightfall, I was crazed with grief. I left the monastery in a daze, still clutching the belongings of my friend.

"I climbed a nearby hill and stood at the top, in utter despair. How could God have let such goodness die? How could he take my teacher from me, when I had so much to learn? When I'd already lost so much?"

William cursed in Latin, the blasphemy echoing inside the library.

"He was too young to die. His writings were unfinished. His work wasn't done. It was such a waste. So unjust.

"I'd fled York when Alicia was murdered. Now that my teacher was dead, where could I go? The thought of staying with the Dominicans, of devoting my life to a God who wouldn't even bother intervening to save a saint, was repugnant to me.

"I considered suicide, but the only thing that stayed my hand was the thought that it would grieve my teacher. He'd written about it, of course, arguing it was a mortal sin. And in that moment, I was more averse to his sorrow than to the fate of hell."

"William," Raven murmured, approaching him.

He held out his hands, warding her off.

"But I wanted to die. I begged God to kill me because I couldn't do it myself.

"It was then, at my lowest point, I heard something rustling in the copse of trees behind me. I turned and saw a man dressed in white, coming out of the darkness."

"An angel?"

William's upper lip curled. "My crisis of faith didn't warrant the sending of an angel. But in his own way, God answered my prayer.

"At first, I thought the man was one of my brothers, sent to bring me back to the monastery. I knew I would never return. My belief in God's justice died with my teacher. I could no longer serve him.

"The man stood at a distance, watching me for some time. At length, he addressed me in Latin. His Latin was archaic and spoken with a strange accent. It wasn't the language of the Church, but he spoke slowly and simply so I could understand. He said he could scent my despair and he asked why I, a novice dressed in the robes of a Dominican, would have given up hope.

"I explained that my teacher had died. That I was lost. That God had forsaken me. The figure smiled and said he could give me life. He could give me power and riches and purpose. He promised to be my teacher and my father." William gritted his teeth. "He called me his son.

"He said he'd been alone for many years, that he was wealthy and had a large estate. All he lacked was an heir. 'Put away the playthings of the old religion and become my son,' he said. 'I can take away your pain.'

"On impulse, I dropped the things I'd inherited from my teacher. I took off my Dominican robe and stood in my underclothes. He beckoned me. I walked toward him and he hugged me like a son.

"I wept. He kissed my forehead and turned my head to the side, then he sank his teeth into my neck."

Raven shivered. "He was a vampyre?"

"Yes. At the time, I had no idea there were such things. I'd heard rumors of strange beings in Paris, but we thought it was the work of the devil. We didn't think there was a different race of beings hidden among us.

"When he was finished drinking from me, he whispered in my ear, asking if I wanted the life he could give me." William's eyes fixed on Raven's. "I said yes. In that moment, I felt his power. I felt the pull to join him. And I felt relief from my suffering. He placed my mouth on his neck and told me to drink.

"At first, I was horrified, but he kept whispering, 'I will give you life. I will take your pain away. You will be my son.'" William shuddered, turning toward the gardens. "I drank."

Raven placed her arms around his waist from behind, hugging him. He stood stiff and still, not touching her.

"What happened next?" Her voice was muffled by his jacket.

"The transformation takes time. It's painful and confusing. I was barely conscious through most of it. No sooner had I swallowed the first taste of his blood than I felt regret. But I kept drinking." His hands clenched into fists. "I was angry, I was in despair. Yet, even as I knew I was making a terrible mistake and unwilling to stop making it, I sent a feeble prayer to my teacher, begging his forgiveness, begging for him to pray for me."

William placed his hands against the glass, head bowed.

"When I awoke, my body was as you see it now. My maker was standing over me with a look of triumph. He pulled me to my feet and said that he would show me my new gifts. And that's how my life as a vampyre began."

She hugged him more tightly, not knowing what to say.

"My maker was extremely powerful, which probably explains my strength."

"Could he walk in the sun?"

"No."

"But you can."

"Yes."

"You're a mystery."

"Perhaps. I spent time with my maker, who, true to his word, treated me as a son. One day I realized the normal things that deterred vampyres had little effect on me. I was wise enough to realize my discovery was something I should keep secret. On that day, I went to my maker and took my leave, saying I wanted to make my own way in the world. He gave me a father's blessing and I left."

"Where did you go?"

"I returned to the place where my teacher died—out of sentimentality, perhaps. I don't know. I traveled up the hill and found that the items I'd left behind were still there. It was as if they were waiting for me. Without thinking, I picked them up. It was only later I realized they had power over other vampyres, but not me."

"The relics," she whispered. "They belonged to your teacher."

"Yes." His posture softened and he placed his arms around her.

"They are all I have left of him. I don't know why they have no effect on me, but they don't."

"If I were a superstitious person, I'd suggest they were a gift."

William's eyebrows drew together. "From whom?"

"Your teacher."

"He wouldn't give a gift to a creature like me."

"He had compassion for your suffering when he was alive," she said softly. "I don't believe in an afterlife. But if I did, I would expect your teacher to have compassion on you still."

"He'd be like the Curia—nobly disapproving."

"Nothing you've told me about him and nothing I've read about him suggests he was that kind of person."

William gave her a half smile. "You've read about him?"

"You forget, I went to a Catholic college. Your teacher was—"

William pressed his fingers to her lips. "Don't."

"Why not?"

"In my present state, I am unworthy to speak his name or to hear it."

"I don't believe that. I don't think he'd believe that, either."

William's gaze bent to the floorboards and all at once, he looked like a boy. "He'd be ashamed of me for losing hope."

"You were young. You'd experienced a great loss. I understand this. Why wouldn't he?"

"I accepted what my tempter offered, knowing it to be wrong. That means I committed a mortal sin."

"You were overwhelmed by grief. And even if you weren't, in that moment you asked for your teacher's help. You must have regretted your decision."

William lifted his eyes to study her. For a moment, his guilty expression faded. Then, like a cloud determined to block out the sun, it returned.

Raven reached up to kiss the edge of his frown.

"Now I understand why you were so upset when I told you the feral called him a pedophile."

William's teeth ground together. "I would have killed it for the insult. Fortunately, by the time you told me, it was already dead."

"Did you come to Florence once you'd retrieved the relics?"

"No. My memory of my human life was beginning to fade. But I remembered everything about my teacher and about Alicia. I returned to York as a vampyre, determined to exact justice."

"And did you?"

"I didn't rest until I'd found her killers. They were a band of brutes who'd been passing through the city. I hunted them, tortured them, and threw their bodies on a pyre. But it was too late for Alicia. I thought that as a vampyre I might have had the power of resurrection." He closed his eyes. "I was wrong."

He peered down at Raven sadly. "I'd spent time in Florence with my teacher. It was a beautiful city—full of artists and intellectuals. I decided to return. The Prince allowed me to join his principality and I've been here ever since."

"I understand how it feels to lose a father. I'm sorry about your teacher."

"Your surrogate father has returned." William's tone grew ominous. "Would that my teacher would make the same trip."

"Father Kavanaugh told me to leave you. He said it was dangerous for me to be with you."

"He's right." William withdrew from her embrace and looked out over the gardens. "If the Curia comes, you'll be caught in the middle."

"Father Kavanaugh said he'd protect me."

"He will side with the Curia." William gave her a look filled with resolve.

"Then we have to keep the Curia from coming."

"No," said William harshly. "*I* need to keep the Curia from coming. If they come, you must flee the city."

"No. You tried to get me to leave before, remember? And I refused. I'm not leaving you or the city. I love you, William Malet. I'm staying with you."

William's eyes burned with gray fire. He pulled her into his arms, penetrating her mouth with his tongue. She clutched his shoulders, holding on desperately as his kiss claimed her.

Without warning, he backed her up against the nearest bookcase, pressing his body against hers.

Chapter Thirty-two

William's left hand cupped the back of Raven's head, cushioning her against the bookshelf. He licked at the inside of her mouth, his tongue teasing hers before withdrawing. She followed, eagerly tasting him, her fingers creeping up his neck to twist in his hair.

There was no space between them. His unyielding body pressed against her soft curves, the contact enticing.

She hummed as his hand slid to her waist, tracing the band of her jeans before popping the button. Raven took that opportunity to tug his dress shirt from his pants, undoing buttons and pushing the shirt over his muscular shoulders.

With a growl, William tossed the shirt to the floor.

In the flickering candlelight, she pulled back to examine him—his defined chest and abdominals, his strong deltoids and biceps. Her finger made a lazy circuit around his navel, and she smiled as he closed his eyes and groaned.

Feverishly, he took her mouth, unzipping her jeans and dragging them over her hips. He knelt before her, tearing at her underwear until it fell. Carefully lifting her injured leg to his shoulder, he nuzzled the inside of her upper thigh with his nose.

When his tongue made contact with the flesh between her legs, her head snapped back, slamming against the bookshelf.

"Ow," she cried, not quite seeing stars.

William lifted his face, his perfect lips glistening in the semidarkness. "Are you all right?"

She nodded sheepishly, placing her hands on his head in an effort to steady herself. She toyed with his blond hair as he continued to lick, teasing and tantalizing with every stroke.

The leg she was standing on began to shake. William's cool hands cupped her backside, bracing her against his mouth.

Her head moved from side to side mindlessly as inchoate noises escaped her throat, echoing in the cavernous room.

He slowed his pace once she climaxed, but continued to caress her, until the sensation was too much and she tried to push him away.

Abruptly, he stood, eyes like glittering embers with a face fierce with longing. He picked up his discarded shirt and passed it over his face before throwing it aside once again.

Raven trembled against the bookshelf, her legs like rubber. He lifted her, pulling her legs to encircle his hips. His left hand cradled her head, shielding her from harm.

He brought his nose to hers. "When I am alone, I long for your taste. You are like honey on my tongue. I could feed on you for eternity." He tugged at the buttons of her shirt.

Soon her shirt and bra joined his clothes on the floor, a tangle of discarded fabric.

She kissed the side of his face as his mouth dropped to her breasts, embracing the round, full flesh before drawing a nipple between his teeth. She clasped his head to her chest, savoring the sensation of his cool tongue.

He laved her nipples, alternating between them. His hand moved to her backside, supporting her as he positioned himself between her legs.

With one quick, deep thrust he was inside her. She gasped at the exquisite fullness, clutching his shoulders.

His mouth moved to her neck as he moved eagerly in and out.

It was almost too much, the feeling of him rubbing against her sensitive flesh. Without warning, she felt her excitement crest and she bit down on his shoulder.

With a growl, William's teeth sank into her neck and he began to suck, drinking the warm, flowing blood from her artery.

She seemed to float away from her body as another wave of pleasure overwhelmed her. He drank as she floated, swallowing her life down his throat as he thrust into her.

His hips stilled as he found his release. He withdrew his teeth from her neck and gently licked at the wound.

Raven's breathing grew shallow and her heart rate began to slow. Then her body began to convulse.

William's eyes snapped open.

"Cassita?"

Chapter Thirty-three

S trong hands surrounded her, pulling her into a tight embrace. Raven relaxed against cool, smooth skin, unable to translate the mysterious words being whispered in her hair.

She murmured, satisfaction thrumming through her, and felt William's palm cover her heart.

He was feeling her heart beat.

When she opened her eyes she found herself cocooned by William's naked body. His eyebrows were drawn together, his eyes dark and distressed.

"You're all right." His tone sounded like a question.

She smiled. "You could say that. You're very generous with your attentions."

William's face was grim. "I thought I'd taken too much."

"I feel light-headed, but I always feel that way when you make me come."

He returned her smile, albeit hesitantly. "I'll try to remember that. Nevertheless, I need to be more careful. It will be difficult because I love how you taste—every part of you."

She nestled in his arms. "What would happen if you drank too much?"

William stiffened, the tendons in his arms rising below the surface of his skin.

"You'd die."

Raven froze. She thought back to a nightmare she'd had not long before—a nightmare in which William had fed from her until he'd drained her.

She cringed.

"I'll be more careful, I swear. It's just that you—I feel—" He faltered, his grip on her tightening.

"I feel it, too," she responded quietly. "If I could consume you, I would. I want you that much. Sometimes it feels like I'm drowning and you're the only one who can save me."

He nodded once, grinding his teeth together.

"I don't want to be separated from you, William. When you left me with Father Kavanaugh, I was afraid you wouldn't come back."

"I shall always come back," he whispered.

"Do you promise?" She gazed up at him in earnest.

"Insofar as I am able, I promise."

"Good." She kissed the space over his heart, relaxing in his arms once again.

"I need to take you to bed. You have to work in a few hours."

Raven sighed. "Work. I forgot."

He kissed her ear. "Come, my love. Come to my bed."

Still naked, he carried her to the hall and up the grand staircase to the second floor.

"If this is what it is to be damned," he murmured, "then may I never be forgiven."

Chapter Thirty-four

Raven appeared for work at the Uffizi the following morning, having had only a few hours' sleep.

Not that she minded.

She still had misgivings over the fact that William had left her when confronted with Father Kavanaugh. A niggling feeling in her stomach challenged her acceptance of his explanation. She didn't want to see conflict between the two men she loved. But she felt abandoned, just the same, and was still feeling its aftershocks.

William had been vulnerable to her, laying bare his past grief and fears. It was an especially intimate experience, even before they'd made love. For the rest of her life she would remember his beautiful, young face and haunted eyes as he told her about standing on the top of a hill, overcome with grief. Indeed, her mind could focus on little else that Monday morning.

And that was why as she neared the employees' entrance to the Uffizi, she dropped her guard, allowing someone to surprise her.

"Signorina Wood."

Raven jumped.

She turned and found Ispettor Batelli standing nearby. He was not wearing a happy expression.

"It's time for us to talk, Signorina Wood. You've avoided me long enough."

Raven favored him with her back. "You aren't supposed to talk to me. You were reprimanded for harassing me."

"I'm still in charge of the investigation. Despite what the newspapers say, I know Agent Savola wasn't murdered by the Russians."

Raven forced herself to keep going, leaning heavily on her cane. Batelli followed, dropping his voice so only she could hear. "Savola worked exclusively on cases involving stolen art. He had no connection with organized crime."

Raven ignored him, moving closer to the door.

"He was murdered near your apartment, after you were investigated by us in connection with the robbery here. He'd been following you for some time. Tell me, how long have you been sleeping with William York?"

Raven somehow lost her footing and pitched forward. Batelli caught her elbow, keeping her upright.

"Don't touch me!" She yanked away from him, nearly toppling over.

"Interesting," he said, his eyes calculating. "Interesting how you and Gabriel Emerson seem to be the only persons who recognize that name. Yet, neither of you wish to discuss him."

The inspector moved to block her path. "Are you fond of Switzerland?"

"If you don't get out of my way, I'll make a scene. Leave me alone." Raven gripped her cane tightly.

"William York made a large donation to the Uffizi two years ago. It was wired from a Swiss bank that, of course, refuses to disclose any information. The Mercedes that drives you around is registered to a Swiss diplomat. And Professor Emerson bought his illustrations from a family in Cologny, Switzerland."

"I'm leaving." Raven skirted the inspector and placed her hand on the door.

He pressed his palm flat against the door, holding it shut.

"I know whatever I tell you will be conveyed to him. So give him this message. I learned from Savola's mistake. If anything happens to me, William York will be exposed."

Against every instinct to suppress a reaction, Raven looked up at him, eyes wide.

Batelli leaned closer. "Tell him to place the illustrations, undamaged, in a secure location. He can have someone send an anonymous tip and we will retrieve them."

Raven tugged on the door and he stepped back, allowing her to open it.

"This is far from over." His voice followed her into the gallery as she quickly shuffled away from the door.

Chapter Thirty-five

"And then there were four," Niccolò remarked dryly, surveying the remaining Consilium members, excluding the Prince.

Niccolò, Lorenzo, Aoibhe, and Stefan of Montréal assembled in the council chamber underground, awaiting their ruler. He'd cut short their normal rest during daylight for urgent matters pertaining to security.

"Any news from Pierre and Max?" Aoibhe trained her dark eyes on Lorenzo, the second in command.

He reacted with visible annoyance, his hand tightening on the staff of Florence he always held during formal assemblies. "We received a message they'd reached Paris, but nothing since."

Aoibhe's gaze moved to Niccolò. "That's a bit odd, don't you think? How long would it take to kill a few humans and throw their bodies under the Eiffel Tower?"

"A bit of finesse is required in these matters." Niccolò's voice echoed in the large, almost empty chamber. "Not that you can appreciate such things."

With a snarl, she flew at him, teeth bared. He stepped to the side and, with a flick of his foot, swept her legs out from under her. She crashed to the ground with a loud cry.

Niccolò looked down at her, making eye contact before he spoke. "Not all of us are blinded by your beauty, female. You'd best remember that."

Aoibhe huffed and leapt to her feet, rearranging her skirts and her hair. She returned to her seat, wisely electing not to turn her back to him.

At that moment, the Prince threw open the doors to the council chamber and strode down the aisle. The Consilium members stood, bowing their respect and waiting until the Prince was seated before regaining their seats. Lorenzo tapped his staff on the floor to call the meeting to order.

The Prince pushed the folds of his black velvet cloak aside, resting his hands on the arms of the gold throne. "Niccolò, you're head of security. What have you to say?"

The Florentine stood and bowed. "As I reported to you earlier, a member of the Curia was spotted in the city yesterday evening."

The remaining Consilium members sat silently, dumbfounded.

"And?" The Prince's eyes revealed barely tempered fury.

The security adviser coughed, clearing his throat. "I spoke with the patrols, my lord. The Curia member in question arrived during the day, wearing ordinary clothes. Since he's American and new to Rome, he was not identified. However, our intelligence network reported he stayed at the Jesuit house inside the city and he returned to Rome by car shortly after midnight."

The Prince's expression became blank. "What about his movements inside the city?"

"I have nothing to report, my lord. It seems he was only noticed when he left. The patrols reported that you were surveilling them that evening, which they found curious."

The Prince waved his hand casually. "A surprise inspection. Instruct the patrols that I will continue those inspections, sometimes delegating the activity to a Consilium member. I want them on the highest alert. Order our spies in Rome to send photographs of any new Curia members so we are not surprised again. Any suspicious movement outside the Vatican is to be reported to me personally, immediately."

"Yes, my lord." Niccolò bowed, obviously shaken.

"A member of the Curia infiltrated my city and I was only notified after the man left. Am I to remove you over this offense?" The Prince's question was not truly a question.

"My lord, I would be in favor of exactly that." Aoibhe stood, her tone carefully calculated to sound less than triumphant.

"What say you, lieutenant?" The Prince turned his attention to Lorenzo.

Lorenzo bowed, restraining a smile. "Previous security advisers have been beheaded for less, my lord."

"True." The Prince's gaze moved to the French Canadian. "And you, the newest member of our august assembly?"

Stefan stood, nervously rubbing at his chin. "My lord, it would be premature for me to weigh in on such a matter when I don't know all the facts."

The Prince's lips turned up. "I appreciate your candor. You may be seated."

Stefan bowed and sat down, noticeably relieved.

The Prince regarded Niccolò for a long time. The Florentine was silent and unmoving under his ruler's watchful gaze. His expression gave away nothing, but closer inspection revealed the closing and opening of his right hand, an expression of nervousness.

The Prince tapped his hand on top of the armrest. "Sir Machiavelli, you've served the principality for centuries and have done so honorably. Although it is my right to execute you for your failure, I am excusing you. I need your service to this body and to the principality for a little longer.

"Security has become the responsibility of every citizen. I want the patrol patterns varied and the number of patrols increased. I want everyone, especially the plebes, to be on the highest alert. Nothing is to be done that will incur the Curia's ire.

"Now that Maximilian and Pierre are in Paris, a diversion should be forthcoming. However, we must prepare ourselves in case they fail.

"Lorenzo and Aoibhe, the Bacchanalia is to be postponed. Perhaps the delay will impress upon everyone the need for increased vigilance. Every citizen is to make preparations for war. The army is to be at its highest readiness.

"This body is dismissed. Lorenzo, I need a word." The Prince gestured to his lieutenant, nodding absently at the other members as they bowed before taking their leave.

As they approached the door that led to the corridor, Niccolò turned to Aoibhe. "You've made a grave mistake."

She stopped, her pretty face pensive. "Really, Sir Machiavelli? Tell me more."

He had just opened his mouth to do so when she kicked the side of his knee, felling him. She stood on his forearm with both feet, preventing him from drawing the long sword that he always carried at his side.

"Aoibhe," the Prince growled, noticing her display of strength.

She forced a smile. "Just a bit of harmless fun, my lord." She stepped to the side, leaning over her captive with a triumphant look. "You're getting reckless in your old age, Nick."

He swept to his feet. "Not likely."

"I'm more valuable to you as an ally than as an enemy. You'd best remember that, as your list of allies has grown surprisingly short." She brushed past him, her eyes meeting Stefan's. Under the intimidating gaze of the much-older vampyre, Stefan dropped his gaze to his feet.

With a pleased toss of her red hair, Aoibhe walked to the exit.

❊ ❊

Sir Machiavelli waited until the corridor was empty before slipping into the Prince's private study, which was located down the hall from the council chamber. Gregor, the Prince's assistant, was away on an errand and the Prince himself was deep in conversation with his lieutenant down the hall. Now was an excellent time for the head of security to make his move.

Niccolò disliked surprises. He disliked being embarrassed even more. His anger and resentment toward the Prince burned blue. But he'd learned from his conflict with the Medici long ago not to allow his anger to overtake his reason.

He quickly surveyed the contents of the study and moved to the desk, picking up reports and missives, reading them quickly, then returning them to their positions. But there was nothing of interest. He continued his search, hoping to find something that would either implicate the Prince or support his own position, but soon gave up. Time was not on his side.

He was just about to exit the study, when he noticed a book protruding slightly from one of the bookcases. It seemed strangely out of place among all the neatly shelved volumes.

He pulled it from the shelf, noting with some interest that it was an edition of one of his own works. He flipped through the pages idly, watching in silent fascination as something fluttered to the floor.

If he'd been human, his heart would have quickened when he realized the parchment bore the imprint of the King of Italy. With almost trembling hands, he unfolded the letter and read it.

The message itself was unremarkable and signed by the Roman's lieutenant. But there was an appendix to the message, penned in a different hand.

His Renaissance profanity was swift as his world tilted on its axis.

Niccolò refolded the parchment exactly as it had been before and placed it back in the book. He reshelved it, taking great care to make sure its appearance was precisely as it had been before he'd touched it.

Then, with eager feet, he exited the study, closing the door carefully behind him.

Chapter Thirty-six

The Prince needed a diversion.

Maximilian and Pierre had not been heard from. As Lorenzo suggested, it was possible they were hiding in Paris and awaiting the appropriate time in which to create a spectacle worthy of the Curia's attention. It was equally possible they'd been found trespassing and had been destroyed.

Which was why the Prince needed a diversion, something to distract the Curia from Florence and Raven.

He sat in his private quarters in the underworld and fished a small envelope out of his pocket. The letter had been delivered to him early that morning, with some urgency. He removed the single piece of paper from its envelope and read it for the tenth time.

To the Prince of Florence,

I have known Raven Wood since she was a child. I am writing to you in deference to your control over her, demanding that you release Raven from your possession and deliver her safely to me at the Vatican.

In exchange, I am prepared to persuade my brethren to over-

look your principality. You have been in control of Florence for several centuries, and in that time, we have never had a reason to engage in open conflict with you. Peace between our peoples is in the interests of all. I will work to ensure the peace continues, provided my demand is met immediately and the previous quietude of your principality continues.

Of course, if you are unwilling to meet my demand, I am equally prepared to persuade my brethren to take an immediate, avid interest in Florence.

I look forward to hearing your decision on this matter.

Father Jack Kavanaugh, S.J.

William folded the letter and placed it back in the envelope.

Over the centuries, his ability to be surprised had waned until it was almost nonexistent. Yet, the priest had surprised him.

The Curia was not known for placing the good of one human being over the good of humanity. In fact, it was legendary for trying to protect the greatest number of people to the greatest extent possible, hence its willingness to enter into a treaty with vampyres.

But Raven's priest was different. He'd flouted Curia convention and opened a direct negotiation with the enemy. He could be expelled from the Vatican and defrocked for that.

He hadn't promised he'd be able to convince the Curia to leave Florence alone, even if Raven was delivered to him. But the fact that he was willing to try was remarkable.

William held in his hands the promise of a diversion—the means of retaining control over the principality and ensuring the Curia fought its battles elsewhere. All he had to do was surrender "his pet" to her surrogate father.

He knew what the Consilium members would say if he were to share the missive with them. There would be no question. Raven should be sacrificed for the security of the city.

Human beings are disposable.

Pets are replaceable.

Don't forget what happened to Faustus, the Prince of Sardinia.

The voices of his brethren rang in his ears. They wouldn't hesitate to deliver Raven to the Curia, in exchange for the possibility of peace. In fact, they'd likely kill anyone who opposed the exchange.

William placed the letter in his jacket pocket and strode out of the room.

Chapter Thirty-seven

Raven waited until Monday evening to tell William about her encounter with Batelli.

William was upset but distant. He spoke to Raven only on Ambrogio's telephone, instructing her to stay indoors for the evening. He insisted he'd see to it Batelli was dealt with, promising his measures would not include execution. There was no need to court the Curia's attention with the murder of another policeman.

Raven asked William what was troubling him but he refused to confide in her, saying only he was worried about the city. He insisted he had to go and turned the telephone over to Ambrogio without another word.

Raven was greatly disquieted by the conversation but, short of tracking William down and confronting him, there was little she could do.

She sent another e-mail to her sister and went to bed early, gazing through her bedroom window at the sky and worrying.

❀ ❀

The following evening, Raven went to the orphanage after work. She spent time with the children, including Maria, the girl who was likely to be adopted by Gabriel and Julia Emerson, helping them with their reading. She ate dinner with the children, too, since Ambrogio had responded to her text by saying that his lordship was engaged that evening and would speak to her Wednesday.

After dinner, she returned to her lonely apartment and spent the rest of the evening listening to music and reading. But not even *Prince Caspian* could keep her mind entirely occupied, distracted as it was by worries about William and his city.

Just before bed, she received an e-mail from Father Kavanaugh. He hadn't sent a reply to her previous message, but rather, had initiated a new exchange.

She found the decision curious.

> Dear Raven,
>
> I was relieved to receive your message.
>
> There is a new restoration project beginning in the Pontifical Palace this September. The team will be working on Raphael's frescoes in the Room of the Segnatura. I've already spoken to the director of the project and passed on your résumé. If you want the job, it's yours.
>
> Vatican City is the safest place on earth. Certain beings cannot set foot inside our borders. I can ensure that you have a job and a place to live here. You will be under our protection.
>
> It took some effort, but I persuaded Cara to speak with me. I confirmed what you said to her and I encouraged her to contact you. We are supposed to speak again by telephone tomorrow. I pray I'm successful in helping you two repair your relationship.
>
> I remember you and your family in my prayers, praying that you all will find peace. Even more, I pray for your safety.

If you want to be free, all you need do is step inside a
church. You will be safe there.

I will text you my new cell phone number. You can call me
at any time, day or night, and I will ensure you safe passage
to Rome.

Your situation in Florence is precarious. I hope to hear from
you soon.

Father Jack

Raven lifted her gaze from the computer screen and stared into
space.

She was relieved to discover that Father didn't know that holy
ground made no difference to William. She took this to be a sign that
William's secrets had not been uncovered by the Curia.

She wasn't sure William would be able to enter Vatican City. But
it didn't matter. She had no intention of going to Rome. She had
no intention of leaving William. Not even for one of the greatest
restoration opportunities the world had to offer—Raphael's Vatican
frescoes.

She sighed. For a man of the cloth, Father Kavanaugh was perfectly adept at tempting her. She typed a brief reply, thanking the
priest for defending her to Cara and reiterating her eagerness to speak
with her sister again. She made no mention of the restoration job.

Raven considered sending Father Kavanaugh's e-mail to William
but decided she'd speak to him about it in person. Then she crawled
into bed, tossing and turning until just before dawn.

Now that she knew the wonder of sleeping in William's arms, it
was painful and difficult to sleep alone. She didn't even have an article of his clothing—a shirt perhaps—to wrap herself in while they
were apart.

Raven's loneliness was made greater still by his cold demeanor the last time they'd talked. After being so close to William on Sunday evening and early Monday morning, it now seemed there was an interminable distance between them.

A distance made all the more sinister by the recognition that several forces were trying to tear them apart.

Chapter Thirty-eight

"It's beautiful." Patrick squeezed Raven's shoulder appreciatively as they admired the newly restored *Birth of Venus*.

It was Friday afternoon. The Uffizi had closed early and invited its entire staff to the restoration lab in order to admire the finished piece before it was returned to the Botticelli room upstairs.

"Professor Urbano is very pleased." Raven nodded in her supervisor's direction. He was beaming with pride, shaking hands and clapping people on the back.

"Everyone is going out for drinks to celebrate." Patrick touched her shoulder. "Are you coming?"

"Yes." Raven smiled. "I wouldn't miss it."

"What about your boyfriend? Gina and I would like to meet him."

"He's busy." Raven's smile faded.

Patrick squeezed her shoulder. "Trouble in paradise?"

"No." Raven toyed with the bracelet on her wrist. "He's just busy this week."

"What about Batelli, is he still bothering you?"

"I haven't seen him since he cornered me on Monday."

"Good. The guy's a jackass."

Raven nodded, neglecting to mention that William's reaction to her tale about Batelli had been much, much stronger. Gina walked over to them and, instantly, Patrick took her hand. They smiled warmly at one another.

Raven felt a sudden pang of envy.

"Are you two coming to the gala tomorrow night?"

"*Si, certo.*" Gina leaned against Patrick and he smiled widely. "What about you?"

"Yes. The restoration team is going to be introduced by Dottor Vitali."

"Dottor Wood." Professor Urbano approached her from the side, shaking hands with her and exchanging pleasantries with Patrick and Gina before asking if he might speak to Raven privately.

"I'll see you tonight." Patrick nodded at her before she moved away.

Raven tried not to be nervous at the thought of speaking to her supervisor privately. They walked toward the painting and, as they did so, the small crowd of people parted.

"The restoration is beautiful." He gestured to the artwork, his face expressing satisfaction.

"The colors are so vibrant," she said. "It's like a completely different painting."

"Yes." He gave her an appreciative look. "I have good news. The gallery has been awarded funding to undertake a complete restoration of Artemisia Gentileschi's *Judith and Holofernes.*"

"Really?" Raven breathed. "That's wonderful. It hasn't been restored before, has it?"

"No. The painting is very dark. There are multiple coats of varnish that will have to be removed. I have the chance to pick the members of my team. I would like you to be part of it."

"Yes," Raven replied without hesitation. "Thank you."

He laughed. "Perhaps you would like time to consider? It is another year contract here at the gallery. Perhaps you'd like to return to the Opificio?"

"No. I like working here and it would be a great honor to restore that painting. I've always admired her work."

"Good. As you probably know, Artemisia's paintings have only recently been given some of the recognition they deserve." Professor Urbano stuck out his hand. "Welcome to the team."

"Thank you, Professor." She shook his hand.

After that exchange, Raven's smile returned, even though it was somewhat smaller than before.

❈ ❈

The black Mercedes waited behind the Uffizi, alongside a few other luxury vehicles. Raven was just exiting the gallery with Gina and Patrick when she saw the car. She stopped short.

"What is it?" Patrick eyed her reaction with concern.

"My boyfriend is here." She gave her friends an apologetic smile. "I haven't seen him all week. Go ahead without me. I might meet you later."

"We can wait," Patrick offered, his eyes narrowing at the Mercedes.

"Give Raven time with her boyfriend." Gina tugged on his hand. "Raven, we can meet you there."

"Thanks." She gave Gina an appreciative look.

"Bring him with you," Patrick called over his shoulder.

As her friends walked in the direction of the bar, Raven made her way over to the car. She opened the door and climbed in, closing the door carefully behind her.

Chapter Thirty-nine

"I'm surprised to see you. I haven't spoken to you since Monday night." Raven clutched her knapsack, making no move toward him.

William turned to address the driver. "To the villa, Luka."

"Wait." Raven fidgeted with her knapsack. "My friends are going for drinks to celebrate the completion of the restoration project. I'm going with them."

William blinked. "Very well."

"That's it?" She frowned. "That's all you have to say?"

William adjusted his cuff links, avoiding her censorious look. "You wish to be with your friends. I understand. I'll see you tomorrow night."

"But you won't see me," she protested. "Tomorrow night is the gala celebrating the restoration. I have to go."

William's eyes met hers. "Then I'll see you afterward. Ring Ambrogio and let him know when to send the car. I'll meet you at the villa."

Raven turned to look out the darkly tinted window.

"I'm luggage," she muttered.

"What's that?" William's tone was sharp.

"I'm something to be picked up and dropped off." She lifted her knapsack to her shoulder and placed her hand on the door. "I haven't seen you all week, after—after . . ." She faltered, suddenly fighting tears.

"Luka, get out of the car." William's tone was low and commanding.

The large man exited the vehicle and closed his door, affording the couple some privacy.

Without a word, William picked Raven up and placed her sideways on his lap, tossing her knapsack to the floor. He ran his thumbs under her eyes, gathering the moisture.

"What am I to do with you?" he whispered.

"Nothing, because I'm leaving." She tried to move off his lap, but he placed an arm around her waist.

"Luka will drive you to meet your friends, after you explain the tears." He dried her eyes again.

"If I have to explain it, then we have more trouble than I thought."

William winced.

When it became clear he was waiting for her to speak, she huffed. "I swear, you are the most infuriating male I've ever encountered. Why are you avoiding me?"

William passed his hand over her hair. "Affairs of state have taken more than their share of my attention. I know I promised to see to it you had access to a swimming pool for your leg, but I haven't had time. I shall have Ambrogio arrange it."

"I don't care about swimming! What I care about is you and how you're treating me."

William appeared confused. "How I am treating you?"

"When we spoke Monday night, you were cold to me."

"I am cold." He pressed his palm to her cheek.

"William." Her tone was anguished. "When we're apart, I miss you. I want to be with you. I want to talk to you. And when you're cold, it hurts."

Realization seemed to dawn on his expression. He pulled her against his chest, enveloping her in his arms. "My enemies will pay for every one of those tears."

"I don't want revenge. I just want you."

His lips found her forehead and he held them there. "I love you a great deal. I'm sure it's cruel of me to love you at all since we can't have a normal life. Yet, I can't bring myself to stop."

"I know you worry about the city. But I worry about you. Please, don't shut me out."

"There are things in motion that I should tell you about. But not tonight." His nose brushed the side of hers. "Dry your tears, Cassita. I regret every one."

She wiped at her face and kissed him, looping her arms around his neck.

"We'll take you to your friends. Tomorrow night, we shall be together."

She smiled and the change was reflected on William's face as his expression eased.

"I am not an easy being to love, Cassita. But I swear my sins of omission are in reality sins of love. I'm trying to protect you and the city. I'm failing."

"I'm sorry about the city. I don't understand what it would be like to be responsible for so many people." She touched his face, tracing his knitted eyebrows and proud mouth. "I just wish we had more time together."

He kissed the side of her hand. "However did I come to be the slave of so magnanimous a lady?"

Without giving the opportunity for Raven to reply, William knocked on the ceiling of the car. Luka opened the door and slipped into the driver's seat. Soon the Mercedes was wending its way from the gallery and down the street.

Chapter Forty

William carried in his pocket the means to save his city. The procedure was simple enough—deliver Raven to the Curia and Florence would be spared.

He'd spent centuries protecting his principality. He'd devoted his entire vampyric existence to it, constantly striving to ensure his citizens enjoyed an easy, comfortable life, secure in the knowledge the Curia would never march through their streets the way they'd done in Prague and Paris and Budapest.

He'd never allowed anyone to come between him and the city he loved, which was why he'd always been alone.

Then a wounded lark had flown across his sky and changed it. Forever.

As the first rays of sunrise illuminated the city streets, William exited one of the secret doors that led to the underground near Santa Maria Novella Station. He was disguised as a tourist, in sunglasses and a Panama hat, a cloth doused in an old vampyre's blood pinned to his shirt. If anyone were to track him, he hoped they'd be confused.

He ignored the headache and discomfort he felt the moment he stepped on holy ground, entering the church of Santa Maria Novella and moving swiftly and almost invisibly to the Spanish Chapel. He approached the famous fresco and bowed his respect.

"Hail, Brother." He greeted the image of his teacher in Latin, as had been their custom when he was alive. As ever, the saint stared at him impassively.

"It has been some time since I've visited. You're looking well." William tore his eyes from the painted wall and began to pace. "I find myself in some difficulty, which is why I have returned.

"Your Church has taken an interest in my city. There are rumors of war. I find it difficult to believe such conflicts fail to disturb your rest, since you clearly taught the clergy should be pacifists."

William paused. "Yes, I know. They battle against principalities and powers, and the forces of darkness. I've resigned myself to the darkness. But there's someone close to me who has not.

"There's a woman." William watched his teacher closely, fancying that, just perhaps, the visage had changed. "A young woman, very lovely. Brave and generous and fierce. The stuff of poetry and dreams.

"You'll laugh at this, old friend. The woman loves me."

The image's eyes seemed to burn into his. The Prince continued his pacing. "She was the protégée of one of the Curia's priests. He's demanded I deliver her to him in exchange for peace."

William straightened and crossed to the fresco, facing it.

"If I accede to his demand, I save my city but I lose her. I'll break her heart and the Curia will break her spirit. If I keep her, the Curia will come. They'll kill as many of us as they can, including me. So you see, old friend, no matter what I choose, I will lose her.

"What would be worse, to lose her voluntarily but know she will be protected by my enemy? Or to keep her, knowing the war will eventually separate us?"

William rubbed his eyes with both hands, blotting out the holy imagery that confronted him.

"It's exactly the kind of dilemma our colleagues would have posed to you in Paris. So what say you, magister? What is the virtuous decision?"

The Prince stared at his famous teacher.

"Yes, of course it's a false dilemma. I could send the woman—my woman—away. But that would only hasten the Curia's arrival. They'd assume I'd killed her.

"I could kill the priest. It would be difficult to do since he lives on holy ground, but assassinations have been carried out in the past." The Prince ran his fingers through his hair. "Yes, I know what happened as a result. The Curia marched on Budapest and massacred the covens there. The principality has never been the same."

He paced, back and forth and back and forth, fists shoved into his pockets. "I could attempt to negotiate with the Curia. But why should they negotiate a treaty with me, when one of their own wants his protégée safe from my control?

"No. There are myriad possibilities, all equally vicious."

The Prince cast a baleful look at the personifications of virtues that surrounded his teacher. The Virtues, of course, remained silent.

"You and I spoke many times of the beauty of goodness. This young, extraordinary woman is so beautiful, so noble in her character, you would have been entranced. She's read your works. I told her of you and she thinks you'd have compassion on me, despite . . ." He cleared this throat.

"I don't hope for compassion. I made my choice; I accept my fate. But for her, for her beautiful, brave soul, I shall hope." William lifted his face. "I love her. And because I love her, I come to you now to ask for your help.

"I know better than to try to bargain with you. Either you will come to my aid or you will refuse. I have nothing to offer in exchange, no way to expiate my sin, no virtue to recommend me.

"But I ask you, teacher, whatever compassion and love you had for me, for the boy I once was, that you would extend the same to her. Whatever grace has been given unto you, I ask you to pray that same grace will rest on her."

William extended his arms, his figure like a cross, and bowed very low. "Once again, I am sorry for disturbing your rest. I ask one favor in memory of our friendship—only remember my woman, that her beauty and goodness may not die."

Without a backward glance, the Prince left the chapter house, his body tight, his heart beating an uncertain tattoo in his chest.

Chapter Forty-one

"Ladies and gentlemen, I give you the *Birth of Venus.*"

With a flourish, Dottor Vitali removed the large tarp covering the newly restored painting. The crowd gathered in the Botticelli room at the Uffizi burst into loud and enthusiastic applause.

Vitali introduced Professor Urbano, who offered a few prepared remarks on the restoration process. He introduced Raven and the other members of his team to thunderous applause.

While he was thanking the donors and organizations who had funded the restoration, including Professor and Mrs. Emerson, who were not in attendance, Raven stood to one side, appraising the work.

An excellent restoration job allows a painting to present its best self. In her careful estimation, this was precisely what Professor Urbano's team had done. The colors of the painting were brighter and more vibrant. The details of the figures and the other elements were much easier to see. Indeed, the skill of Sandro Botticelli was more visible now that the layers of darkened, discolored varnish had been removed. The *Birth of Venus* would now enjoy a second life.

Raven was proud.

She stood with her friends Patrick and Gina, leaning against her cane. The full skirt of her new blue silk dress swished whenever she moved. She'd spent a great deal of time on her appearance, even going to a hairstylist to have her long black hair done in an elaborate, elegant twist. She'd covered the bite mark still visible on the side of her neck with makeup, its presence hardly noticeable except upon very close scrutiny.

The Botticelli room was full. There were patrons and politicians, journalists and professors, and the staff of the Uffizi, all standing in appreciation of the beautiful painting.

And Ispettor Batelli, watching the proceedings from a spot a few feet in front of *Primavera*.

Raven ignored him.

"I can't believe that asshole is here." Patrick jerked his head in the direction of the policeman.

"It makes sense, no?" Gina shrugged. "Perhaps the thieves are here. Perhaps they will try to take the *Birth of Venus*."

Raven glanced furtively in Batelli's direction and found him staring at her. She turned her back on him to address her friends. "They'd need ten men to do it and possibly a crane. We had a terrible time moving the painting from the lab."

"It's a masterpiece." Gina smiled at her as they applauded the conclusion of Professor Urbano's speech.

Dottor Vitali ended the formal part of the evening by inviting everyone to enjoy the Botticelli room. The crowd moved forward, eager to have a closer look at the restoration, and Raven and her friends discreetly moved aside to allow the guests a better view.

Patrick gave a low whistle. "I saw the photographs from before the restoration. You guys did a fantastic job."

"Thank you." Raven bowed.

"I think this calls for wine. Ladies?" Patrick lifted his eyebrows. Raven and Gina nodded and he excused himself in order to find a waiter.

Raven's gaze followed him as he moved to the far side of the room. For no reason in particular, her eyes flickered to the doorway that led to the corridor.

Standing in the hall, partially shadowed, was a young, handsome man dressed all in black.

His eyes locked with hers.

Raven fumbled an excuse to Gina and began to weave through the crowd. But there were a lot of people and she was not swift of movement. By the time she reached the door, he was gone.

Frustrated, she continued down the empty corridor, looking for him. The rest of the second floor of the Uffizi was cordoned off. She paused next to the velvet rope and sign that instructed guests to stay out.

Someone grabbed her arm and pulled her in between a pair of statues.

Before she could scream, she looked up into a familiar face. Her heart skipped a beat.

"You have to stop doing that!" She shook off his grasp. "You nearly gave me a heart attack."

William smirked. "I can hear your heart. It's perfectly sound."

"I think vampyres are capable of recognizing a figure of speech." She fanned a hand to her chest, trying to catch her breath.

William grew solemn. "I didn't mean to frighten you." He leaned forward and pressed a light kiss to her cheek. "You are beautiful."

Raven's face flamed. "Thank you."

"The painting is lovely, but its beauty pales in comparison with yours."

"Could you see it from the hall?"

He caressed the side of her face. "I slipped in earlier and peeked under the tarp. Your work is exceptional."

Raven fidgeted with her purse. "I was part of a team. Why are you here?"

"I came to see you." His eyes grew shuttered. "Am I not welcome?"

"Of course you're welcome." She moved so she could see past the statues toward the Botticelli room. "But there are cameras everywhere. And Ispettor Batelli is here."

"I know. I saw him." William's mouth moved to her ear and he kissed its shell. "Let's move to a place that is more private."

He took her hand and led her to the octagonal Sala Tribuna, which was only three doors down from the Botticelli room. He led her inside the space, which was lined with paintings and sculptures. "There are no cameras in here."

The room was dark, lit only by a series of small, high windows that filtered the starlight from outside. The sculptures seemed like ghosts to Raven's eyes. William, on the other hand, navigated the space as if it were bathed in sunlight.

They stopped in the center of the room, before an octagonal table. Without a word, he tossed her purse and cane aside and lifted her by the waist, seating her on the edge.

"This isn't a good idea. I don't want to break it." She gazed at the table doubtfully, wondering if it would hold her weight.

William placed his palm on the table and pressed, as if testing its sturdiness. "I wouldn't worry."

"I don't want to damage anything." She moved as if to stand.

"We won't."

He placed his hands on her knees, subtly lifting the skirt of her dress. His cool fingers slid under the silk to part her legs, then he was standing in between them, bringing his hips in contact with hers.

"William, I—" Raven was interrupted by William's lips, which touched hers reverently.

As if a flame had been ignited he began to kiss her deeply, urgently, his hands cupping the back of her head.

"What have they done to you?" he murmured, his thumb tracing the twist in her hair.

She spoke against his mouth. "I thought it would look nice."

"You're lovely, but lovelier, I think, naked and with your hair streaming down." He kissed her again, this time exploring her cheek, and jaw, and neck. When he began nibbling at her throat, she placed a palm to his chest. "Stop."

"Why?" He continued his ministrations, his hand sliding between her legs to trace the edge of her panties.

"Something is wrong."

William lifted his head, but he kept his hand where it was, angling it so he was cupping her over her underwear.

"What is wrong?"

She shook her head. "Not with me. With you."

She plucked his hand from between her legs and cast it aside.

He tried to move closer but she kept him at bay with a hand over his heart. "This week you were distant and cold. Now you're all over me. What's happening?"

"Excuse me. I didn't think I needed a reason to touch you."

He withdrew immediately and adjusted his trousers, turning from her to tug on the cuffs of his shirt. His gold cuff links, which bore the symbol of Florence, glittered as he moved.

Instinctively, she touched her bracelet.

"William," she breathed, her face crumpling. She turned away from him and wrapped her arms around her chest.

"There's no avoiding it," he mumbled. "I have to tell her."

He wound an arm around her waist, resting his forehead on her shoulder, and heaved a great, shuddering sigh.

"I am undone." His words were muffled against her dress.

"How?"

When he didn't reply, she turned and touched his head. "I'm right here. Talk to me, William."

He lifted his face, his expression tortured. "It will be a long conversation."

"I don't have anywhere else to go." She scratched at his scalp.

"What about the celebration? You should be with your friends."

"I am with a friend, I think." She gave him a searching look.

"Then it's best we leave." He picked up her purse and her cane and extended his hand.

She took his hand, hopping inelegantly from the table. Without further explanation, William accompanied her out into the corridor and down one of the side staircases.

Once they reached the outside, he lifted her into his arms and began to run, gaining enough speed to scale a nearby building and ascend to the roof. From rooftop to rooftop he leapt, while Raven kept her eyes tightly shut. A few minutes later, he landed on a terrace on top of one of the structures near the Duomo.

He placed Raven on her feet.

"I don't dare step on holy ground, not when the night has so many spies."

She nodded her understanding. "Please tell me what's wrong."

William crossed to the edge of the roof and placed his hand on the stone battlement. He was quiet for a moment as he gazed out over the city he loved.

"I received a letter from your priest."

Raven's heart leapt into her throat. "What? Why?"

"Because you are with me. Did you really think he'd let you go? If he didn't give you back to your mother the night he found you and your sister, why would he allow you to stay with a demon?"

"You aren't a demon." Raven's tone was fierce. "He's misguided. He thinks he has to save me. He wrote to me this week and asked me to come to Rome to work on one of the restoration projects in the Vatican."

William turned his head. "It's a ruse."

That pricked Raven's pride.

"Perhaps." She shrugged.

"To you he offers the promise of a prestigious project. To me, he offers peace. If I deliver you to him, he will persuade the Curia to stay away."

"Why would he do that?"

"Because he loves you. Because he's afraid for you. He thinks I'll kill you, or worse, I'll make you like me."

The Prince gazed out over the city again, his body tense.

"Father told me he spoke with Cara. I'm grateful for that."

"I'm glad for you, if it's true."

Raven stiffened. "He's never lied to me. What did you tell him?"

William leaned heavily on the battlement. "I haven't replied. That, in itself, is a kind of answer, but I doubt he'll act preemptively. . . . I have been trying to figure out what I'm going to do."

"What *you're* going to do?" Raven repeated.

He continued to look out over the skyline. "Yes."

"What about me? Shouldn't I have some say about what happens to me?"

William's eyes cut to hers. "I am responsible for my city and for you."

She limped toward him. "I didn't ask you to take on that responsibility."

"You asked me to love you," he said, reproaching her. "How can I love you if I don't ensure your safety?"

Raven shut her mouth abruptly.

William ground his teeth. "The Vatican is the safest city on earth, at least from vampyres."

"I don't want to be safe from you." She leaned on her cane, shifting her weight off her injured leg, which was beginning to throb.

William didn't respond.

"Do you want me to go?" Raven's voice trembled.

"No." His grip tightened on the stones. "But what I want doesn't matter. With one letter, he's destroyed everything I've built."

She reached out and grazed his sleeve. "You have to explain it to me, because I don't understand."

William flexed his arms, moving back from the battlement.

"If I deliver you to him, I shall lose you. He'll deprogram you or whatever it is they do to those who were in thrall to a vampyre. You'll forget me and he'll ensure I never see you again."

His expression tightened. "If you remain here, the Curia will come, if not for you then to ensure my reign ends. No single principality has ever been able to fight off the Curia. I'll be destroyed and you'll be rescued, if you aren't killed by accident."

She gripped his arm, leaning on him. "We can leave. We can flee the city tonight."

He gave her a look that was grim in its resolution. "I can't."

"But they'll kill you! If we leave, the Curia will stay away."

"I won't leave my people to be butchered. Even if I cared nothing for the city I have loved and ruled for centuries, I still wouldn't leave. Your priest is determined to save you. He'll hunt us. Eventually we'll be found."

"Isn't there another city you can appeal to? Can't the other principalities band together?"

"And risk massacres on their own city streets? No. There was a time when all the vampyres stood together. That was how we were able to broker a treaty with the Curia. But times have changed. Many of the covens are weak and all are selfish. No one will come to my aid.

They'll simply watch, relieved Florence is being attacked and not them."

"So you're just giving up?" She pushed him in the chest. "You can't give up!"

William retreated a step, his eyes sparking in anger. "Tell me, if you're so wise, what should I do? Kill him?"

"I didn't say that. I don't want you to kill him. I don't want him to kill you."

"But that's precisely what will happen. One of us will die and it will likely be me."

She searched his eyes. "I could go to him, beg him to leave Florence alone."

"No. I don't know what they'll do to you." He lowered his voice. "If you go to them, I may as well hand over the keys to the city. I'd rather find myself in hell than remain here without you."

She looked down at her shoes. "I never believed in hell. But I'm beginning to change my mind."

"Hell is knowing your fate and knowing there isn't a damn thing you can do about it." William pushed a lock of hair back from her forehead.

"Father Kavanaugh said he didn't rule the Curia. He doesn't think he has a lot of influence with them."

A muscle jumped in William's jaw. "That may be the case. But since the Curia is already interested in Florence, his pleas will not land on deaf ears. He's given them a reason to march on my city, something they haven't had since the old prince ruled."

Raven turned her head and looked at the Duomo. She looked at the tiled rooftops and buildings, the starry night sky, and the solemn structure of the bell tower that stood nearby.

"I'm not Helen of Troy. The Curia won't wage a war with you over me, not when they risk worldwide panic and exposure. All we need is one bystander with a cell phone, and video of the Curia killing vampyres will be all over the Internet."

"You underestimate their power."

"I don't care how powerful they are. They can't control everyone and everything. War means exposure, for them and for you. That's why Father wants me to come to him voluntarily. He doesn't want a war any more than you do."

William scowled. "I wouldn't compare me to him if I were you."

She lifted her chin. "I may not be able to choose my death, but I can choose my life. And I choose to spend whatever time I have left with you."

"No!" he snapped.

She gave him a look that was more wounded than irritated. "Why not? Don't you love me?"

He rubbed his chin roughly. "Of course I love you. That's the point. I'm trying to save you. You could return to America. I could send for you when it's safe to return."

Raven watched him for a few seconds, the expression on his face, his body language, and the strange emptiness that filled his beautiful gray eyes.

"You're lying. You know that if you send me away, we'll never see one another again. It would be too dangerous for me to return and it's possible the Curia will kill you for outsmarting them."

He sighed his resignation. "I am already dead. The human I was died years ago and this body took its place. I've lived a long life, long enough to hold hope in my arms."

William caught a lock of Raven's hair and tenderly wound it around his finger. His expression grew anguished. "But you, Cassita, you have your whole life ahead of you. If you stay, you could be killed."

Her green eyes flashed defiantly. "Then we die together."

"It's suicide. You can't—"

Raven interrupted him. "What would my life be like, knowing you were still alive but that we couldn't be together? Worrying every day that they could be hunting you or torturing you. Worrying that they were going to kill you. I'd rather spend whatever time we have left with you, than to be safe somewhere across an ocean, suffering because I've lost half my heart."

She gripped his biceps tightly. "You're the other half of me, William. Please don't send me away."

William lifted his head to the heavens and closed his eyes. He clenched his fists and recited a litany of curses.

"I'm too weak to send you away. The night I found you, I saw a vision of what the world would be like without you. That was before I knew and loved you. Now that I do—it would be impossible."

She buried her face in his chest. "I would go to the Curia to save your life."

"I know." He kissed the top of her head. "*Defensa*. But it's possible they'd destroy me anyway. And what kind of life would I have without you? Without light? Without hope?"

Her lower lip trembled. "I was so afraid you would send me away."

"No," he whispered, enveloping her in his tight embrace. "I may as well walk into fire and let the flames annihilate me. That fate would be preferable."

She shivered in his arms. "What are we going to do?"

He hesitated. "We can hope your priest has little influence on those in power. We can hope the Curia will direct its attention to a different principality."

"Is that likely?"

William sighed. "I don't know. I tried to organize a distraction but it seems to have failed."

"I can try to delay Father Kavanaugh. I can say that I'm thinking about it."

"I wouldn't antagonize him, Cassita. That might hasten their arrival."

"It's so unfair," she whispered, fighting back tears. "I waited my whole life to find you, and now that I have, I'm going to lose you."

"Do not give up hope. I couldn't bear it if the light of your hope was extinguished." He held her tightly and she clung to him as if she were falling.

Chapter Forty-two

In the aftermath of their shared decision, William and Raven's love-making took on a new dimension. William spent the evening hours slowly adoring Raven's body, and in her turn, she did the same for him. They lay awake in each other's arms almost until dawn, when Raven finally succumbed to sleep.

William spooned Raven, his eyes drawn to Botticelli's depiction of Allegra while his mind whirred with preparations for war and for the protection of his beloved.

❊ ❊

The following morning, Raven was seated on the balcony, drinking coffee and sunning herself, when her cell phone chirped with an incoming text.

> I'm in Rome. Dan and I flew in last night. We're staying
> with Fr. Jack. Come and see me and we'll talk.

Raven nearly dropped her phone.

She stared at Cara's message, reading and rereading it, a feeling of dread falling over her. She wanted to see her sister and reconcile with her. But not in Rome. Not now.

Could it be that Father Jack is using Cara to get me away from William?

The answer to her own question was clear.

She hadn't expected this. She hadn't expected any of this. And she had no idea what to do.

"I scent anxiety." William spoke from the doorway, his nose wrinkled. He was dressed all in black, as was his custom, and his hair was still damp from the shower.

Raven looked up at him sadly. "Read this." She handed him her phone.

He scanned the words. "And so it begins." He returned the phone to her.

She looked down at the screen. "I can't believe he'd use her like this."

William didn't comment.

Raven looked up at him. "What should I do?"

"I think it best to leave all talk of the Curia and of me out of it. Perhaps you could reply, saying that you're just finishing up your project and you can't get to Rome. Invite her to come here."

"If Father is pulling the strings she'll see through my excuses."

William leaned over and kissed her forehead.

"And if Cara is anything like her sister, she'll stubbornly insist on deciding for herself what to think."

"That's true," Raven admitted.

She typed out a quick response and showed it to William.

> Hi, Cara. Glad you and Dan are here. I can't leave work
> this week. Could you come to Florence? Love, Rave.

He nodded tersely. She sent the text and placed her phone aside, turning back to her breakfast.

William's hand rested on her neck. "How are you this morning?"

"I'm tired," she confessed.

His thumb traced the patch of skin around the place where he'd fed from her. "I've taken too much. I'll instruct Lucia to bring you an iron supplement."

She shook her head. "It isn't that kind of tired. I'm just anxious because of everything and—and I'd like to make peace with my sister before . . ." She couldn't bring herself to speak the words.

William nodded his sympathy. "I am sorry."

"I know." She leaned into his touch. Just then, her cell phone chimed. Her worried eyes met William's. She picked up the phone.

> I'm sorry about what I said to you. I flew across an ocean to get here. Why can't you take a couple of hours to see me in Rome? You don't have to stay all night.

William read over her shoulder.

"I'd offer to bring her here, but that would only exacerbate things."

"I have to persuade her to leave Rome."

Raven quickly typed out a response.

> I can't. It's a couple of hours by train each way and I have to work early tomorrow.

She was lying and Cara probably knew it. The conclusion of the restoration project had been international news, especially on the heels of the robbery at the Uffizi.

Even if Cara hadn't seen the news, no doubt Father Kavanaugh would have told her.

Raven sent her lie quickly and within a few minutes, she received a reply.

> Right. Work is more important than me. Why the hell did
> I bother coming. . . .

Raven resisted the urge to throw her phone from the balcony into the rose garden below. She tossed the offending item on a vacant chair instead.

William pulled up a chair beside her. "This may not be what you want to hear, but Cara might still be in America."

"You think Father Kavanaugh stole her phone and texted me? The texts are coming from her number."

"I think he wants you in Rome and he's willing to do whatever it takes to get you there."

"I'm going to call her landline in Florida." Raven pressed buttons on her phone and held the device to her ear. It rang a few times and shifted to voice mail. She ended the call and dialed Dan's cell phone number. The same thing happened.

Taking a deep breath, she called her mother's house. The telephone rang and rang and then she heard a sleepy voice. "Hello?"

"Mom."

There was a long pause and then the sound of movement and footsteps. "Jane? Is that you?"

Raven gritted her teeth. "It's Raven. Where's Cara?"

"What do you mean?"

"I called her house. She isn't home and Dan isn't answering his cell."

"That's because she's in Italy. Isn't she with you?"

"We had a fight. What makes you think she's coming to see me?" Raven tried her best to sound convincing.

"She wanted to talk to you. I thought she told you she was coming."

"So she's on a plane?"

"She left last night." There were inchoate, muffled sounds and the sharp click of what could have been a light switch. "It's five o'clock in the morning here. According to the itinerary she gave me, they would have arrived in Rome a couple of hours ago."

"Really." Raven sat back in her chair.

"Ja— Raven, what's going on?"

"Nothing, Mom. Go back to bed."

"Wait! Don't hang up." Her mother sounded panicked. "I want to talk to you."

Raven screwed her eyes shut. "I can't talk now. I have to find Cara."

"I'm sorry." The words were barely above a whisper.

"What's that?"

"I'm sorry." Her mother coughed. "I—I heard about David. It made the news. I—I'm sorry."

"It's too late for that." Raven's tone was harsh. "Why weren't you sorry when he touched Cara?"

There was silence for a moment.

"What happened with Cara was a misunderstanding. But of course I'm sorry about how he treated you. I'd like to see you."

"A misunderstanding?" Raven counted to five in order to control her anger. "It's pretty difficult to misunderstand an adult male with a little girl who's naked from the waist down."

The sharp intake of breath on the other end of the line whistled through the air.

"I don't need this shit, Mom. Forget I called."

"Don't hang up!" Her mother sounded frantic. "Please. Just give me a minute. We haven't spoken in years. I've missed you."

Raven tapped her thumb and her middle finger together, trying very hard not to yell.

Her mother continued. "You don't have to call me. I can call you. Just give me a chance, when you're ready."

"I make no promises."

Her mother sighed. "Okay. At least we're talking now."

"I have to go." Raven's eyes met William's. He was gazing over at her, looking protective but confused.

"Okay. Good-bye, Raven. I love you."

"Good-bye." Raven ended the call and curled into a ball on top of her chair.

William plucked the phone out of her hand and put it aside. He lifted her and sat in her chair, pulling her onto his lap. When he'd wrapped her in his arms as tightly as possible, he spoke. "I take it that was your mother."

Raven resisted the urge to say something flippant. "Yes."

"Human beings are the strangest creatures. I can never anticipate what they'll do next."

"Does she expect me to talk to her? When she still won't admit what happened?"

"If she does, she's mad."

"Why did she say she was sorry if she denies the truth?"

"She's a human and a woman. Such mysteries are beyond me."

Raven gave him a half smile. "You sell yourself short."

"I doubt it. Is it possible your sister is in Rome?"

"Yes, unless she fabricated the itinerary and lied to my mother. I can't see her doing that."

William hummed. Raven leaned against him. "I can't deal with my mother right now. I spent years in therapy trying to get her out of my head."

"I can send a message to her, if you wish." William's tone had an edge to it.

Raven shifted so she could see his eyes.

"What? Like a parcel of dead fish?"

William's gray eyes twinkled. "Since viewing the film you showed me, I've been wanting to send a Sicilian message. Although in this case, it would be a Tuscan message, which means we'd need to send pieces of a wild boar."

"Please, no." She rubbed her eyes. "It was a mistake showing you *The Godfather*. Promise me—no dead boars on their way to my mother's house in Miami."

"As you wish." He pressed his lips together.

"What should I do about my sister?"

"Nothing. She contacted you; you answered. Let's wait and see what she does next. It will give us an indication of the Curia's next move."

"I don't like the idea of waiting. It makes me nervous."

"I'm afraid our decision to stay in Florence requires us to wait. But I wanted to mention something."

"What?"

"If anything happens to me, or if for some reason you decide you want to leave the city, go to Via San Zanobi, number thirty-three, and ask for Sarah."

"Who's Sarah?"

"My mother." He gave her a tight smile. "Don't worry. It isn't my mother you'll be seeing; it's simply a password. Go there and they will see that you get out of the city safely."

"Who are 'they'?"

"They've been well paid," he evaded. "Only go to them in the direst of circumstances."

"William, I told you I don't want to leave."

"We have no idea what will happen. This is my peace of mind that you will be safe."

"Okay. I don't promise to use it, but I'll remember it. Thirty-three Via San Zanobi."

"Good." William's body relaxed. "With that matter taken care of, we should probably make arrangements to retrieve your things from your apartment and bring them here."

"Yes." She hugged him close.

"We'll celebrate tonight, once you're comfortably ensconced here in your new home."

"I like the sound of that, even though the circumstances are not ideal."

"Welcome home," he whispered, covering her mouth with his.

Chapter Forty-three

By the time the sun set, Raven had successfully packed her worldly goods in boxes and was sitting at her desk in her bedroom.

William had offered his assistance and he'd also offered the assistance of Lucia and Ambrogio, but Raven didn't want other people handling her things.

It was strange to think that after knowing William for so short a time she would be living with him. Given the uncertainty of their lives, she was throwing caution to the wind. She didn't want to be separated from William for a single evening, so it made sense to share his home as well as his bed. As he pointed out, the villa was one of the safest places in the city.

Raven surveyed the blank walls and the part of her old cane that was still embedded in one of them. She had no idea how she would explain it to the landlord. No doubt she'd have to borrow money from William to pay for the damages. He'd been the one to throw the cane so hard it had lodged inextricably in the wall.

She'd taken down and carefully packed all her artwork and her sketches. She was looking forward to painting in William's garden. She was looking forward to having him pose for her. The thought made her skin flush.

Her phone chimed with an incoming text.

The text was from Cara.

At the train station in Florence. What's your address?

Raven was so surprised, she nearly dropped the phone. She quickly typed the address and added, Is Father Kavanaugh with you?

Within seconds, she received the reply, No, he didn't want us to leave. Fuck that. We snuck out.

Raven snorted and placed her cell phone in the back pocket of her jeans. She was relieved her sister had decided to come to her, but she was also nervous. She didn't know how their conversation would go. And she didn't know how she was going to account for the now-strained relationship between herself and Father Kavanaugh.

She wondered how long it was going to take for him to realize that Cara and Dan had left. She wondered if he'd send the Curia after them. She was about to telephone Ambrogio in order to let William know of Cara's plans, when a knock sounded at the door.

She grabbed her cane and limped through the kitchen. William was being overly formal. She unlocked the door and opened it, swinging it wide.

But it wasn't William who stood in the hall.

The man standing before her looked young, barely twenty. And he had long, curly brown hair that swept his shoulders. His eyes, which were also brown, were narrowed and peering. He was dressed in Renaissance clothes.

He smiled and bowed. "*Signorina*," he said, addressing her. "The Prince has sent me to retrieve you."

"Oh. Where is he?" Raven looked past him into the hallway.

"He is waiting at Palazzo Riccardi."

Raven's brow furrowed. She'd never been inside Palazzo Riccardi with William. And it wasn't like him to send someone in his stead, unless he was busy.

"Where's Luka?"

The man hesitated, but only for a fraction of a second. "He is downstairs."

She looked at the man carefully. He was obviously a vampyre, with pale, perfect skin and an almost ethereal perfection of face and form. She didn't recognize him as one of William's servants, but his voice, and his old-fashioned Italian, was familiar. She must have heard it somewhere before. She wondered why she couldn't identify him by his face.

"I can't come right now. My sister and her boyfriend are on their way here."

"The Prince wants you to come now." The vampyre's tone changed. "Pets obey their masters."

Raven lifted her eyebrows, while resisting the urge to correct him.

"I'll call Ambrogio and explain." She pivoted toward the kitchen table.

"Aren't you going to invite me in?"

Reflexively, Raven stood aside.

She opened her mouth to invite the vampyre in, when something Father Kavanaugh had said flashed through her mind. She turned her head slowly and saw the man watching her, poised on the threshold like a snake, waiting to strike.

She smiled in an effort to disarm him. Then, in one quick motion, she closed and bolted the door.

Something heavy slammed against the door and the wooden object sagged on its hinges. The sounds of Italian curses filtered through the air.

She pulled out her cell phone, fumbling with the buttons. The man pounded on the door, demanding to be invited inside. Raven waited impatiently for her call to connect.

"Ambrogio?" she almost shouted into the phone. "A strange vampyre is here. He says he works for his lordship. He's pounding on my door, demanding to be invited in."

"Don't invite him in," Ambrogio responded coolly, as if she were merely giving him a weather report. "His lordship is not at home but I will get a message to him. Stay where you are. I'll send Luka and Marco."

"My sister is on her way here. She's taking a taxi from Santa Maria Novella."

"Stay where you are. The men are coming."

Raven ended the call, dropping her phone on the kitchen table.

Luka and Marco, who were merely human, would be no match for the angry, pounding vampyre. And what if he was lurking around when Cara and Dan arrived?

Raven inclined her head toward the door, but the vampyre had ceased. Quietly, she stepped over to the peephole and looked outside. The hallway was empty.

Cautiously relieved, she entered her bedroom and walked to the window, pushing the curtains aside so she could look down at the piazza.

There were patrons sitting at the café across the square and there were a few tourists and students milling about. But there was no vampyre. She wondered where he'd gone.

Thirty minutes later, Raven was sitting on her bed, clutching her phone and waiting for Luka and Marco to arrive. There was still no sign of the vampyre. Unfortunately, there was no sign of Cara and Dan, either.

Her apartment buzzer rang. She looked out her bedroom window and was relieved to see Cara and Dan standing outside with their luggage.

She placed her phone in the back pocket of her jeans and approached the door to her apartment. The hallway was still clear.

She unlocked the door, opened it a crack, and poked her head out. Satisfied the hall was empty, she locked the door behind her and descended the stairs, gazing over the railing as she descended to make sure no one was hiding on the staircase.

Once she reached the front door, she opened it and quickly pulled her visitors indoors.

Raven was about to close the door behind them, when a man's hand clamped onto the door frame.

Chapter Forty-four

Before Raven could push the door shut, the man swept inside the building, slamming the door behind him. He stood, blocking the exit, his size menacing, his expression severe. When his gaze alighted on Raven, he leered.

In a horrifying instant, Raven recognized him as the vampyre who had attacked Bruno some months before. William had called him Max.

"Dan, take Cara to the back door." Raven placed herself between the vampyre and her family, tossing her house keys to Dan. He caught them handily.

With a growl, Max grabbed her by the arm and began to drag her toward the door.

"Hey, let her go!" Cara reacted immediately, moving to Raven's side.

Raven struggled, twisting and turning in an attempt to free herself. But he held her in a bruising grip.

Cara struck him with Raven's cane, but her blows seemed to have little effect other than to irritate him. He wrenched the cane from her grasp and threw it several feet away. When he lifted his hand as if to strike her, Dan intervened, grabbing the vampyre's meaty arm and pulling it backward. With a snarl, the creature released Raven and she fell to her knees. The vampyre reared back and punched Dan in the face, causing a sickening crunch to echo in the hall. Dan slumped to the floor amid Cara's screams.

"Dan!" she cried, kneeling at his side. She placed a hand on his chest. "He isn't breathing!"

The vampyre ignored her outburst and grabbed Raven by the hair, pulling her to her feet.

"Cara, run," Raven managed, wincing in pain. "Get help."

"Let her go." Cara stumbled to her feet, wiping her boyfriend's blood on her black jeans. She was shaking with anger.

"No, Cara. Run!"

Cara ignored her sister's pleas and picked up the discarded cane, brandishing it like a club in the direction of the vampyre.

"Run!" Raven screamed, panic overtaking her.

"Let my sister go." Cara advanced determinedly.

The vampyre spat at her feet. "My orders were to limit the mess. Stay where you are or I'll kill you."

"No." Raven gripped Max by his shirt. "I'll go with you. Leave her alone."

Max grinned.

He opened his mouth to voice a retort but Cara caught him in the side of the head with the cane.

Momentarily stunned, he released Raven and she pitched forward, slamming against the wall.

"Cara, get out of here!"

Her sister kept swinging the cane at the vampyre, striking him where she could, but Max just batted the cane away, his face split into a broad grin. When he'd tired of Cara, he backhanded her and she crashed to the ground, blood spurting from her nose. She grew still.

"No!" Raven cried, crawling toward her sister.

Max interrupted her movement and picked her up by the waist.

"I belong to the Prince of Florence." Still struggling, she showed him the bracelet William had given her. "I'm his pet."

"I know who you are," he snarled. "Shut your mouth or I'll kill the other one, too."

Raven's gaze darted over to Cara. She wasn't moving and neither was Dan.

Perhaps the vampyre could sense Dan was already dead.

Raven grew quiet.

As Max carried her through the back door and into the alley, she turned to him.

"Where are you taking me?"

He shook her like a cat shakes a kitten. "Silence." He brought his nose to her neck and inhaled deeply. "I'm taking you somewhere private enough for revenge. Then I'm going to find out exactly what kind of pet you are."

He laughed at her show of fear and tucked her under his arm, grabbing hold of the side of the building as he prepared to climb.

Chapter Forty-five

"What news from Switzerland?" The Prince stood at the Piazzale Michelangelo after sunset with Gregor, his assistant.

The younger vampyre bowed. "On your orders, I went to Cologny and met with the family who sold your illustrations to the Americans. I told them I was an Interpol agent assigned to investigate the robbery."

"What have you to report?"

Gregor produced a small valise and handed it to his ruler. "The family provided me with notes and pages from a diary that was kept by one of their ancestors—the man who purchased the illustrations in the nineteenth century."

The Prince tucked the valise under his arm. "And the person who sold them?"

Gregor cleared his throat. "He was described as Italian. He sold the illustrations for much less than they were worth, saying that they had belonged to his family, who'd fallen on hard times."

The Prince's eyebrows drew together. "Did this Italian have a name?"

"The gentleman insisted he remain anonymous." At this, Gregor pointed to the valise. "But the diary describes the man. He wore old clothes, spoke Italian fluently, and had pale skin."

"A vampyre?"

"The family did not identify him as such, but the description suggests it. The man who purchased the illustrations was warned that he should keep the transaction secret and never make them public, or he would risk some kind of curse."

"Subterfuge, of course." The Prince looked off into space for a moment. "It's possible whoever stole the illustrations from me enlisted the aid of the Italian to sell them."

"Possible, my lord, but there is more to report."

The Prince's eyes moved to his assistant. "Proceed."

"It seems, my lord, that the recipient described the man as young, with dark, curly hair that fell to his shoulders."

The Prince moved abruptly to the stone railing. "Thousands of vampyres answered to that description at one time. And we all appear young to some degree."

Gregor shifted his weight uncomfortably. "Yes, but this individual claimed to be related to the Medici."

The Prince turned his head, pinning Gregor to the spot with his gaze.

"Are you certain?"

"It's in the diary, my lord. It's penned in French but translating it was easy enough."

"So the shadow reveals himself," the Prince muttered, turning to survey his city once again. "Rather than exposing himself as a worthy adversary, he shows he is a petty thief and a coward. Have you mentioned your journey to anyone?"

Gregor shook his head vigorously. "No, my lord."

"Have you spoken about your findings to anyone else?" The Prince's tone was deceptively calm.

"I serve only you, my prince."

"Good. You have done well, Gregor. Your service shall be rewarded. I am elevating you to the Consilium."

Gregor's nervous expression lightened into a smile. "Thank you, my lord."

"Last century, a shadow fell over my principality. Tonight that shadow shall be extinguished. Come, Sir Gregor. I shall have need of you at the Consilium meeting."

The assistant bowed low and the two vampyres vaulted the stone railing, running in the direction of the Arno.

Chapter Forty-six

Maximilian's feet were still on the ground when something wet splashed over him and his prisoner. He howled in pain and released her, leaving her to hurtle to the ground.

Raven landed hard on her backside, pain radiating from her tailbone up her spine. The impact of her fall was so great she just sat there, stunned.

Max was on his knees, rubbing his face and cursing, while a man tried to encircle him with a ring of salt.

Raven recognized the man as Marco. A pair of hands reached under her armpits to lift her. She struggled, rolling to the side and trying to escape.

"It's Luka," a voice said.

She peered up into a familiar face.

Without another word, William's chauffeur threw her over his shoulder and began running, heading out of the alley that ran behind the buildings and to a nearby street. William's Mercedes was parked at the curb.

Luka quickly opened the rear passenger door and placed her in the backseat, then climbed into the front seat, locked the doors, and fired up the ignition.

"My sister," Raven choked out. "She's in my apartment building. We have to take her to the hospital."

"My orders are to take you to the villa."

She grabbed his shoulder. "We can't leave her. Her boyfriend was attacked, too. They need an ambulance."

"My orders are to take you to the villa," he repeated.

Raven tamped down her incredulity at his intractability and hastily unlocked the door. Luka reached over the front seat and caught her arm.

"It isn't safe. We don't know how many others are out there."

"I'm not leaving her."

Luka observed her expression for a moment. He swore and put the car in park. "Just wait."

He pressed a button. The sound of a ringing telephone filled the vehicle before the call connected. Luka announced to Ambrogio that he had Raven and was bringing her to the Prince. He asked that an ambulance be dispatched to her building for her sister and her friend.

Ambrogio ordered him to bring Raven to the villa immediately, but she interrupted. "His lordship doesn't want me to leave my sister. I'm following his orders and they are always obeyed."

There was silence on the other end of the line. Finally, Ambrogio spoke. "Luka, retrieve the sister and bring them both back to the villa. I'll see that a medical doctor is summoned."

Luka ended the call, and with another loud curse he exited the vehicle, engaging the locks before he closed the door.

She sat in the backseat, scanning the dark area around the car. Seconds became minutes and one minute became ten. She was just about to get out and return to the building, when something heavy landed on the roof of the car.

The vehicle groaned, but held fast.

Raven turned to look through the windshield and saw Maximilian standing in front of the car.

His face and head were disfigured, as if he'd been doused with acid. His hair and skin had been stripped away, leaving open, gaping wounds that oozed black vampyre blood. One of his eyes was shut, as if he'd been blinded.

But it was what he held in his arms that caused Raven's heart to stop.

Without hesitation, she unlocked the door and stepped out of the car.

Chapter Forty-seven

There was something unsettling in the air.

Aoibhe stood high atop the Palazzo Vecchio, surveying the city with her face pointed south. She closed her eyes and inhaled, allowing her mind to sort through the myriad scents that swirled around her.

In other respects, it was a perfectly normal evening in summer. Tourists and locals strolled in the piazza below and nearby at the Uffizi Gallery. Vampyres moved with stealth among them, sometimes watching from rooftops, sometimes melting into the shadows.

But Aoibhe's senses, which had been honed by various events over her long life, were piqued.

She opened her eyes and saw movement atop the buildings near the Arno—a great hulk of a vampyre running and carrying a body under each arm. The scent of one of them hit her nostrils with force. Her lips curled back in a snarl and she flew to the roof of a lower building, running as soon as her feet made contact with the tiles.

Several more leaps and she'd successfully cut him off, waiting with anticipation as he landed in front of her.

"Hunting, Max?" she greeted him, her smile calculated to disarm.

"Go fornicate yourself." Max adjusted his grip on his charges, preparing to fly to the building adjacent.

He held a young woman under each arm. The first was a blond with an attractive but unremarkable scent. Her face was bloodied and she was barely conscious, her moans lifting and falling with every breath.

But the other woman was easily recognizable. She was the reason Aoibhe's interest had been roused.

Aoibhe clucked her tongue. "I'd drop the black-haired one, if I were you. She's the Prince's pet."

Max merely growled and held the woman more tightly. Aoibhe's eyes met Raven's and in them she read a silent plea. Aoibhe averted her gaze.

"He'll kill you for touching her."

"The Prince is dead, or will be shortly." Max chuckled. "I'd see to your own head. You may not keep it long."

He ran to the edge of the building and dropped to the next one. Aoibhe watched him run until he disappeared out of sight, near the Duomo. A stab of fear pricked her insides.

She wondered if he'd spoken the truth—if something had happened to the Prince. Surely, if there'd been a coup she would have seen or heard something.

She was about to follow him when she heard a loud noise behind her. She turned and was surprised to find five of her brethren standing near the edge of the roof. They were all armed with swords.

She straightened herself. "I am Lady Aoibhe of the Consilium. What is the meaning of this?"

"We know who you are," one of the soldiers grunted, rattling his sword.

She sighed and rolled her eyes heavenward. This was not how she imagined meeting her demise.

She pushed up the sleeves to her dress and spread her feet. Then, with an arrogance born of many victories, she drew a curved, slim samurai sword from behind her back. She gripped the weapon with both hands.

Three soldiers advanced, one in the center and one on each side in an attempt to flank her. She disposed of the soldier on her right first, beheading him with a single stroke.

Aoibhe's movements were quick and elegant, her red hair swirling in the air, as she faced the other two soldiers. She dueled with each, avoiding their blows until she was able to unsword one of them. She killed him swiftly before turning her weapon on his companion.

The largest solider approached her next. He had more skill than the others and knew better than to give her the slightest opening.

She tried to sweep his legs, but was thwarted. She tried to unsword him, but he was able to land a blow to her left side, stabbing through the crimson folds of her dress to make contact with her body.

The wound surprised her.

Instinctively, she placed her palm against it. But this was a mistake, since the sword she preferred required two hands.

The swordsman slashed at her wrist and she dropped her sword, black blood pouring from her veins.

"Lady Aoibhe." As he spoke, he pointed the tip of his blade in the direction of her throat. "You are sentenced to death for treason."

"Treason against whom?" She clutched her wrist with the opposite hand. "I've been loyal to the Prince."

"Exactly. The Prince has been disloyal to Florence, allowing his control to wane while the Curia lies in wait. For these crimes, you will be executed."

"On whose authority?" she stalled, her dark eyes scanning the roof for any possibility of an escape.

"On the authority of the new prince." The soldier lifted his arm, preparing to strike.

"Am I not to learn the name of the new lord?" She bent her knees.

"No," the soldier replied. He lifted his arm still higher.

And then his arm and his sword flew through the air, landing with a wet and tinny thud on the roof.

The soldier cried out in surprise as blood gushed from the gaping wound. He turned to seek his attacker, but a sword whistled through the air, separating his head from his torso.

Aoibhe watched in silent fascination as a figure dressed in dark robes quickly dispatched the two remaining soldiers before moving to face her.

She took a step back. The figure's scent was muddled and unfamiliar. She looked around wildly for her sword, but it was too far away.

"I will not go quietly," she said, baring her teeth and moving into a crouch.

The figure threw off his hood.

"Ibarra," she breathed, placing a hand to her throat.

"I've just saved your life, my lady. Is that all the praise I'm to be given?" He flashed a devilish smile.

With a cry, she wrapped her arms around him and kissed him.

"Much better." He bent to examine her side and her wrist. "You've been injured. Are you all right?"

"A flesh wound." She lifted the fabric of her dress from her skin and poked her fingers through the tear. "It's already closing."

She made a similar move with her wrist, wiping the blood from her pale skin.

"I'm glad." Ibarra moved to kiss her again but she pulled away, wrinkling her nose.

"You stink."

"Thank you." He bowed mockingly. "I've been using various bloods to mask my scent."

"Must you bathe yourself in undesirables? I can barely stand the stench."

He laughed. "Which is why I was able to surprise the killing party that targeted you."

"I thought you were in the Basque Country."

"I decided to stay close and see what I could discover." Ibarra gazed at the bodies of the five soldiers. "It would seem the Prince has been deposed."

"I can scarce believe it. Niccolò isn't powerful enough to best him in a fair fight."

"The army is. Who said anything about the fight being fair?"

Aoibhe shook her head. "The army is loyal to the Prince."

"Niccolò's forked tongue could easily sway them, especially with the rumors of an invasion by the Curia." Ibarra surveyed the adjacent rooftops, looking for any sign of movement. "He must be killing off his rivals from the Consilium."

"Stefan isn't worth bothering with. Max is in good health. I saw him carrying the Prince's pet a few minutes ago. He's supposed to be on a mission to France. Clearly, he failed."

"Then Max must be allied to Niccolò. A strange alliance, indeed. The Prince must be dead if Max was able to secure his pet. Why would he bother with it?"

"Because Max covets pretty things."

Ibarra's dark eyes met hers. "Unless it's a trap."

"The Prince is intelligent enough to value Florence over a pet." Aoibhe reached up to kiss him once again. "I owe you my life."

"A debt I am pleased to own." He kissed her back, wrapping his arms around her waist. "Should we clean up this mess? It's sure to attract attention."

Aoibhe gazed at their fallen brethren scornfully. "I want Niccolò to know that he failed."

"They'll send more soldiers."

"They'll have to catch me first. I'll be more adept at hiding now." She released him and picked up her sword, sheathing it before disguising it behind her back.

"Don't die until I have a chance to taste you again." Ibarra smirked, cleaning his sword on the clothes of one of the fallen soldiers.

Aoibhe dropped into an exaggerated curtsy. "The same to you, Sir Ibarra."

Chapter Forty-eight

The Prince felt a sense of relief as he ran through the secret metro of underground passages that led to the central chambers of the underworld.

He knew the kingdom of Italy and its vampyre inhabitants. Age and political connections had furnished him with that knowledge. There was only one vampyre still in existence who claimed to be related to the Medici, and he'd served the Prince of Florence for hundreds of years. For how many years had he planned to betray him?

Armed with a valise full of evidence, the Prince was eager to confront and execute the traitor, making him an example for others.

For the sake of security and surprise, the Prince led Gregor through a passage that only he knew about, passing through a hidden door that led into his study, which was situated near the council chamber.

They could see in the dark, but for convenience more than anything else the Prince lit a candelabra, illuminating the dark room that had been hewn out of stone. What he found disturbed him.

Papers were strewn over the desk and across the floor. Books had been pulled from their shelves and tossed haphazardly. Documents, scrolls, and manuscripts littered every surface.

"Fetch a detachment of ten soldiers and return here immediately," the Prince barked. "Someone will pay for this outrage."

"Yes, my lord." Gregor bowed and exited into the main corridor.

The Prince moved to the bookshelf and was momentarily panicked when he failed to find the volume he wanted. A quick survey of the books on the floor yielded the prize.

He picked up the copy of Machiavelli's writings and carefully removed a handwritten missive. He hid it in the pocket of his jacket, near another important document. Then he reshelved the book.

Within minutes, Gregor returned. He opened the door quickly, entered the study, and closed the door behind him. Without warning, he strode over to the desk and blew out the candles.

"What is the meaning of this? Where are the soldiers?" The Prince scowled at his assistant in the darkness.

"My lord," he stammered, visibly shaken.

"What is it?"

"The army is assembled in the gymnasium."

The Prince straightened. "On whose authority?"

"A new prince. Someone seized your throne and has already sent out smaller detachments to execute the Consilium members."

"Aoibhe." The Prince breathed, gripping the edge of his desk tightly.

"She may already be dead, my lord. General Valerian addressed the assembly, saying they're awaiting further orders. He was extolling the virtues of the new leader."

"If cowardice and pettiness are virtues." The Prince's eyes narrowed. "Where is the traitor?"

"The general didn't say. I don't know, my lord."

"He's probably situated himself on my throne already. Steer clear of the council chamber, but see if any of the Consilium members have survived. Tell them and all you come in contact with that the

true prince is very much alive and preparing for war. Those that oppose me will be slain. Those that are loyal will be rewarded."

"Yes, my lord."

"Gather the loyal at Palazzo Riccardi, but do so cautiously so as
to avoid an ambush. There is a cache of weapons and Kevlar vests in
a room beneath the palazzo. Theodore has the keys. Arm those loyal
to me and await further instructions." The Prince pointed to the concealed door. "Make haste. But do not lose your head."

With a bow, the assistant disappeared through the secret passage,
leaving the Prince to contemplate his more pressing concern.

Raven.

By now, Ambrogio should have ensured that she'd returned to the
villa, where she would be safe. Since the Prince was not in possession
of a cell phone, he had no way of confirming this. In any case, cell
phones did not receive signals in the underground passages.

He'd done his best to keep his relationship with Raven as private
as possible, confident his brethren would view her as a temporary
amusement. Given the traitor's pettiness, however, even a toy was a
potential target. Since he no doubt knew where her apartment was . . .

The Prince removed one of his swords from a weapons cabinet
that stood at the far wall. He concealed the blade under his jacket and
quickly exited the study, hoping his beloved Raven was already waiting safely in his bed.

Chapter Forty-nine

"Cara?" Raven stroked her sister's face. "Can you hear me?"

When she'd seen Max holding the unconscious body of her sister, Raven hadn't hesitated. She'd gotten out of the Mercedes and pleaded with him to leave Cara and take her instead.

The vampyre had grinned and taken her, too. Now they were in one of the private rooms at Teatro. It was the same room in which Raven had made love with William what seemed like an age ago; a room with dark purple walls and a large bed dressed in black satin. A mirror ran the length of one wall, reflecting the two sisters.

"Cara?"

She moaned in response. Raven interpreted this reaction as a positive sign.

The vampyre had carried them through one of the secret entrances, bringing them down the back hallway, which was empty.

Raven doubted anyone knew where they were. Despite the fact that her cell phone was still in her pocket, she hadn't had a moment of privacy in which to use it. She comforted herself by thinking Ambrogio would use it to track her and that William would rescue her.

She hoped that Dan was all right. Tragically, she was fairly certain both Luka and Marco were dead.

She fingered the bracelet he'd given her. William would come for her. She was sure of it.

Cara moaned again.

"She needs a doctor." Raven shifted her attention to their captor, careful to keep her body in between him and her sister.

"No doctor." Max's Germanic accent muddled his Italian, making him difficult to understand, but she understood his refusal.

Loud techno music thumped inside the club, but with the door closed the noise faded into a distant hum. If Max were to attack them, no one in Teatro would hear their cries.

Raven shuddered.

She tore a strip from the bottom of her T-shirt and began wiping the blood from her sister's face. Cara was positioned on her back, eyes closed. Her nose was broken, her eyes blackened, and there was a large bruise purpling her jaw.

"You're going to be okay," Raven whispered. "I promise."

Holding the soiled fabric in her hand, she glanced at Max. "My sister has a head injury. She needs to be in a hospital."

"No doctor!" His hand shot out and he shoved Raven's shoulder, sending her flying backward on the bed.

Instinctively, she crawled back to her sister and covered her body with her own. "Don't touch her."

The vampyre watched her display with undisguised amusement. "Your blood smells sweeter."

He lumbered toward the door and placed his ear against it. Seemingly satisfied with whatever he did or did not hear, he put his back to the door and stared across the candlelit room.

His body had already begun to regenerate, but slowly. Skin was beginning to grow on his face and neck, closing over the open wounds. His injured eye was no longer swollen shut and he seemed to have regained full sight.

He was, however, still hideous.

Raven met his gaze. "Can I have some ice? It will help with the swelling."

"No ice."

"Ice would help your face, as well. Those wounds must hurt."

The vampyre blinked. "You'd tend my wounds?"

"In exchange for ice? Yes."

He stared. When he offered no further communication, Raven swung her feet over the side of the bed. She walked to a cabinet that held a small bar fridge. While keeping watch on the vampyre, she opened the fridge and was relieved to discover a few ice cubes. She wrapped them in the fabric she was still holding and returned to the bed.

Max watched her movements but did not intervene.

"Why don't you let us go?" She held the ice to her sister's face, alternating between her nose and her jaw. "The Prince will rescue us. Now is your chance to escape."

The vampyre laughed. "The Prince is dead. A new one has taken his place."

Raven froze. "Dead?"

"We seized control of the army. Not even an old one can defeat so many." He chuckled. "Why do you think it was so easy for me to take you?"

Raven pressed her hand over her mouth.

William is dead?

She didn't know if Max was telling the truth. But it would explain why William hadn't come to her rescue. It would also explain why the other vampyre had been so bold as to venture inside her building.

He's lying. William has powers they are unaware of; they won't be able to kill him so easily.

Despite her positive thoughts, Max had introduced doubt into her psyche. She looked at her sister and tears filled her eyes.

A low chuckle came from across the room. The creature was laughing at her, mocking her pain.

Perhaps he spoke the truth and something had happened to William after she'd spoken with Ambrogio. Perhaps the creature was lying, toying with her mind. She didn't have time to grieve. She had to save her sister.

"Rave," Cara whispered, her eyes fluttering open. She slid her hand across the bedspread, her baby finger touching her sister's.

Raven gripped her hand tightly, swallowing back tears. She held the ice to her sister's face.

"If the Prince is—dead"—Raven shivered, barely able to pronounce the word—"there's no reason to keep us. I'm sure the new prince needs your help. The Curia is watching."

Max's angry footsteps echoed in the chamber. "What do you know about the Curia?"

She tried to sound nonchalant. "I am the Prince's pet. I hear things. He was worried the Curia would invade the city."

"What else?" He leaned forward, bringing his hideous face inches from hers.

Raven racked her brain for something she could say, something that wouldn't be too damaging to William, if he were still alive.

"He said there were spies in the city."

Max straightened, stroking what was left of his beard. "Everyone knows that."

"Yes, but these spies are reporting to the Curia. Every time a human is killed in a suspicious manner, the Curia hears about it. Those bodies you left by my apartment are going to attract attention." She leaned forward. "Maybe it's time for you to escape."

"No escape," he said angrily. "Now is time for sport."

"There are beautiful women out there." She gestured to the door. "Why don't you leave us? We aren't going anywhere."

"Not yet. I'm going to enjoy you before I drain your heart. And then I'm going to dispose of your sister."

Raven gritted her teeth. "Everything you could ever want is out there. You don't want to waste your time with us."

The vampyre stood next to the bed and leered at her from head to foot.

"Take off your clothes."

"No." Raven's low voice had steel in it.

"I said, *take off your clothes*." He pulled her from the bed, spinning her toward the wall.

"If the Prince is dead, then I don't care about living." Her voice was low but defiant. "I don't care if you kill me. I'm not taking my clothes off."

Max lifted his hand as if to strike her, then he squeezed her chin roughly, forcing her to look at him.

"Look into my eyes and focus on my voice. I am your master now."

Something niggled in the back of Raven's mind, something disturbing. At that moment, she couldn't remember what it was.

An icy tendril of fear snaked down her spine. She stared back at the vampyre with contempt.

"No," she repeated stubbornly.

Max's eyes narrowed in confusion. He cursed and gripped her head with both hands. "I am your master. You will do as I say. Take off your clothes."

Raven blinked. "No."

He pushed her aside, rubbing a hand across his face where the skin was new. "Then I'll take your sister first."

He moved toward the bed.

"No!" Raven grabbed his arm, trying to pull him back. He shook her off and put a knee to the bed.

Cara lay motionless, eyes closed.

There was no way Raven was going to stand by while this animal touched her sister. She hadn't done so when she was twelve and she wouldn't do so now, not so long as she still had strength with which to fight.

Raven grabbed the vampyre around the waist. "No, please. Not her."

He turned his head, his eyes cold and calculating.

"Then take your clothes off. Slowly. I want to savor this moment.

"I'm going to fornicate you until you can no longer walk, and then I'm going to drink you dry."

Raven released him. She moved away from her sister, hoping he would follow.

He did so, watching in anticipation.

She screwed her eyes shut.

William, she thought, *help me.*

With trembling hands, she lifted the hem of her T-shirt.

Chapter Fifty

By the time William arrived at Raven's apartment building, the police had already cordoned it off.

Ispettor Batelli was visible smoking a cigarette just outside the front door. Two emergency medical technicians walked past him, carrying a black body bag on a stretcher.

Anxiety rolled over William as the scent of death filled his nostrils. But the dead human being was male, not female, and certainly not Raven.

Hope lived.

From his vantage point atop her roof, he could see another set of medical personnel hovering over two bodies that were lying behind the building. He recognized Marco's scent and that of Luka. With that recognition came the chilling realization that whoever had attacked them had probably done so in an effort to steal Raven.

Fortunately, there was no sign of her body.

Not caring if he was seen leaping to the building next door, he flew across the gap and ran to the edge of the roof. Some distance away he could see his Mercedes, abandoned on a side street. Policemen were moving in and out of the vehicle, placing items in bags.

A gust of wind lifted from the street below and with it, a hundred different scents. He shut his eyes and discerned the remnants of blood, including the blood of a young female. Her scent was unfamiliar.

Commingled with that scent was the sweetest aroma he'd ever experienced—light, sensual, courageous, and beautiful.

He inhaled, savoring the fragrance, and began to cough violently. The stench of a vampyre scoured his nostrils, blotting out Raven's scent. The vampyre odor was all too familiar.

Maximilian.

He had returned.

William resisted the urge to give in to fury or to haste, forcing himself to set aside the stench and focus only on Raven. His heart sank when he realized that Max must have extricated her from the Mercedes, carrying her toward the Arno. Puzzlingly, the scent of the unknown female remained linked with the other two.

The scent was fresh—less than an hour old. But that was time enough for Max to have murdered Raven or to have transformed her into a vampyre.

A cry of anguish escaped William's lips as he swung his fist heavenward.

I've lived for centuries and cursed the empty years. Now I have no time.

William ran as fast as he could across the roofs, tracking the scent from building to building before dropping to the street in order to cross the river.

He climbed a building near the Ponte Santa Trinita in his pursuit, pausing atop a roof strewn with vampyre bodies. They were dressed in the uniform of the Florentine army, their swords discarded nearby. If this was one of his rival's hunting parties, it had failed. No Consilium members were to be found among the dead.

And yet two familiar vampyre scents were discernible—one belonged to Aoibhe. And the other . . .

"I knew it." A triumphant voice sounded beside him.

Aoibhe was standing a few feet away.

He gestured to the bodies that lay behind them. "Is this your handiwork?"

"A stranger came to my aid. But I killed my share." She smiled. "I see rumors of your death are exaggerated."

William sniffed. "A stranger, you say?"

Aoibhe appeared uneasy, but only for an instant. "Yes. I'm fortunate he happened by."

"I am not so fortunate." William walked to the edge of the roof. "I am in haste and cannot dally. I'm glad you're well."

"If you're looking for your pet, Max has her."

William hesitated. "Where are they?"

"They headed in the direction of the Duomo, but of course that cannot be his destination."

William leapt to the ground and Aoibhe followed. He gave her a sour look.

"Your life is in danger. They're hunting the Consilium. You should leave the city."

She tossed her hair. "And be killed somewhere else? No. I'm too old to join another principality. They'd never admit me."

"It's your head."

He took off at great speed, running in the direction of the Duomo and, once again, Aoibhe stayed at his side. He scowled in her direction. "If you're found with me, they'll kill you."

"If I'm with you, there's a chance I'll survive."

"Then be useful and gather the loyal citizens. We may have to fight our own army."

She set her teeth stubbornly. "After I've paid my debt."

William turned a corner, following the scent to the building that housed Teatro.

"What debt?"

"You saved my life. Your pet defended me from the hunters. I'll help you retrieve her, then see to my own skin."

William stopped. "It isn't like you to take an interest in others, let alone a human."

"It isn't like you to take an interest in a woman, yet you're running as if your existence depended on it. Clearly, you value her. In helping you, I'll discharge my debt. Besides, I've wanted to kill Max for close to a century. He's a rapist. It would be a pleasure to end him."

William's expression hardened. "If he's touched her, I shall be the one killing him."

Aoibhe grinned. "Then allow me the luxury of being present at his execution. I'm in need of a new decoration for my front door. His head shall do nicely."

William shook his head but didn't bother to discourage her further.

"He's taken her inside." William gestured to the side door. "It could be a trap. We'll have to enter through the tunnel."

He strode off in the opposite direction, Aoibhe trotting at his heels.

"There isn't a tunnel that leads to Teatro."

"Prepare to be surprised."

He entered a nearby building and descended a staircase, twisting and turning in the darkness until he came upon a wooden door, locked with an iron padlock. With a flick of his wrist he broke the lock and swung the door open.

Aoibhe lifted her skirts distastefully as they walked down a dark, damp passage that was crawling with rats. "I've changed my mind. I'm not noble enough to pay my debts."

William ignored her, increasing his pace. Without explanation he made two left turns and then stopped in front of another locked door.

"This will lead us to one of the rooms."

"Pray it's not in use," Aoibhe muttered as he broke the lock.

They ascended a winding staircase that led to a trapdoor. Loud, pulsing music swirled around them, signaling they were under the club.

"There may be soldiers. Are you armed?" William whispered, moving his attention to his companion.

"Yes. You?"

"Yes." He lifted the trapdoor a fraction of an inch, bracing himself as the hinges of the door creaked. He could see dim candlelight but little else. The trapdoor opened underneath a bed.

"Allow me to enter first," Aoibhe whispered. "I frequent Teatro and will not garner attention."

"You're wanted for treason. They'll execute you on sight."

"Which is why you must follow me closely, my prince." She touched his face. "These may be my final moments."

"It isn't like you to be sentimental."

"Death has strange side effects." She nodded at him and he lifted the door higher. She crawled through it onto the floorboards.

Then she peeked from underneath the bed.

Chapter Fifty-one

The room was empty.

"Follow me." Aoibhe crawled out from under the bed and stood, dusting her crimson dress off and clucking to herself. "What a pity. I liked this dress."

William followed her to the door, opening it a crack.

Other rooms ran the length of the empty hallway. He'd have to enter it and make haste to pick up Raven's scent.

He hoped he wasn't too late.

"Let me." Aoibhe ducked under his arm. "If I'm seen, I may be able to talk my way out of danger."

Reluctantly, William stood back, watching through the crack as Aoibhe tiptoed down the hall, finally pointing to a closed door. Before he could join her, she'd already knocked.

"Aoibhe!" he hissed.

She gave him a knowing smile and turned to face the door.

Nothing happened. She knocked again.

"Be gone!" Max bellowed from inside.

She knocked a third time, somewhat impatiently.

"What is it?" he cried, flinging the door wide.

Aoibhe had already drawn her sword and as soon as she saw his face, she swung at it. Unfortunately, her weapon glanced off his spine, leaving his head only partially severed.

William wasted no time but flew past her and knocked over the great, hulking beast.

Aoibhe closed the door firmly and blocked it with her body.

"William!"

He lifted his head to see Raven standing by the bed. She was clad in only her underclothes. William's anger ignited.

He landed a blow on Max's jaw while the larger vampyre still lay on the ground. "What did you do to her?"

Max jumped to his feet. "You aren't the master here. Your reign is over."

Aoibhe intervened, slashing at his legs with her sword and toppling him. William took hold of his head and, with a quick tug, caused the flesh that had been opened to rip further.

"What did you do to her?" he hissed.

Max began to laugh. "He was right. You care more for your little pet than you do for the city. That's why he was able to take over the army. You're so busy rutting with your crippled human, you ignored what was going on under your nose."

Aoibhe wiped her hands on her dress. "Let's kill him and be quick about it. We need to leave before someone scents us."

Max stumbled to his feet but she evaded him, landing a swift kick in his ribs. He groaned and bent over, clutching his side. "You won't survive," he gasped. "You'll lose everything."

"One last question." William lifted Max's chin with his sword. "Where's Pierre?"

Max's eyes took on a strange light. "Dead. We never reached Paris."

"May I?" Aoibhe asked, holding her sword.

William nodded.

"Finally," she breathed. She swung her sword with both hands, decapitating Max completely.

She walked over to his head, which was still dripping black blood, and lifted it. "Yes, this shall do nicely. Now that I have my prize, I'll leave you." She bowed to William.

"Don't leave, Aoibhe. I have need of you."

A strangled cry filled the room as Raven collapsed on the bed, covering her mouth with both hands. William moved to her side, draping his jacket over her shoulders. He sheathed his sword.

"Are you injured?"

She shook her head.

"Did he . . ." William trailed off, his gray eyes darting to her lower body, which was noticeably absent trauma.

"No," she managed. "He said you were dead."

He cupped her face in his hands. "But I'm not. I'm here and you're safe."

He kissed her firmly, his cool breath commingling with hers.

"The city has fallen into the hands of a traitor. We must return to the villa." William's gaze moved to the woman on the bed. "Is that your sister?"

"Yes." Raven turned on the bed, examining her sister's pale form. "I think her nose is broken. Will she be all right?"

"Her heart is beating and she's breathing well. She'd do better with vampyre blood."

William turned to look at Aoibhe, who shook her head. "I've discharged my debt. It's time for me to leave before someone realizes we're here."

"She'll heal more quickly if you help."

"Then feed her."

"Aoibhe." His voice was just over a rumble.

A long look passed between the two vampyres.

"If I do this, I want a favor in return." Aoibhe sniffed.

"A modest favor in exchange for what will be a modest amount of blood." William's expression grew threatening.

"Do I have your word?" she asked, still holding Max's severed head.

"So long as your request is modest, I won't refuse."

"Fine," she snapped. She walked to the bed and held out her wrist.

"Wait." Raven held her hands over Cara protectively. "William, I'd rather she had your blood."

"No," he said firmly.

"Why not?"

"Because he doesn't want your sister to bond with him." Aoibhe gave Raven a withering look.

"Is that true?" asked Raven.

William nodded.

"I don't like the idea of Cara bonding with her." Raven grimaced.

"You'll like it well enough when her wounds are healed," Aoibhe retorted. "You ungrateful wench."

"Aoibhe," William rumbled.

He took Raven's hand and passed his thumb over her palm. "It will be all right, I promise. I'll only feed her a little—enough to heal her wounds and perhaps her mind. She'll probably sleep peacefully for several hours."

"Okay." Raven squeezed his hand.

William looked up at Aoibhe, and when she nodded, he took his thumbnail and sliced open her wrist. Opening Cara's mouth, he positioned Aoibhe's wrist over it.

Raven turned her back on the scene.

"Now that's done, I'll be taking my leave," Aoibhe announced a few minutes later. "You're welcome, pet."

Raven turned and found Aoibhe looking at her contemptuously before she swept out of the room, carrying her prize. Cara was still on the bed, eyes closed. Slowly, her bruises began to fade and her breathing deepened.

William examined her. "She's healing. The blood will continue to work for some time. She may not remember what happened, but that's probably a mercy."

"Thank you."

"I understand why you didn't want Aoibhe's blood in your sister's system, but it's best this way." He pulled Raven into his arms. "I've never shared my blood with anyone but my maker."

"Why?"

William's brow wrinkled. "The exchange of blood bonds the pair. I'd be hesitant to share my blood even with you. We already have an extraordinary connection. I think if you tasted me, you wouldn't be satisfied until you'd drunk enough to transform. I would be unable to refuse you."

Raven looped her arms around his neck, resting her chin on his shoulder. "Being separated from you is worse than the thought of becoming a vampyre. But I can't resign myself to a life of hundreds of years. I just don't want to live that long."

William held her more tightly.

Tears pricked at the corners of her eyes. "I was so afraid I wasn't going to see you again. I was more afraid of that than of Max killing me."

William crushed her to his chest. "Every bruise, every wound is my fault."

"Don't take on the faults of others, but please, don't ever leave me alone. We have to stay together."

"I will protect you. I swear it." He reached down and kissed her, their lips melding together until she was breathless.

Raven leaned against him. "My sister's boyfriend was with us at my building. Is he all right?"

William looked at her gravely. "I saw the police there, removing bodies."

Raven covered her mouth with her hand, her gaze moving to her sister.

"Both Luka and Marco were killed. I don't know about the boy-friend."

"They were going to get married."

William squeezed her hand. "He may be alive. I shall find out. But right now, we need to get you and your sister to the villa. Can you walk?"

"Slowly, but yes. What about you? Where will you be safe?"

"The traitor has taken control of the army. I'm going to have to fight him to regain the city. But I'm not doing anything until you're safe."

William lifted Raven off his lap and they both stood.

"There's a secret tunnel. It's a long walk but it will lead us straight to the villa." He lifted Cara into his arms.

William walked toward the door, waiting while Raven turned the doorknob for him. As they stepped into the hall, they saw Aoibhe, flanked by several vampyres dressed in uniform.

"I'm sorry," she whispered.

Chapter Fifty-two

"Aoibhe betrayed you," Raven whispered as she marched at William's side down a long corridor. "She summoned the soldiers."

He was holding a sleeping Cara in his arms and had been divested of his sword. "I doubt it, unless they were posted at Teatro. There was barely time to summon them from the underworld. Besides, the traitor tried to have her killed earlier this evening. It's not in her interest to be caught."

"Why didn't you fight?"

William held Cara more tightly. "I couldn't dispatch them and save you and your sister at the same time."

"I'm sorry."

William gave her a sharp look. "Don't be. Stay close, but if we're separated, remember what I told you about Sarah. Take your sister with you."

Raven hesitated. Then she remembered their previous conversation. She nodded.

The soldiers marched them through the underworld, along with Aoibhe, to a set of large wooden doors, which opened to reveal an immense, cavernous space. Raven had seen glimpses of it from beneath her blindfold on the single occasion William had brought her into the council chamber.

Only this time, someone else sat on the throne. Someone who had stood at Raven's apartment door hours earlier, asking to be invited inside.

"At last, the traitor is apprehended." Lorenzo applauded slowly.

The soldiers accompanied the captives to the base of the steps that led to the throne, then half their number moved to flank Lorenzo.

"Humans aren't allowed at council meetings unless they're part of the catering," he announced.

"Sitting on a throne doesn't make you a prince. I am the Prince of Florence and you are a traitor." William growled.

"My control of the army says differently." Lorenzo gestured to the troops. "And I am prince by birth. I am a Medici; you're only an Englishman."

Raven stared with shock at the pretender to the throne.

"You're a right bastard, whatever spawned you," Aoibhe spat out. "Why did you try to kill me?"

"I'll deal with you later. Don't think you've escaped execution; you've merely delayed it." Lorenzo spoke over her sputtering. "Where's Max?"

"Dead." Aoibhe lifted Max's head triumphantly. "I'm going to use this as a door knocker."

"I doubt that, since you'll be dead also." He gestured to the soldiers who were guarding William. "Remove the pets to Palazzo Riccardi. I'll dispose of them later."

"That would be unwise." William's voice was deceptively calm.

"I think you overestimate your strength. With a snap of my fingers I can have the entire army assembled in this chamber. Not even you can defeat them singlehandedly."

"Perhaps. But these human beings belong to the Curia."

Silence rang out in the large room.

"You lie." Lorenzo clenched his fist.

William turned to Raven, who was standing next to him. "In the jacket's inner pocket on the left is a letter. Hand it to me."

Raven did what she was told, rummaging in the jacket she was wearing and retrieving a folded piece of paper. William took the letter with the hand that was wrapped around Cara's back as he cradled her.

"This message was sent to me by a priest of the Curia. He has known these humans since they were children. He threatens war if they are not delivered safely to him in Rome."

Lorenzo signaled to one of the soldiers, and he took the letter from William's hand, delivering it to his master.

Lorenzo scanned the letter. "He mentions one human, not two."

"They are sisters." William lifted Cara slightly. "This one just arrived to accompany the other back to Rome. But you know this already, since you sent Max to capture my pet."

"Your pet is a security risk. Isn't that correct, Stefan of Montréal?"

The French Canadian had been standing off to the side in the shadows. He moved forward now, bowing nervously before the throne.

"By the Prince—ah—I mean the former prince's admission, his pet has psychiatric problems that caused him great concern."

"That's not true," Raven whispered.

William shook his head at her. She gave him a wounded look and averted her eyes.

"I spoke with Stefan about the fragility of her mind," William admitted. "But that is an ancillary issue. The Curia wants her and her sister. Immediately."

"The letter is dated several days back." Lorenzo tossed the paper to the ground. "Are you telling me you refused?"

"No. My servants were supposed to deliver them this very night.

Unfortunately, you interfered." William's tone was stunningly indifferent.

Raven inhaled loudly, eyes wide. She examined William, trying to determine how much of his presentation was artifice and how much was truth. He'd promised he wouldn't leave her. He'd promised they wouldn't be separated.

Under her scrutiny, William stood statue still, his eyes fixed on the traitor.

"I suppose my ascension to the throne was dreadfully inconvenient for your pet." Lorenzo sneered. "Max operated on my orders. I needed some way to ensure we had your attention.

"You made an agreement with the Curia but since you are no longer prince, that agreement is void," Lorenzo continued. "I shall dispatch a messenger to the Vatican, inform them of the change in power, and reopen negotiations."

"Do so at your peril and at the peril of the city." William's tone grew ominous. "The Curia wants the humans. They avoided Florence for centuries, knowing I was a worthy adversary, but they threatened me with war in order to force compliance. With what shall they threaten you?"

Lorenzo's expression twisted. "I am the one who will be making threats!"

"Then your reign will be the shortest in Florentine history." William spoke evenly. "Honor your ancestors and the house of Medici by protecting the city. Deliver the humans safely to the Curia and avoid a war."

Raven placed her hand on William's arm, cautioning him. She was terrified the traitor was going to agree with his words.

Lorenzo glanced between the couple. "This is the pet you killed three men for some months ago. You healed her with your blood and have been protecting her ever since. How do I know this is not a ploy to spare her life?"

"Are you not familiar with the fate of Prague? Who would choose a pet over annihilation?" William's expression remained impassive.

Lorenzo's dark eyes fixed on Raven. She withdrew her arm, unable to hide her distress.

"Perhaps the letter is a forgery," Lorenzo observed.

"The priest who wrote to me visited her some time ago. His presence was confirmed by security."

"He may be a member of the Curia, but he isn't a high-ranking one. His attempt at persuading his superiors to invade us may fail."

"Not even you are foolish enough to take that kind of risk," William said.

"I am the Prince of Florence!" Lorenzo snapped. "You will address me with respect!"

William scoffed. "What respect should I have for a lieutenant who betrays his prince? For a petty thief who stole from me and sold my treasures to humans? You sold secrets to the Venetians and colluded with them to have me assassinated on Florentine soil. You let hunters into the city, allowing them to maim and kill, so you could gain the throne."

William turned to make eye contact with the soldiers, one by one. "Do you wish to serve a prince who is so quick to sacrifice his citizens at every turn? Do you not know what happened to the principality of Prague? If the Curia marches on Florence, all of you will die."

"Enough!" Lorenzo hammered his fist on the armrest. "You did not deserve to be prince of this great city. I am a prince by birth; you are merely a foreigner."

William spat on the ground. "You were a bastard at birth in the sixteeth century and only a distant cousin to the reigning Medici.

Your father barely acknowledged you, and then only because your mother's family threatened him with violence."

"Those are lies!"

"I've been Prince of Florence since the fourteenth century. I knew the true Medici and what they thought of you. You cannot whitewash your history to me."

Lorenzo spoke over him. "Guards, take the humans away. I'll decide what's to be done with them later."

"No!" Raven cried, clinging to William. Two large vampyres grabbed her by the arms.

"No," she begged again, but the soldiers pulled her away.

Two more soldiers approached William cautiously, eyeing the woman in his arms.

"You'd condemn us all to death at the hands of the Curia because of your vanity?" William lifted his voice incredulously. "You are a coward."

Lorenzo opened his mouth to respond, but before he could speak the doors to the chamber crashed open.

A lone figure appeared in the doorway, his clothes spattered with blood.

Chapter Fifty-three

"Next time you send a detachment to kill me, double their numbers." Niccolò swept into the chamber, his torn robes fluttering behind him.

Lorenzo stared in shock.

The former head of intelligence strode up the aisle, nodding stiffly at Aoibhe. "I see you survived execution. What a pity."

"Go to hell," she snarled.

Niccolò gazed around the council chamber. "It would appear I am already there."

"Guards." Lorenzo pointed at his rival. "Remove Machiavelli and kill him."

"A moment, please." Niccolò lifted his hands in surrender. "It appears I'm interrupting something important. Does anyone care to enlighten me before my execution?"

Aoibhe angled her head in the direction of Raven and her sister. "The Curia wants the human females. Lorenzo is refusing to give them up."

"Ah," said Niccolò. "Another tactical error on the part of the new prince. It isn't his first and, sadly, it won't be his last."

"Guards!" Lorenzo barked.

"Just a moment." Niccolò stood to Aoibhe's left, facing the throne.

He observed Raven and Cara, then shifted his attention to the new prince. "The black-haired one is sweet enough, but hardly worth a war. Why not give them to the Curia in exchange for a peace treaty?"

"If I'd wanted your opinion, old man, I wouldn't have sent a hunting party after you."

"Centuries of opportunities came and went and you learned nothing." Niccolò sighed. "You're the last of your family—the last of the famed Medici. You've disgraced them with a sloppy coup, leaving the old prince still alive and courting disaster with the Curia."

"What's happening?" Raven whispered, lifting fearful eyes to William.

"When one's enemies are at war with one another, it's best to be silent," he murmured. The edge of his mouth turned up slightly.

Raven bit at her lip, struggling to remain calm.

Niccolò moved to address the soldiers. "This one is not worthy of allegiance. He attempted to unseat his rival, while leaving him alive. Now he risks the ire of our most powerful enemy."

A murmur rippled through the ranks.

"I said, enough!" Lorenzo shouted. "I am prince here, by birth and by power. Guards, seize Machiavelli and take off his head."

At this Niccolò smiled. "You're just like your ancestors—arrogant, small-minded, and ignorant. You wouldn't recognize greatness if it ran you through with a sword."

Lorenzo began to clap, exaggeratedly. "Pontificating even at the end. I've never met a man who loves the sound of his own voice more than you."

"A voice you ignored."

"You had every opportunity to seize the throne for yourself but were too cowardly to do so. What's the old adage? Ah, yes. *Fortune favors the brave.* Today, I am favored and you are dead."

Niccolò's smile widened.

"Yes, fortune favors the brave. If you'd paid attention to the history of your family, you'd know that fortune abandoned them long ago. I witnessed the exile of your family in 1494. I saw them return to power only to lose it. I learned my lesson—never pin your political aspirations on a Medici."

He made a low, slashing motion with his hand, and a long line of soldiers entered the chamber, marching down the aisle and assembling behind the chairs that were reserved for the Consilium members.

Lorenzo appeared confused. "Guards, seize him."

One of the soldiers stepped out from behind the throne, sword raised. Lorenzo caught sight of the sword and moved to the side, but another soldier slashed at his head.

His corpse fell to the ground.

"Someone should have read *The Art of War*." Niccolò stepped over the head with distaste, lifting his robes as he kicked the headless body.

Soldiers continued to file into the chamber until it was full. It appeared that the entire Florentine army had been assembled—all three hundred of them.

Machiavelli nodded at the commanding officer, who bowed to him.

"You there." He gestured to the soldiers who were holding Raven. "Release her. Take three of your brethren and carry the Medici dog's body outside the city. Burn everything and report back here."

The soldiers bowed and obeyed.

Raven pressed herself close to William and Cara, eyes wide.

"I didn't expect that," Aoibhe muttered, cursing in Irish.

"I didn't live this long to have my life ended by a Medici." Niccolò favored her with his back as he ascended the throne.

He arranged his robes and looked down at Raven and William.

"Now, what's to be done with the two of you?"

Chapter Fifty-four

"The letter from the Curia regarding the humans is at your feet." William nodded toward the paper.

A soldier picked it up and handed it to Niccolò. He read it and returned it.

"If the Curia want the females so badly, it's tempting to keep them in order to negotiate a more detailed, protracted peace."

William cursed.

Niccolò lifted his hand. "But for a new prince, that would be unwise. The females have no value to me except as political pawns, and so it's better to send them as a gift to our enemy and then negotiate the peace."

"No," Raven protested.

"It isn't safe here," William cautioned her in English, speaking under his breath.

"How long, Niccolò?" William lifted his voice, speaking now in Italian. "How long have you been waiting in the wings?"

"I'd like an answer to that question, as well," Aoibhe interjected.

"Neither of you are in a position to make any demands." Niccolò straightened on the throne. "But since I am in a mood to be magnanimous, I'll reveal that I discovered Lorenzo's activities some time ago.

I kept my discovery to myself. Not even he knew I was aware of his duplicity. He took the risk, while I bided my time. But he was supposed to destroy you."

"We could duel for the throne." William barely restrained a smile.

"We both know I cannot best you face-to-face."

"Face-to-back, then?" William taunted him.

"I doubt you'll find it amusing when I set the army against you."

"I may not be able to defeat them"—William's tone grew menacing—"but I shall die trying. If you're certain the army is loyal to you, then you won't mind putting that to the test."

"The odds are in my favor."

William's smile widened. "You can't know what lies in their hearts, Niccolò. We've enjoyed centuries of prosperity and peace under my command. Even now I have negotiated a way to keep the Curia at bay."

A murmur rippled across the assembly of soldiers.

William nodded appreciatively. "It would seem I still have friends in the ranks."

"You assume much. Perhaps I shall force you to surrender by taking your pet and enjoying her for a while."

William pressed his lips together, restraining his reaction. "Any harm that comes to her will be reported to the Curia by their spies."

"Yes," Machiavelli mused. "I am well aware of that. Your pet smells sweet, but she's infirm. I don't find her tempting."

He gestured to the commanding officer of the army. "General, choose ten of your best and most trusted soldiers to accompany the humans to Vatican City. They are to deliver the females unharmed and unspoiled."

"No," Raven cried in English. "I don't want to go. William, do something!"

"Cassita," he whispered. His eyes held a warning.

"You promised," she said accusingly. "You promised we'd stay together."

"It's the only way."

Raven bowed to Niccolò and switched to Italian. "Please don't send me to Rome."

He ignored her and spoke to William. "Is your pet addressing me?"

"Yes," she replied.

The new prince scowled. "Your pet is spoiled and needs to learn its place."

"I'm not deaf. You're discussing my fate in front of me. I should be allowed to say something," Raven countered.

"Human beings don't have status in this chamber except as food."

"I didn't think the great race of vampyres would be speciesist." Raven's hands clenched at her sides.

Machiavelli's eyes flickered to hers. "I'll indulge you for a moment, but only because you have an enviable vocabulary. Be brief."

"Thank you." Raven took a deep breath, trying to slow the rapid beating of her heart.

"In your book *Il Principe*, you wrote that when there is no tribunal to appeal to, we look to results."

At this, Machiavelli leaned forward. "You read *Il Principe*?"

"I read it in English, but yes."

His chest puffed out. "Interesting. Proceed."

"I can provide you with the results that you want, without being delivered to the Curia."

"How?"

"Father Kavanaugh is my friend." Various whisperings filled the chamber, but Raven ignored them. "He thinks I'm in danger, which is why he wants me in Rome. If you would let me write to him, I can persuade him I'm safe and that the Curia should leave Florence in peace."

"While I appreciate the gesture, the priest has demanded your presence. What makes you think you can change his mind?"

"War isn't in the interest of the Curia and it isn't in your interest, either. Let me broker a peace."

Niccolò chuckled. "A human girl brokering a peace agreement between the Curia and us. Oh, this pet is a delight. Truly. I almost want to give you the opportunity to try your hand at peacemaking simply for the sake of amusement. But that would not be judicious.

"The Curia want you. Perhaps they want your sister. Neither of you have any worth to me so I'm gifting you to them. What they decide to do with you afterward is their concern. The fate of your master is a separate case. But it's fair to say he will not live long."

Raven stared the vampyre in the eye. "Send him with us."

Niccolò smiled triumphantly at William. "It would seem your pet's affections have been alienated. She wishes the Curia to execute you."

"If you won't send him with us then let me stay with him. Please."

Machiavelli's eyes bored into hers. "Tell me, would you still be willing to write to the Curia and ask for peace, after I execute him?"

Raven flinched. "I don't think sentient beings should be killed indiscriminately—whether the being is a vampyre or a human. Peace between you and the Curia is better for everyone, including humans.

"I know you know this, Signor Machiavelli. I've read your works. You reject tyranny. But if you execute William for no purpose other than to show your political power, you will become what you despise—a tyrant. And after everything I've read, I can't believe you'd do that."

Machiavelli scowled. "I have evolved. The human I was no longer exists. I'm flattered you read the works I wrote when I was human, but I'm not convinced by your argument. The action most likely to yield results is the one I've described. You will go to the Curia. And the former prince will be executed.

"General, choose the soldiers who will be escorting the females to the Vatican."

Ten soldiers moved forward at the general's indication, and William handed over Cara to one of them.

"William, please." Raven clung to his arm, even as a soldier began to pull her away.

He gestured toward her and lifted his voice. "May I have my jacket?"

Raven's jaw dropped. "Your jacket?"

"Think of Cara," he whispered, in English.

A soldier helped her out of the jacket and delivered it to William, who put it on, discreetly patting the pockets.

"Stefan," Niccolò said, addressing him. "You will accompany the humans to the Vatican, ensuring they arrive in good health. Take the letter from the priest with you."

The physician stood and bowed. "With respect, my lord. We don't have permission to travel through the intervening territories. Our neighbors will see the soldiers and kill us."

"Couriers will be sent before you, offering an explanation. I'll see to it a messenger is sent to the Curia tonight, announcing your arrival."

"But what about hunters," Stefan protested, "or ferals?"

"You will be traveling with a detachment of Florentine soldiers. I trust they can handle a few predators." Niccolò beckoned to one of the soldiers who were guarding him. "Remove the signet ring from the hand of the former prince. I have need of it."

The soldier approached William warily, sword at the ready. William grimaced and removed the signet ring symbolizing the principality of Florence. He relinquished it without a word.

Niccolò smiled triumphantly, placing the ring on his own finger. "Stefan, leave for the Vatican at once. I'll pen letters for the couriers when I've disposed of the former prince. The couriers will overtake you."

"William, you promised we'd stay together." Raven struggled against the soldier who had hold of her arm. Her mind spun wildly in several different directions, trying to think of a way she could stay in the city. She was furious with William for agreeing to her removal and for placing her and Cara in the hands of their enemies.

"William!" Raven pleaded, hoping she could change his mind even as she was dragged to the door. "How could you do this?"

His eyes never left hers as his lips moved silently. *"Je t'aim."*

"If you love me, then help me," she cried. "William!"

Raven and her sister were taken into the corridor and the large chamber door was shut behind them with a resounding crash.

Chapter Fifty-five

"Now that the minor problem is solved, the major problem remains." Machiavelli stared down at William.

"Your problems are only beginning," William responded. "Have you checked the borders recently? Tonight I scented an old enemy who somehow infiltrated the city."

At this, the new prince straightened. "Who?"

William's eyes flickered to Aoibhe and back to the new prince. "That is for you to discover."

Niccolò lifted his hand, and a line of soldiers moved forward, surrounding William. "It is time for me to solve this problem."

William turned, surveying the soldiers' faces.

"Then let me offer you a fresh solution—I appeal to the Roman."

Once again, silence rang out in the large chamber.

Niccolò scowled. "Your appeal is pointless. I am lord and master here."

"The King of Italy allows principalities at his pleasure. When the Prince of Palermo insulted him, Roman soldiers marched on the city and executed him. Even now, Palermo remains under Roman control."

"That was three hundred years ago. The Roman no longer interferes in the affairs of city-states."

"When he learns of the circumstances of my death, he will make an exception."

Something flickered in Niccolò's eyes. "That is a bold claim."

"One I am prepared to defend." William rummaged in one of the inner pockets of his jacket and withdrew a missive.

A soldier carried it to Niccolò, who opened it. "I've seen this before."

William's eyebrows lifted. "How?"

"As head of intelligence I searched your rooms and found it. I don't doubt its authenticity. Lorenzo delivered it himself from Rome. But just because you have a connection with the Roman, doesn't mean he'll trouble me."

"You are not Lorenzo," William observed quietly.

Machiavelli's eyes glinted. "Indeed, I am not."

"If you are intelligent enough to avoid a war with the Curia, you should be intelligent enough to avoid one with Rome."

"The Roman is never seen and communicates only through his lieutenant. I was stunned he'd bother with you."

"A sign of his regard for me," William rejoined. "You've read the history of Florence. I was young when I killed the old prince, yet who supported my ascension to the throne?"

Niccolò pressed his lips together and said nothing.

William continued. "Neither of us want a war—not with the Curia, not amongst ourselves, and certainly not with Rome."

"If you expect me to hand over the throne and submit to execution, you're mad."

"I'll decimate the army before I succumb, leaving you vulnerable to an attack. News of my death will spread, and in addition to the Roman, you'll be dealing with Tarquin of Venice and potentially Simonetta of Umbria. They've long envied this territory. Allow me to leave the city."

"What?" Machiavelli's tone was sharp.

"I will join the Roman at his court, praise your leadership, and live out my days at his side."

Niccolò's eyes narrowed. "You'll go to Rome, secure his army, and march it here."

"If I leave Florence voluntarily, I will have abandoned my claim to the throne. You can send messengers to the Roman stating that fact."

"What assurances have I that he won't decide to gift you with the principality, since you are his favorite?"

"I would have no reason to return to a city I fled, especially when I can enjoy the luxuries Rome provides."

Machiavelli stared at William for some time.

"You are an old one. The Roman is older still, but he cannot live forever. If I let you go, there's a possibility you'll overthrow him. That would only increase my peril."

"The Roman has escaped the Curia's curse. He's the most powerful vampyre alive and absolutely unassailable." William leveled cold eyes on his rival. "All the more reason not to anger him."

Machiavelli drummed his fingers on the armrest, apparently deep in thought.

"All I ask, Niccolò, is that I be allowed safe passage from the city and that Aoibhe be allowed to accompany me."

She looked over at William, her face an expression of shock.

"Aoibhe is slated for execution," Machiavelli announced.

"I'd rather speak on my own behalf than have either of you decide my fate." Aoibhe glared at each vampyre in turn. "Your list of allies grows short, Nick. You have no Consilium and no friends. Send William to the Roman to live out his days, of which there are few, and allow me the role of lieutenant."

"Lieutenant?" Niccolò sputtered. "You must be mad."

"Who will guard your back? Stefan?" Aoibhe laughed. "If you exile William, I'm the oldest citizen of this principality, next to you. You need me. Or else you'll find yourself with a reign the length of Lorenzo's."

"On second thought, I'd rather send you to the Roman. You can be a thorn in his flesh, just as you've been in mine."

Aoibhe pursed her lips and exchanged a look with William.

Machiavelli gestured to the sentries who were guarding the two vampyres.

"I had hoped Lorenzo would dispose of you both. Now that he's failed I have no choice. Executing the former prince may earn me censure from the Roman, but I'm willing to take that risk.

"If the Curia has decided to exert more control over the kingdom of Italy, the Roman will have larger problems to deal with. I will argue that you lost the principality due to carelessness."

At this, he stood and extended his hand. "I, Niccolò, Prince of Florence, hereby condemn William of Britannia and Aoibhe of Hibernia to death for acts of treason. Execution will take place summarily by the Florentine army."

"Are we not to be afforded a moment to speak in our own defense?" William challenged him.

Machiavelli regained his seat. "There is no judge or jury here. I've already pronounced sentence."

William turned away from the new prince to address the army, arms spread wide.

"Brothers and sisters, you know me. I am William and I've served the principality of Florence since the fourteenth century.

"For hundreds of years, I kept the city safe from the Curia, while other cities fell. I ensured food was plentiful and that ferals and hunters were kept out of the city. I protected us when the Venetians attempted to invade us.

"But years of peace and prosperity are insufficient for someone like Niccolò." William gestured dismissively toward the throne. "He will only be satisfied with tyranny.

"Look to your swords, brothers and sisters. Look to those who serve with you. Will you give your sword and your life to this interloper? This tyrant who whispers sweet lies in the shadows while the true prince is fighting to keep danger at bay?"

A few echoes of support were heard.

"He cannot best me in combat so he summons my army to take his place. Are you willing to give up your existence to feed his vanity?"

"Make no mistake." Aoibhe aimed her dark eyes at the general. "He'll have your head. Anyone who is a threat will be eliminated, and that means anyone above the age of youngling." She pointed at the row upon row of soldiers. "That means all of you."

"That is quite enough," Machiavelli growled. He gestured to General Valerian, who was already positioning his soldiers so that they encircled the condemned prisoners.

"You may begin, General."

The soldiers lifted their swords.

"There is still time to surrender," William cautioned them. "Drop your sword and your life will be spared."

He placed his back to Aoibhe's so that they were both facing their executioners.

"I can't believe I've lived this long only to end my life at the end of a Florentine sword." She lowered into a crouch, watching for the first sign of an attack.

"Surely the Prince of Florence is not so stingy as to leave us without weapons." William lifted his eyes to the throne.

Niccolò waved a hand at the general. "Give them each a sword."

Two swords flew through the air, each caught handily by the captives.

"This is your last chance, Niccolò." William's voice rang out. "End this conflict before I diminish the army."

"If I lose soldiers, I'll make new ones." Machiavelli nodded at the general. "Begin."

Aoibhe lifted her sword with both hands, poised to strike. "Did you hear that, army? You're no better than humans to your new prince. Each of you is disposable."

The general barked out an order and the army advanced on all sides.

Chapter Fifty-six

William and Aoibhe were a whirlwind of movement, striking and blocking at every turn, but they were hopelessly outnumbered. For every soldier killed, another took his or her place. All the while, the new prince sat on his throne, watching his army shrink.

William knew there were too many. There were too many for him and he was an old one. Aoibhe was stronger than any of the soldiers individually, but taken together, they'd overwhelm her and then he'd have no one at his back.

He'd let Raven go without kissing her. Without persuading her he was keeping his promise to protect her and her sister, even though that meant sending her to his enemy. Now he'd never have the chance to look into her eyes and explain.

With renewed vigor, William went on the attack, forcing the line of soldiers to retreat.

Behind him, Aoibhe stumbled. She fell to the ground, her sword careening across the floor and coming to rest out of reach.

A line of soldiers advanced and one lifted his arm in preparation to take her head.

His blow was caught inches from Aoibhe's neck by William's sword.

A soldier saw the opening and ran up behind him, aiming for his head. Lightning fast, William turned, leaning backward to avoid the metal that flashed through the air, narrowly missing his throat.

He lifted his sword, but before he could strike, the soldier's head flew from his shoulders and his body crumpled to the ground.

Gregor stood behind him, sword in hand.

It was then William saw an influx of his citizens, armed and battling with the soldiers who surrounded him. Beyond them, half of the army had already fallen back, disengaging from the conflict.

A female tossed a sword to Aoibhe and she was on her feet, swirling like a red-haired dervish.

"Down with the traitor!" William cried. "To arms, citizens of Florence!"

The loyal civilians cheered as he battled his way to the throne, taking the steps two at a time before standing in front of the one who had unseated him.

"Guards, kill him!" Niccolò shouted.

But the guards ignored his order, throwing down their swords. The metal clattered on the stone floor.

William paused as he stood over his former head of intelligence.

"You should have granted my appeal, Niccolò."

"It was a calculated risk."

Machiavelli looked out over the hall. The skirmishes had ended as everyone watched the scene unfolding at the throne.

"I have lived a long life, with some regrets." He gazed at William's sword bitterly. "I regret underestimating the citizens' loyalty to you."

"A mistake you will not make again."

Machiavelli looked up at his prince. "I don't suppose you can be persuaded to be merciful?"

William pressed his lips together. "I know no such word."

Machiavelli's head flew to the floor and a great series of cheers filled the hall.

William tugged the signet ring from the headless corpse's finger and pushed the body aside. He replaced the ring on his finger and stood, arms raised.

"Citizens of Florence, the traitor is dead."

Chapter Fifty-seven

"It's fortunate the Curia have a prize being sent their way," Aoibhe declared, standing with the Prince in the empty council chamber. "They would have marched on us for certain. The hunting parties wreaked havoc across the city, and Max killed three humans in Santo Spirito, leaving their bodies to rot."

The Prince kept his own counsel as he surveyed the aftermath of the battle. They'd been able to regenerate much of the army—reuniting bodies with their severed heads and borrowing vampyre blood in order to effect the reanimation. The corpses and heads of those the Prince despised had been removed from the chamber and were now burning on a pyre outside the city.

He'd executed General Valerian and his officers, replacing them with lower-ranked ones who'd sworn fealty. He would be keeping a closer eye on the army henceforth.

At the mention of the Curia, William grew agitated. Niccolò hadn't had time to send couriers to the rulers of the neighboring principalities. William had dispatched messengers as soon as he could but it was still possible Raven and Cara could fall into the hands of another coven on their way to Rome. They'd escaped one danger only to be thrust into another.

"I know better than to believe our kind worthy of miracles,"

Aoibhe observed, moving so the Prince could no longer ignore her. "Yet I cannot help but believe you were favored with one today."

He stiffened. "I make no such claim."

"It seems I'm destined to remain in your debt." She touched his arm. "Thank you. Now comes the difficult task of rebuilding the city."

The Prince regarded her stoically. "You fought at my side today and for that I'm grateful. But you concealed your contact with Ibarra. I should execute you for that."

Aoibhe withdrew her hand as if she'd been burned. "Ibarra is dead."

"Ibarra's amalgam of scents might be strong enough to fool many, but it isn't strong enough to fool me. I scented him atop the building where you were attacked. He came to your aid."

"It was a stranger. I didn't recognize him."

"You lie as you fornicate, Aoibhe: artfully and forcefully. I have no time for either." He strode down the aisle, carrying his sword in one hand and the missive with the Roman's signature in the other.

"Wait." She lifted her skirts and followed him. "Why would you think Ibarra is still alive? We watched him die."

William glared at her. "Don't insult me. An armed detachment is already hunting him."

Aoibhe flew to his side. "I've been your ally. I helped secure your pet. I gave my blood for her sister."

"That is why you are still alive," he replied. "I promised you a modest favor. Electing not to execute you for treason is hardly modest but I don't have time to deal with you at the moment."

Aoibhe scowled. "I've done nothing but show my loyalty, again and again, while the other members of the Consilium plotted your demise. I argued with Nick for your life. I fought at your back. This is how you repay me?"

William's jaw clenched and unclenched, as if he were barely controlling his anger. "Did you summon the soldiers at Teatro?"

"Of course not! They were already posted in the club. They'd scented us in the hall and when I left the room, they fell on me."

"You're adept at lying, Aoibhe. Did you not think to lie in order to lure them away?"

"They knew Max had your pet. They knew you were inside the room. Lying would have accomplished nothing. You saw me when you came into the hall—they'd already disarmed me. I have yet to retrieve my sword."

William's eyes narrowed as he concentrated on the sound of her heart, listening for any indication of duplicity.

"We've been allies, Aoibhe. But alliances change. If you betray me, I'll kill you."

Aoibhe swept into a curtsy, averting her eyes. "Understood, my lord."

William approached the door and was just about to walk through it, when she called after him.

"What was in the letter you showed to Nick?"

William considered her question for a moment before he answered.

"The Roman wrote a postscript in his own hand."

"A postscript isn't enough to have given Niccolò pause."

"He wrote, 'Greetings, my beloved son, with whom I am well pleased.'" William's gray eyes glittered. "The Roman is my maker."

Her eyes widened. "Truly?"

"Yes."

She took a step back, her expression fearful. "Is it true the Roman is past his thousand years? That he escaped the curse?"

"He was past his thousand years when he made me."

"How is that possible? The curse affected everyone—those who were past their thousand years were struck with madness immediately."

"Our existence seems to be riddled with—exceptions."

She looked at him with new eyes. "You have so much power. Why didn't you take over the principalities in America?"

William pressed his lips together. "You forget my age. America wasn't desirable at that time."

"You could have made of America what you wanted."

"I came to Florence in search of beauty and hope."

"Beauty?" She frowned. "Perhaps you didn't look hard enough."

"On the contrary, I was rewarded with both. Now I must save her." He strode toward the door.

Aoibhe raised her voice. "Florence doesn't need saving, my prince. Florence is already saved."

William exited into the corridor, his footsteps quick and sure. Yes, he'd saved the city he loved, but in trying to protect his woman, he'd placed her in grave danger. He'd done so even as she begged to stay with him, knowing they would both likely die.

The woman with the great green eyes and the maddening, courageous soul.

His teacher had not heard his prayer to keep her safe. It was clear. There was only one being who could help him battle the Curia with any hope of success.

It was time to see his maker.

It was time to visit the Roman.

Fin

List of Terms and Proper Names

(NB: This List Contains Spoilers)

ALICIA—William's fiancée from the thirteenth century.

ALLEGRA—Fifteenth-century woman who loved the Prince.

AMBROGIO—William York's servant.

AOIBHE—*Pronounced "A-vuh."* An Irish member of the Consilium.

ISPETTOR BATELLI—Police inspector in Florence.

THE CONSILIUM—The ruling council of the principality of Florence. It consists of six members: Lorenzo, Niccolò, Aoibhe, Stefan, Maximilian, and Pierre. The Prince is an ex officio member.

THE CURIA—Enemy of the supernatural beings.

GABRIEL EMERSON—The professor is a Dante specialist who teaches at Boston University. He is the owner of a famed set of Botticelli illustrations of Dante's *Divine Comedy*, which he lent to the Uffizi Gallery in 2011. His story is told in the Gabriel's Inferno trilogy: *Gabriel's Inferno*, *Gabriel's Rapture*, and *Gabriel's Redemption*.

JULIA EMERSON—Doctoral student at Harvard University. She is married to Gabriel and the co-owner of the Botticelli illustrations.

FEEDERS—Derogatory term for human beings who offer themselves up as a food source to supernatural beings.

FERALS—Supernatural beings who live and hunt alone. They display brutal, animalistic behavior.

GREGOR—Personal assistant to the Prince.

HUMAN INTELLIGENCE NETWORK—Human beings who are contracted to provide information to the supernatural beings. They also provide security and perform specific tasks.

HUNTERS—Humans who hunt and kill supernatural beings for commercial purposes.

IBARRA—A Basque former member of the Consilium.

FATHER KAVANAUGH—Former director of Covenant House in Orlando, Florida, and friend of Raven Wood.

LORENZO—A member of the Medici family and second in command in the principality of Florence. Also a member of the Consilium.

LUCIA—Ambrogio's wife and servant to William York.

LUKA—Servant to William York.

DAN MACREADY—Cara's boyfriend.

NICCOLÒ MACHIAVELLI—Famous Florentine and member of the Consilium. Head of intelligence for the principality of Florence.

MARCO—Servant to William York.

MARCUS—Also known as the Prince of Venice. Former ruler of the underworld principality of Venice, now deceased.

MARIA—A young girl with special needs who lives at the Franciscan orphanage in Florence. She is introduced in *Gabriel's Redemption*.

MAXIMILIAN—A Prussian member of the Consilium.

THE MEDICI—Famous ruling family of Florence during the Renaissance.

GINA MOLINARI—Friend of Raven Wood, employed in the archives of the Uffizi Gallery.

OLD ONES—A special class of supernatural beings who, by virtue of having attained seven hundred years in their supernatural state, enjoy tremendous power and special abilities.

GIUSEPPE PACCIANI—A professor of Dante at the University of Florence. His backstory is given in the Gabriel's Inferno series.

KATHERINE PICTON—Retired Dante specialist and former professor at the University of Toronto. Her backstory is described in the Gabriel's Inferno series. Friend of the Emersons.

PIERRE—A French member of the Consilium. Oversees security and liaises with the human intelligence network as well as the police services.

THE PRINCE—Ruler of the principality of Florence, the underworld society of supernatural beings.

RECRUITS—New supernatural beings, formerly human.

THE ROMAN—Ruler of the principality of Rome and also the head of the kingdom of Italy, which includes all the Italian principalities.

AGENT SAVOLA—Interpol agent assigned to Florence.

SIMONETTA—The Princess of Umbria.

STEFAN—A supernatural physician of French Canadian origin.

TARQUIN—The current ruler of Venice, under the authority of the Prince of Florence.

PROFESSOR URBANO—Director of the restoration project working on the *Birth of Venus*. Raven Wood's supervisor.

GENERAL VALERIAN—Commanding officer of the Florentine army.

THE VENETIANS—Supernatural beings living in the principality of Venice.

DOTTOR VITALI—Director of the Uffizi Gallery. He appears in the Gabriel's Inferno trilogy.

PATRICK WONG—Canadian citizen and friend of Raven Wood. Works in the archives at the Uffizi Gallery.

CAROLYN (CARA) WOOD—Raven's younger sister. Carolyn is a real estate agent in Miami, Florida.

RAVEN WOOD—American citizen and postdoctoral restoration worker at the Uffizi Gallery.

WILLIAM YORK—A wealthy Florentine and patron of the Uffizi Gallery. He appears briefly in *Gabriel's Redemption*.

YOUNGLINGS—Supernatural beings who have yet to attain one hundred years in their supernatural state.

Acknowledgments

I owe a debt to the city of Florence, its citizens, and the incomparable Uffizi Gallery. Thank you for your hospitality and inspiration.

I've used poetic license in locating Raven's restoration work in the Uffizi itself, since in reality it would be undertaken in one of the labs operated by the Opificio instead.

The quotation in chapter 9 is taken from Miguel de Cervantes's famous work *Don Quixote*. Other texts referenced in this novel include *The Prince* and *The Art of War*, both by Niccolò Machiavelli, as well as *The Art of War* written by Sun Tzu.

I am grateful to Kris, who read an early draft and offered valuable constructive criticism. I am also thankful to Jennifer and to Nina for their feedback and support.

I've been very pleased to work with Cindy Hwang, my editor, and Erin Galloway and Kristine Swartz at Berkley. Thanks are also due to the production and design team at Berkley. I'd also like to thank Kim Schefler and Cassie Hanjian, my agent, for their guidance and counsel.

My publicist, Nina Bocci, works tirelessly to promote my writing and to help me with social media, which enables me to keep in touch with readers. I'm honored to be part of her team.

Elena patiently answered my various questions, and for that I'm grateful. I also want to thank the many book bloggers who have taken the time to read and review my work.

I am grateful to Erika, Deborah Harkness, and Lauren for their kind words about *The Raven*. Thank you.

I also want to thank the Muses, Argyle Empire, the readers from around the world who operate the SRFans social media accounts, and the readers who recorded the podcasts for *The Gabriel Series* and *The Florentine Series*. Thank you for your continued support.

I wish to remember Terry, who was a supportive reader and contributor to Argyle Empire before she passed away. She is greatly missed.

I owe a debt I can never pay to my teachers, who educated and mentored me and set me on a path of curiosity and learning.

Finally, I would like to thank my readers and my family for continuing this journey with me. I'm proud to be your Virgil during this foray into the Underworld.

—SR

ASCENSION 2015

An Outtake from The Shadow

July 1, 2013
Umbria, Italy

"You have to leave. Now." Gabriel entered the bedroom from the balcony, closing the doors behind him. He engaged the locks and proceeded to check them. Twice.

"Leave? It's almost ten o'clock. What are you talking about?" Julia pressed a kiss to the baby in her arms, Clare, whom she'd just lulled back to sleep. She placed the child in the crib they'd set up a short distance from their bed, and gently brushed her hand over the baby's head.

Gabriel drew the curtains over the balcony doors, shielding them from outside. "You, Katherine, and Clare need to leave for Boston at once. It's too dangerous here."

Julia straightened. "We were outside making love a short time ago. Now you say it's dangerous?"

Gabriel's expression tightened and he brushed past her, flinging the towel from his waist onto the floor.

"I'll accompany you to Rome to make sure you get out of the country safely. Then I'll return to Florence to tie up a few loose ends. I'll follow a day or so later."

Julia ignored the distracting sight of her husband's naked body and followed him to the closet.

"I just put Clare down again. Katherine is asleep down the hall. What's going on?"

Gabriel thrust his legs into a pair of jeans, sans underwear, and turned to her, leaving the fly open. His face was grim.

"There's someone out there. He surprised me on the balcony."

"Who?"

"The man from the gallery. William York."

Julia gazed at her husband incredulously. "What's he doing here? How did he get on the balcony? We're on the second floor."

"Obviously, the man was on a mission." Gabriel cursed. "Although I hesitate to call him a *man*."

Julia touched her throat absently. "What would you call him?"

Gabriel set his teeth. "Let's just say whenever he's around, I feel darkness."

"*Gabriel*," she whispered, glancing back to look at her sleeping child. "Can't we just call the police?"

"There's nothing they can do. He's like vapor, disappearing into the night." Gabriel zipped up his fly and fastened his jeans. "And there's something else."

"What?" Julia wrapped her arms around her waist.

Gabriel hesitated.

His sapphires eyes fixed on hers.

"He told me you're ill."

Julia blinked.

She shook her head. "That's a lie. This man, whoever he is, is trying to scare you. I'm fine." She gestured to her body, which was encased in a long satin robe. "Look at me. I've never been healthier."

"I pray that's true," Gabriel whispered. "But I'm not leaving anything to chance. As soon as you get to Boston, I want you to have every test known to medicine."

She huffed. "But I'm fine."

He placed his hands on her arms, forcing her to look at him. His eyes blazed. "I'm asking you to trust me, Julianne. I know it strains credulity, but I believe him.

"It's possible he's put something in your food or your drink, or he infected you with something. We are all in danger. We need to go and we need to go now."

Julia searched his eyes, becoming even more frightened by what she saw. Gabriel, her fearless husband and protector, was afraid.

She nodded shakily. "All right. We'll go."

He closed his eyes in relief. "Thank you."

He opened his eyes and pressed his lips to her forehead.

She leaned against his chest. "Is he the one who was in our room at the Gallery Hotel Art?"

"Yes."

Julia shivered. "And you think he's not human?"

Gabriel shook his head tersely. "No."

"Oh, my God," she breathed.

"I won't let anything touch you—you or Clare." His voice, like his expression, was very fierce. "I swear on my life."

Julia's grip on her husband tightened. "I don't understand why he's threatening us. We don't even know him."

"'For we are not contending against flesh and blood, but against the principalities, against the powers, against the world rulers of this present darkness,'" Gabriel quoted, his expression ominous.

"Get dressed. Start packing. I'll go explain things to Katherine."

He released her to rummage in one of the drawers in the closet, withdrawing a simple gold necklace. He placed it around her neck.

"Wear this. And whatever you do, don't take it off."

Julia clasped the cross with both hands and nodded, her gaze moving to their sleeping child.

The Carrel

An Outtake from *Gabriel's Inferno* with an
Alternative Universe Twist...

Gabriel saw light spilling from underneath the door of his library carrel, but since Paul had pasted brown craft paper over the narrow window in the door, Gabriel couldn't peer inside. He was slightly surprised to find Paul working so late on a Thursday night. It was ten thirty in the evening and the library would be closing in thirty minutes.

Gabriel fished around in his pocket for his keys and opened the door without knocking.

And what he saw inside completely floored him.

Curled up in a chair was Miss Mitchell, her head resting on folded arms that were poised elegantly on the desktop. Her eyes were closed, her mouth partially open but not quite smiling. Her cheeks were flushed with sleep, her body rising and falling slowly, soothingly, like the waves of the ocean against a quiet beach.

Gabriel stood in the doorway, entranced, thinking that the simple sound of her breathing would make an excellent relaxation CD. One he could imagine falling asleep to again and again and again.

Her laptop was open and Gabriel saw her screen saver, which was a slide show of hand-drawn illustrations of what looked like a children's story; something with animals, including a funny-looking white bunny with long ears that fell to its feet.

The strains of music filled the air and Gabriel realized that the sound was coming from her computer. He saw a CD with a rabbit on it.

Gabriel began to wonder why Miss Mitchell was so obsessed with bunnies.

Perhaps she has an Easter fetish?

Gabriel was halfway through a very elaborate imagination of what an Easter fetish might include before he came to his senses.

He quickly entered the carrel and closed the door behind him, taking care to lock the door. It would not be good for the two of them to be caught together like this.

Gabriel regarded her peaceful form, not wishing to disturb her or to intrude upon what looked like a very pleasant dream. Now she was smiling.

He located the book he had been looking for on the bookshelf and turned his back to her, preparing to leave her in peace.

"Gabriel," she breathed. "*My* Gabriel . . ."

The sound of her voice, husky with sleep, heavy with want, floated over to him like a soft Siren call and sent a thrill coursing up and down his back.

He was momentarily frozen, his hand on the doorknob. No one had ever pronounced his name like that before. Ever. Not even in the most intimate moments in his memory. Such as it was.

He knew that if he turned around everything would change. He knew that if he turned around, he wouldn't be able to resist the urge—the undeniable and primal urge to claim the beautiful and pure Miss Mitchell.

She was there, waiting for him, calling to him, singing for him, her scent heavy in the small, too warm, confined space.

My Gabriel. Her voice laved across his name the way a lover's tongue moves across the skin. . . .

His mind traveled at light speed as he imagined pulling her into his arms. Kissing her, embracing her.

Lifting her onto the desk and pressing himself between her knees, her hands tugging at his hair, his sweater, his shirt, undoing his pretentious bow tie and flinging it to the floor.

Tangling, tugging, fisting.

His fingers would explore her wavy hair and trace gentle lines across her neck, causing every space, every pore to explode into scarlet— his nose nuzzling her cheek, her ear, her perfect milk-white throat.

He would feel her pulse at her neck and find himself strangely calmed by the gentle rhythm of her blood, and he would feel connected to the beating of her heart, especially as it would begin to quicken beneath his touch.

He would wonder if they were close enough, would their hearts beat synchronously . . . or was that simply a poet's fancy?

They would kiss and it would be electric—intense—explosive. Their tongues would tangle and tango together desperately. As if they had never been kissed before.

She would be shy at first, hesitant. But he would be gently insistent, whispering words of sweet seduction into her hair. He would tell her whatever he thought she wanted to hear and she would believe it.

His hands would drop from her shoulders and inch over her lovely and still innocent curves, marveling at the changes that emerged in response to his touch.

For no man would have touched her like that before. And she would be eager and responsive to him. Oh, so responsive.

He would be her first. And he would be glad.

She would be wearing too many clothes.

He'd want to tease her out of them and spread feather-light kisses against every blushing inch of perfect porcelain skin. Especially her lovely throat and its metro of bluish veins.

She would blush like Eve, but he would kiss away her nervousness and distract her so that she would be naked and open before him before she even knew where she was; she would be thinking only of him and his rapt admiration. And not the feel of the carrel air against pale, pink flesh.

He would praise her with oaths and odes and soft murmurings of sweet pet names and she would not feel shame. *Honey, sweet girl, dear, my lovely* . . . He would make her believe in his affection and her belief would not be entirely false.

Eventually the teasing and tingling would be too much and he'd lean her back gently, cradling the back of her head in his hand. He'd keep his hand there throughout, for he would be worried he might hurt her. He would not have her head banging against the desk like an unloved toy; he'd sacrifice his knuckles and the back of his hand before he would allow that to happen.

He was not a cruel lover. He would not be rough or indifferent. He would be erotic and passionate, but gentle. For he knew what she was.

And he would wish her to be pleased as much as him, her first time.

But he desired her spread out under him, breathless and inviting, her eyes wide and unblinking, blazing with desire. Even though . . .

His other hand would flex across her lower back, the sweet expanse of arched skin, and he'd gaze into her large and liquid eyes as she gasped and moaned.

He would make her moan. Only him.

She'd bite her lip, her eyes half-closed as he slid toward her, willing her with whispered words to *relax* as she gave herself to him.

It would go easier for her that way, the first time. He would still and not rush. He would pause and not tear. He would stop, perhaps?

His beautiful, perfect brown-eyed angel . . . her chest rising and falling quickly, the flush of her cheeks blooming across her entire body. She would be a rose in his eyes, and she would blossom beneath him. For he would be kind. And she would open.

He'd love her firmly but gently. And when her pleasure crashed over her, he would kiss her lips firmly, then sink his teeth into her neck.

The sharp canines would penetrate her flesh, exposing her wondrous sweet vintage. He'd turn his tongue in it, tasting it before drinking deeply.

The sudden loss of blood would only prolong her orgasm, potentially causing her to climax a second time.

He would drink and drink as her body trembled, then he'd plant himself deeply within her and release.

A final swallow, a final taste, and he'd withdraw his teeth from her flesh. He'd lick the wound clean, waiting for the punctures to heal, then, firmly seated within her, he'd watch.

She wouldn't become a vampire like him. Not from so one-sided a feeding.

No. Her transformation would be of an entirely different order— from maiden to matron through loss of maidenhead. All because of him.

Maidenhead?

There would be blood of a different kind. For the price of sin was always blood.

And a little death.

❊❦

Gabriel's heart, which beat but rarely, stopped.

It lay silent for some time, then thudded twice as a new awareness overtook him and metaphysical poetry, long forgotten from his days at the side of John Donne, sprang to memory.

For in that instant, he saw very clearly that he, Professor Gabriel O. Emerson, would-be seducer of the lovely and innocent graduate student, was more than just a vampyre.

He was a flea.

Here are the words his mind whispered to him as he stared breathlessly at the carrel door,

> *Mark but this flea, and mark in this,*
> *How little that which thou deniest me is;*
> *It suck'd me first, and now sucks thee,*
> *And in this flea our two bloods mingled be.*
> *Thou know'st that this cannot be said*
> *A sin, nor shame, nor loss of maidenhead;*
> *Yet this enjoys before it woo,*
> *And pamper'd swells with one blood made of two;*
> *And this, alas! is more than we would do.*
>
> *O stay, three lives in one flea spare,*
> *Where we almost, yea, more than married are.*
> *This flea is you and I, and this*
> *Our marriage bed, and marriage temple is.*
> *Though parents grudge, and you, we're met,*
> *And cloister'd in these living walls of jet.*
> *Though use make you apt to kill me,*
> *Let not to that self-murder added be,*
> *And sacrilege, three sins in killing three.*
>
> *Cruel and sudden, hast thou since*
> *Purpled thy nail in blood of innocence?*
> *Wherein could this flea guilty be,*
> *Except in that drop which it suck'd from thee?*

Yet thou triumph'st, and say'st that thou
Find'st not thyself nor me the weaker now.
'Tis true ; then learn how false fears be;
Just so much honour, when thou yield'st to me,
Will waste, as this flea's death took life from thee.

He'd known Donne in life; he mourned him in death. He'd known the mistress for whom Donne penned those words. She'd been a virgin when Donne met her, and he'd plied her with his seductive trade, arguing that the loss of her virginity was less consequential than the swatting of a flea. She should give herself to him quickly without a second thought. Without hesitation. Without regret.

Donne's words took on new meaning as Gabriel reflected on the past centuries. Indeed, the poem was an apt description of his existence. An apt description of what his primal self was contemplating doing to her.

Tasting.

Taking.

Sucking.

Sinning.

Draining.

Abandoning.

She was pure. She was innocent.

He wanted her.

Facilis descensus Averni.

But he would not be the one to make her bleed the first time. He could not, would not make another girl bleed for the first time.

All thoughts of seduction and mad, passionate feeding on desks and chairs and floors, against walls and bookshelves and windows immediately gave way.

He would not drink from her.

He would not claim her.

He would not mark her and take what he had no right to take. *Not her.*

❀ ❀

Gabriel Emerson was a trite and only semi-repentant sinner. Preoccupied with the fairer sex and his own physical pleasure, he knew he was governed by his thirsts. And only rarely did that thirst give way to something more, something approximating love, but never in the bedroom.

Nevertheless, despite these and other moral failings, despite his constant magnetism for sin, Gabriel still had one last moral principle that governed his behaviour. One line he would not cross.

Gabriel Emerson did not seduce virgins.

He did not take virginity, *ever*, even if it was freely offered.

He did not slake his thirst with innocence; he fed only on those who had already tasted and who in tasting wanted more.

And he was not about to violate his last and only moral principle for an hour or two of salacious satisfaction with a delectable graduate student in his study carrel.

He was a monster, but he had principles.

He would leave her virtue intact. He would leave her as he found her, the blushing brown-eyed angel, surrounded by bunnies, curled up like a kitten in her little chair. She would sleep unruffled, unkissed, untouched, and unmolested.

His hand tightened on the doorknob, and just as he was about to unlock the door, her voice floated over to him once again.

"Gabriel . . . *you hate me.* Why?"

Julia's tone was no longer brimming with desire; Gabriel heard only desperate resignation and deep, deep sorrow.

The sound of sorrow was something he was strikingly familiar with. And her whispering sounded so upset, so defeated.

Now he had to turn around, if only to convince her that he did not hate her. That she was far too good and too perfect to be despised. And that he wasn't foregoing a night of pleasure with her out of hatred.

But out of love—for the goodness he craved and wished his life had been. And perhaps, out of love for the memory of his former self, before all the sin and vice took root and grew, like a patch of thorns turning and twisting and choking out his virtues.

Gabriel's hand left the doorknob and he drew in a very deep breath. He straightened his shoulders and closed his eyes, wondering how he would explain himself. What he would say . . .

He slowly turned around and was stunned by what he saw.

For Miss Mitchell was not sitting upright, chewing her plump lower lip, swimming in rejection.

Miss Mitchell's head was still resting on top of her arms. Her eyes closed. Her lips parted.

"Gabriel . . . *my* Gabriel." Despite the whispered protestations that fell from her ruby mouth, landing squarely on his trepidatious heart, Miss Mitchell was still very much asleep.

Gabriel frowned as the realization passed over him.

Even while dreaming she thinks I hate her. How could anyone hate so sweet a creature? She would be so easy to love.

He should leave her to her dreams, and pray she dreamed of someone else. Assuming he was the Gabriel of her dreams—*her* Gabriel.

He formed this intention and was ready to leave for the second time when Miss Mitchell groaned slightly and stretched, mewling like a kitten.

Her eyelids fluttered and she stifled a yawn with the cup of her hand.

But her eyes flew open when she saw Professor Emerson standing open-mouthed in sudden surprise by the door.

Startled, she let out a yelp and flew backward out of her chair and against the wall.

She cowered in confusion and it almost broke Gabriel's heart.

(Which would have proven that he had one.)

"Shhhhh. Julianne, it's just me." He held his hands aloft in complete surrender. He tried to smile in order to disarm her.

Julia was dazzled. She'd been dreaming of him moments before. And now he was here.

She rubbed her eyes. He was still there, staring.

She pinched her skin on her arm between her fingers—he was still there.

"It's just me, Julianne, Professor Emerson. Are you all right?"

She blinked rapidly and began rubbing her eyes again. "I . . . don't know."

"How long have you been here?' He lowered his hands.

"Um . . . I . . . don't know." She was trying to wake up and remember all at the same time.

"Is Paul with you?"

"No."

Somehow, Gabriel felt relieved.

"How did you get in? This is my carrel."

Julia's eyes flew to his.

She moved forward rapidly, knocking the chair over in the process and tipping over a stack of books that had been resting near her hands. A ream of loose paper was thrown aloft by the general upheaval and began falling about her like massive, ruled snowflakes.

Gabriel thought that she looked like an angel—an angel in a child's snow globe, with whiteness fluttering all around her. Beautiful.

She began scrambling about, trying to put everything back into order. She was repeating an apology over and over again like a decade of the Rosary, mumbling something about borrowing Paul's key. She was sorry. So very, very sorry.

In one stride, Gabriel was next to her, his hand gently but firmly on her shoulder. "It's all right. You are welcome here. Be still."

Julia drank in the electricity of his touch and hummed softly. She closed her eyes involuntarily and willed herself and her heartbeat to slow. It was very difficult to do; she was so afraid he would lose his temper with her and banish Paul from his precious carrel. Forever.

Gabriel inhaled and Julia's eyes flew open.

"You're bleeding." He was holding up her right hand and folding all her fingers down but one, her pointer finger.

Julia saw blood trickling from the tip of her finger. The room began to feel slightly warm and she felt light-headed.

He brought his head close to her face and peered into her suddenly vacant eyes.

"Julianne? Can you hear me?"

Gabriel didn't know what to do. It was only a small wound, why was she reacting so strongly to it? Perhaps she was weak from hunger or not quite awake. And the room was very warm. She'd left the heater on.

He caught her as she swooned, wrapping her tightly and pulling her into his chest. She was not unconscious, at least, not yet.

"Julianne?" He pushed the hair out of her eyes and brushed the back of his hand across her cheek.

She murmured something and he realized she hadn't fainted, but she was leaning against him as if she did not have the strength to stand.

He held her to keep her from hitting the upturned chair or the floor.

She raised her finger to her face and stared at the blood that was beginning to flow downward. "Oh no . . ."

"What, Julianne? Are you going to faint?"

"It needs to go away . . . the blood . . ." Julia held her finger in front of his face like a panicky child just before her eyes rolled back into her head.

Her legs weakened and Gabriel felt her begin to fall. He needed to hold her with both hands. There was no way he could shift her to one arm without the risk of dropping her to the concrete floor.

So Gabriel did something impulsive. Something he'd sworn not to do.

He became the flea.

He scooped her up into his arms and, watching the blood seep from the wound, which she held aloft so stiffly, he did the unthinkable—he took her finger into his mouth. He closed his lips gently around her flesh and slowly drew his tongue across the pad of her finger, sucking it.

Thankfully, Julia was too out of it to realize what he was doing.

Sucking on her finger sent shivers racing up and down his spine, for her blood was sweet and only mildly spiced—the true evidence of her character and virtues.

Mercifully, for himself and for his career, he released her finger from his mouth before Julia realized what he was doing, swirling his tongue around it one last time as he ejected it, just to ensure that it was clean.

Now I am a blood-sucking thesis advisor. Great.

Julia moaned into his chest and opened her eyes.

"Does blood make you sick, Julianne? Are you all right?"

He was going to move her so that she was sitting down, but she clung to him, wrapping her little arms about his neck as if she were a toddler. He liked the feel of her pressed against him and so he hugged her tightly and leaned his head down to sniff her hair somewhat surreptitiously.

Vanilla.

Her body pressed against his perfectly, as if they were made for each other. It was astonishing.

"What happened?" she mumbled against his cashmere sweater, which was a brilliant green calculated to contrast with the striking blue of his eyes.

"I'm not sure. You cut your finger, but you're all right now. The bleeding has stopped."

She looked up at him and smiled weakly, a smile that melted his heart.

Julia desperately wanted to kiss him. He was so close. So very, very close. Two inches and those lips would be hers . . . again. And his eyes were soft and warm . . . and he was being sweet with her . . .

He pulled back from her minutely, testing her to see if she was going to faint again. And then he placed her gently on top of the desk before righting the chair.

He withdrew to the door of the carrel and raked a hand through his hair. He could still taste the vintage, *her vintage,* in his mouth.

"I don't mind if you use the carrel—not at all. I was just surprised to find you here. In fact, I'm glad Paul suggested you use it. There's no problem."

He smiled to put her at ease, watching as she grasped the surface of the desk for support.

"I was looking for a book Paul borrowed." He held the volume aloft and then turned to look at Julia again.

She was staring at her injured finger and wondered why it was wet. And why Gabriel was staring at the wound and licking his lips . . .